Advance Praise

HOW TO GREET ST

—~~~—

"*How to Greet Strangers* is equal parts spiritual odyssey and gripping detective story, a bold and vibrant work. Read it and fall into a world you will not easily forget."

CAROLINA DE ROBERTIS, author of *The Invisible Mountain* and *Perla*

"*How to Greet Strangers* is suspenseful, spiritual, sexy, and satisfying. It's both a kick-ass mystery and a genuine story of love and the human heart. Thompson creates characters on the far edges of modern life and gives them such humanity that we feel deeply connected to them. *How to Greet Strangers* is one to read and keep."

SCOTT SPARLING, author of *Wire to Wire*

"With Archer Barron, Joyce Thompson has introduced a truly new personality to the world of the murder mystery and this is no mean feat. What is even more remarkable is the world Archer Barron inhabits. Only a writer of Thompson's skill and imagination could do this justice and she puts the reader right in there alongside Archer. The book is filled with keen and pithy insights into the big existential questions: love, death, religion, and what Archer calls being a prisoner in the human zoo. Oh, and you will be amazed when you find out who done it."

KARL MARLANTES, author of *Matterhorn* and *What It Is Like to Go to War*

"With her beautifully imagined and breathtakingly original *How to Greet Strangers*, Joyce Thompson has single handedly rebooted the murder mystery. The prose sings, the story truly thrills, and the detective, Archer Barron, is a hero like no other (and I'm not just talking about the cross-dressing). This is one of those rare, delicious tales you'll want to both cherish and gulp down in one sitting."

KAREN KARBO, author of *How Georgia Became O'Keeffe*

HOW TO
GREET STRANGERS

HOW TO
GREET STRANGERS

a novel by

Joyce Thompson

LETHE PRESS

MAPLE SHADE, NEW JERSEY

Published in 2013 by Lethe Press, Inc.
118 Heritage Avenue • Maple Shade, NJ 08052-3018
www.lethepressbooks.com • lethepress@aol.com
ISBN: 978-1-59021-271-4 / 1-59021-271-1
e-ISBN: 978-1-59021-164-9 / 1-59021-164-2

This novel is a work of fiction. Names, characters, places, and incidents are products of the author's imagination or are used fictitiously.

Set in Baskerville & Bordeaux Roman LET.
Cover art & design: Niki Smith.
Interior design: Alex Jeffers.

LIBRARY OF CONGRESS CATALOGING-IN-PUBLICATION DATA

Thompson, Joyce, 1948-
 How to greet strangers : a novel / by Joyce Thompson.
     p. cm.
 ISBN 978-1-59021-271-4 (pbk. : alk. paper) -- ISBN 978-1-59021-164-9 (e-book)
1. African American gay men--Fiction. 2. Murder--Investigation--Fiction. 3. Santeria--Fiction. 4. California--Fiction. 5. Mystery fiction. I. Title.
PS3570.H6414H69 2013
813'.54--dc23

                              2012036862

FOR SCHUYLER

ACKNOWLEDGMENTS

My husband Schuyler Ingle read Archer's story chapter by chapter as it got written and his enthusiasm for the serial kept me writing. His March birthday gave me the deadline for a completed draft. This book was first of all a birthday present for him in a lean time.

My son Ian Steele answered many questions and provided needed details along the way.

Canny early readers surrendered to the story, raised hard questions, contributed insights and cheered me on: Alexandra Steele, Teresa Miller, Carolina de Robertis, Elisa Williams, Leslie Hall, Kareem Jo Willy.

Ellen Datlow knew just where to send me and Archer: Steve Berman and Lethe Press. I'm proud to be on their list—and awed that one man and one cat can do so much, so well. Thanks also to another one-man show, copyeditor/designer Alex Jeffers.

Lowell B. Denny III gave me the best editorial notes I've ever gotten, period—and this is my sixth published novel.

Finally, my thanks to Yemaya, who is Archer's mother in ocha and my own. This book is a healing and an opening. Whenever I doubted, I heard the voice of the ocean in the center of my brain. The message was, Trust Archer.

———∿∿∿———

For a glossary of Lucumi words and phrases, visit
www.archerbarron.com

PROLOGUE

Some of this part, I wrote in jail.

Jail is different from prison, more like a zoo than another country. All the animals are more or less equal. When you're caged, you need to find some way to pass the time besides jostling the other beasts. Fuses are too short, claws too sharp. You keep to yourself. I did it by writing, trying to make sense of how I ended up where I was, Oakland jail, locked up with a couple of drug dealers, a pimp, a gang-affiliated drive-by shooter and a couple of scruffy college dropouts who still hadn't made bail after Occupying City Hall Plaza in their pup tents. It goes without saying that seven out of the eight of us were shades of black. The second Occupier was probably Samoan.

Did my cage mates make me for a queen? Maybe, but no one had been away from home long enough to be looking for a good time. Everybody was a lot more interested in getting out than getting laid. Me, I was interested in counting up all the ways Michaela de Estrella, now deceased, had promised to save my life and ruined it instead. Sitting there on the hard bench, fingers cramping around the stub of my No. 2 pencil, I tried to write honestly about the sharp exit I'd taken off the interstate of life, following the signpost that said, depending on how you chose to read it—*Authentic Afro-Caribbean Spirituality* or *Beware of the Cult*. Boys, you think I'm weird because I'm writing? Wait until you see me dressed head to toe in white with half a dozen strings of pretty beads—*elekes*—around my neck.

I became an ocha priest, I wrote, then stared at the big gray letters I'd made. By then I knew the plusses and minuses involved in that becoming. I surrendered skepticism, free will, personal autonomy, most of my spare time and a lot of cold hard cash. In return, I received a whole pantheon of African gods, male and female, river goddesses and dwellers on the mountain top, warrior kings and keepers of the crossroads, forest hunters, death defeaters, the power of the volcano, the ocean's tireless fierce bounty. These are all orishas.

Pantheism, good. I still believe that.

Owning personal copies of the gods, ochas, in the form of rocks who live in pots and speak with cowrie shell mouths through divination—this remains a mystery, one that stretches my credulity and just as often touches my soul.

The relationship between these super-charged stones, these otans, and the ritual culture that produces them and binds them to the initiate—that's the hard part. The brochure says, This is the real deal, this diaspora of stones, brought to you straight from Nigeria through Cuba and on to California, and I—I'm speaking for my godmother Michaela here—have both the arcane knowledge and the spiritual power to pass them on to you, so long as you pay me, obey me, work for my spiritual business in an unpaid and on-call capacity and hail as truth everything that comes out of my mouth.

And then there's obi.

Obi, coconut, the handy everyday low-cost way to discern the wants of the orishas and the paths of fortune. Four pieces of the woody fruit, white on one side, brown on the other from the inner lining of the shell. Does Obatala (king of the white cloth) want some rice pudding? Should I wash my car today? Are there blessings to quit my job?

Invoke the ancestors, say the prayers, toss the pieces, read the truth in the pattern of light and dark the pieces fall in. If you've ever struggled with a decision, you can see the appeal of throwing obi. The worm in the coconut is that once you accept obi as your trusted personal advisor, you pretty much stop thinking for yourself. You do get good at parsing even the most complicated issues into binary propositions, since *yes* and *no* are the only words that obi speaks, with a little eau de maybe sometimes leaving wiggle room for interpretation.

"Levon Johnson!"

The desk sergeant hollers into our cage and one of the dealers gets up, adjusts his big pants and saunters up to the cell door. The door opens wide enough to let him out, then clangs shut on the rest of us. Holding his waistband with one hand, Levon raises the middle finger of the other one at the rest of us losers still in the white man's zoo.

"Wait'll I get my hands on those bitches." That's the pimp, stage-whispering, and I'm thinking, Those bitches are taking their sweet time for a reason, asshole.

There are reasons on reasons folks get drawn to Santería, get sucked in and it's possible you get sucked into the house, the ilé, that you deserve. There are Santeros in the world, even in the Bay area, who practice the tradition out of love and not for money. They are spiritual beings and community leaders. I believe that. It's just, those are not the ones I hooked up with, not the ones who read my destiny in the cowrie shells or birthed my stones. For better but mostly worse, I am Michaela de Estrella's godson.

She was my godmother.
Lance died.
I left her house.
Michaela is dead.
I am in jail, a prisoner in the human zoo.

PART ONE

That's me in the corner, losing my religion.
Michael Stipe, REM

ONE

⚜

Faith's a tide. A poet said that and I read it in English class my Freshman year at UC Santa Cruz. I think it's true.

I was totally over Jesus by the time I took up with the orishas, but getting there took its toll. The tides don't turn easily or do it without psychic pain. The second turning hurt much more than the first one. It's natural for a new apostate to feel loss, guilt, confusion. When you're bailing out of Santería, though, it's pretty much unavoidable to spend hard time feeling shit-your-pants afraid. You buy in because you want those magic powers. When you opt out, the folks who gave them to you in the first place are perfectly capable of turning them against you. Or so you spend a lot of sleepless nights believing.

That's why I moved back to Santa Cruz, a beautiful seaside hippie town my godmother cordially despised—for its white faces, its high rents, its eclectic new age earnestness and its academic heart. Even though the first thing Michaela de Estrella would tell you about herself was that she was massively intellectually gifted, she was also a college dropout who trash-talked higher learning every chance she got. Leaving her sphere of influence, I returned to my own roots, to the town where I was a carefree undergraduate with a future before me unlimited by viruses, depressions, addictions or cult behaviors. Because it came with health insurance, I was happy to take a job as a night watchman at the university when I moved back. I've never needed much sleep and working at night leaves me free to pursue my daylight passions, which include surfing, both the ocean and the Internet, with a dash of community service on the side.

The hardest part of recovering from Santería, or any other cult you survive joining is having to look hard at what made you susceptible to joining in the first place. That and how damn much money you handed over along the way. A loose accounting puts me out of pocket about $35K. Not all of that went to Michaela. She bled me, and I bled a lot of chickens and goats so the rocks in my pots would be happy and do what I wanted them to do. Once in a while, it appeared that they did.

When I say that I'm black, understand that I refer to the Africans in my lineage and not the color of my skin, which is a light honey brown not unlike what in slave times the boss caste called "high yellow." This requires a nod to all the white men who contributed bits of material to my genetic profile even if their seed was planted in violence and watered with tears. My driver's license says I am male, stand six foot one and a half inches tall, and weigh 180 pounds. This is true, as far as it goes, but fails to add that in spike heels and a wig, I top out at six foot five and have two of the best legs you'll ever see. I would have signed up to be an organ donor, but since I've been HIV positive much of my adult life, it's hard to imagine someone eager to recycle my kidneys or liver or my heart. I graduated from law school but because the cowrie shells said I should avoid arguments, and Madrina Michaela interpreted that to mean I would have bad fortune if I became an attorney, I got a job as a personal trainer at a 24-Hour Fitness franchise instead. My pecs and abs are steely but I fear that in my time as an ocha priest, my brain has lost some of its tone.

With distance, I can see that everyone who fell under Michaela's spell had one thing in common. I'll simply call it "mother issues," since no two cases were quite the same. In most instances, mom was a meanie, a bitch, a drunk, a derelict, a whore, someone who made Mommie Dearest look like Mother Theresa. I myself grew up in the godawful state of Texas, son of a small-town high school principal and a third-grade teacher. In East Austin, that made them black aristocrats. My mother was so formidable, so beautiful, so utterly and eternally *present* that no attention-seeking organism that moved in her orbit could ever be anything but a dwarf star. As a little boy, I worshipped her. At fifteen, I hated her. When I turned twenty-one, I bought myself a second hand Oscar de la Renta cocktail dress at a designer consignment store and more or less became her. Not too long after that, I was diagnosed. It was an emotional perfect storm, one that ripped me away from all the anchors of my life before and gave over captaincy of my leaky little ship to Michaela de Estrella and the spirits she claimed to command and serve.

~

In my ita, Yemaya took away the ocean.

An ita is a life-reading, one you're given when you become an ocha priest, when all the orishas you've just received speak through their cowrie mouths to give you advice. Some of it makes common sense. Some leaves you scratching your head for years afterward. You may be told you will own a home of your own one day, that you must avoid threesomes, that you should not wear yellow or eat pork chops or go outside when a strong wind's blowing.

I was told to forget lawyering and that Yemaya, the orisha who owns the ocean and crowned my head, loves me so much that if I were to appear in her waters, she would sweep me away and keep me for herself. In the jargon, that constitutes "taking the ocean away," a harsh fate for a man who not only likes the look of himself in a wetsuit but loves to ride inside the curl of ocean waves. During the whole time I was Michaela's obedient godchild, I stayed away from the beach, even though it meant a piece of my soul went numb. Even after I cut myself loose and moved back to Santa Cruz, I was afraid to go near the water for a long time. Once you slip into your cult skin, once you learn to talk the cult talk, certain truths become self evident. If Yemaya has "taken away the ocean," terrible things will happen if you try to take it back.

Suiting up, wading into the surf just as the morning sun lofted high enough to paint the ocean gold, hearing the incessant roar of waves thrusting forward and sucking away from shore, feeling the salt cold on my bare feet for the first time in ten years, I had a profound sense of coming home and an equally deep conviction that I was about to die.

I flew instead.

I had lost a lot of my skill in ten years and the equipment itself had evolved, but after some unceremonious dunkings that were more comical than deadly, I got the hang of it again, caught a wave and melded with it until it threw me off. As if I were a coconut struck by a hammer, my heart broke open, my soul unfurled and tears of joy and liberation rolled down my cheeks. I remember the thoughts that rose up in the middle of my brain: *This is my authentic self* and *My journey is not over.* I played in the ocean until the tide turned and my giddiness gave way to exhaustion.

The return to surfing alone would have made that day memorable but the hits kept coming. When I got back to my car, I found my god sister Rosario perched on the hood. It could have been a year since I'd seen her last. In Santería, priests bump shoulders instead of shaking hands, but I was disengaged from the tradition and so genuinely glad to see Rosario that I caught her up in a big salty hug. Only when we parted could I see how sad she looked.

"Rosario, what's wrong? " I asked her.

For a moment, Rosario simply stared into my eyes, so hard that I began to share her desolation without knowing where it came from. Then she tilted her head a little to the left and said, "Piri is dead. Archer, mi hermano, I need your help."

TWO

In the days when I admired Michaela de Estrella, one of the things I admired most was the racial and ethnic mix of her house. Of the "houses" (read, personally branded religious communities) in the San Francisco Bay Area, most are homogenous, predominantly African American, or mostly Latino, one I know of full of skanky older white people who Love the Music, another, east of the tunnel, where membership is based strictly on skin tone, as in, "I will not put elekes on anyone darker than X," X being the Puerto Rican wife of the house. Some were seeded with black radicals, looking to fill the void of community the collapse of the Black Panthers left behind. At least in the early days, these houses required both racial and political purity as conditions for membership. Michaela, on the other hand, would put her hand in anyone's pocket, regardless of race, sexual preference or national origin.

Rosario was one of the small colony of Salvadorans within the larger nation of Michaela's house. Although the six Salvadorans had not known each other back home, they were all political refugees and had come to the US around the same time. They met in San Francisco, formed fast bonds and eventually ended up as Santería god kin. Rosario was the smallest, plainest and shyest of the Salvadoran women, thus, it was generally supposed, the least likely ever to find a husband. Michaela was not modest about claiming credit for Rosario's marriage to Carlos, who was Mexican, nor for the birth of their son Piri, who was billed as a miracle baby in a house full of miracles. The last time I'd seen Piri he was two or maybe three, a small, good-natured boy who from the moment he was born looked like a very old man.

I put my arm around Rosario's thin shoulders and guided her back toward the ocean with its mother energy—the beach would give us a place to sit and something to look at besides each other. It was a bit of a sacrifice, given that my wetsuit was going dry and starting to pinch and chafe, but I couldn't think of a better alternative. When we were settled behind a sun-bleached log, sheltered from the brisk wind, I asked her to tell me the whole story.

"Piri got sick," she said. "He had no energy. He didn't want to eat anything anymore. I took him to the doctor and they said he had cancer."

I took a deep breath. "Oh, Rosario. The poor little guy."

"The doctor wanted to operate on him, to cut out the tumor on his brain," she said. "We didn't know what to do. We went to Madrina Michaela for a reading." At this point, the tears started. When I dabbed more modest accretions of salty water from the corners of my own eyes, I told myself the wind had put them there.

"Madrina Michaela said Eleggua said Piri didn't need an operation. She said making ocha would save our son's life."

I felt it in the pit of my stomach, the combination of hope, dread and defiance those readings summon up. Every breath Rosario took now sounded like a sob. I waited until she was ready to talk again.

"Carlos was against it. He wanted Piri to have the operation."

"Was he working? Did you have health insurance?"

Rosario shook her head no. "We had some money put away. Carlos wanted to ask his cousin for a loan. He swore he'd work three jobs for the rest of his life to pay it back." She stared out at the implacable ocean. Her head moved side to side in tiny arcs of disbelief. The wind almost swallowed her words. "I believed Madrina. Ocha gave me my husband. Ocha gave us a son. I believed her when she said ocha would save his life."

I waited. There was nothing I could say.

"We had bad fights," Rosario said. "Carlos was crazy mad, not just at me. He went out and got drunk and picked fights he knew he couldn't win. I think he needed to feel pain, you know?

"He left for a while," Rosario said, "but he couldn't stay away from his son. When he came back he was different. Quiet and sad. Carlos said Piri could make ocha to save his life."

"Which, uhm, who...." I wanted to ask which ocha had crowned Piri's head.

"Obatala," Rosario said. "Madrina gave us a special price. Only eight thousand dollars. Our god sisters and brothers bought his pots and his tools and his white clothes and paid for some of the animals."

"Such a deal." I said it under my breath, but I couldn't resist saying it out loud.

"Carlos borrowed the rest from his cousin Antonio. Madrina scheduled the ocha in the middle of the week and kept it secret from most of the house. Piri was very sick and thin by then." Rosario looked haunted and I started to feel hungry, missing the breakfast I'd skipped to surf. The hollow growing in my stomach complemented the look in her eyes.

"I had to hold him most of the time," Rosario said. "During penitencia. During the ceremony. I had to keep my hand over his eyes."

I could see it in my mind and the sight was painful. Rosario was quiet for a moment, then she said, "Iku came."

Inside my rubber suit, the hair stood up on my arms. "Are you kidding me? How? How did you know?" Iku is death.

Rosario turned to look at me and spoke in a small voice. "I passed him," she said. "During matanzas. Madrina passed Aganju. He ate a goat heart and went to war with death." Rosario looked at her hands. "I don't remember anything," she said. "I don't know where I went. But for a little while, while he was on the throne, Piri seemed a little better. He smiled more. He ate a little bit. I stayed there with him and sang him songs." After a long pause, she said, "Madrina was proud. She said she won the battle with Iku."

I let myself imagine my godmother then, beaming with hubris, already crafting the legend of the latest miracle.

"When we took Piri home from Madrina's house, he started to slide backwards. He started to have seizures. We were afraid. One night they got so bad we took him to the emergency room. Carlos carried him inside in his arms. The nurses took Piri away from him. That was the last time we saw our son."

I let a respectful silence grow around the story, then reached over and put my hand on Rosario's small brown one. I noticed then the stripe of paler flesh around the finger where her wedding ring must have been. Maybe she pawned it. "I'm so sorry," I said. "What can I do to help?"

I thought the story was close to over, but it turned out I was wrong.

"Piri died that night. Two days later, the doctors said we killed him. By not getting him the operation. The day we buried him, police came to the cemetery and arrested Carlos for negligent homicide. They say I was his accomplice."

"Where is Carlos now? Is he in jail?"

"Since last Thursday." Now that she'd finished catching me up, everything she'd been through settled on her, rounding her shoulders, making her voice thin as a thread. "He wanted to leave the country," she said, "but he didn't go in time."

For some time we just sat there, staring out at the unremitting ocean. I don't know what Rosario was thinking, but I was trying to figure out why she'd tracked me down. We'd been friendly, even fond of one another back when faith was fresh and we both had some. But we were never close. Why were we together here, now? What did she want?

"My husband needs a lawyer," she said. "He didn't kill our son."

"Rosario, I went to law school, but I never took the bar exam. I'm not licensed to practice, in this state or anyplace else."

"Carlos isn't safe in jail," Rosario said. "Please, you're the only person who can help us."

Her voice was so insistent and her gaze so clear, I started to believe her. Who did I know? What could I do? "Damn girl," I said. "You really know how to get your way."

The smile she smiled at me then went on my life list of the saddest smiles I've ever seen.

THREE

❦

When we were saying goodbye, I told Rosario I was glad she tracked me down, but it wasn't really true. On the way home, I turned the radio up so loud that it was impossible to think, much less feel, a big blast of Teutonic thunder. (Okay, it's true, I prefer opera to hip-hop, one more way that gay trumps black. Get over it.)

As soon as I got home, though, reflection settled in. Home was an attic studio apartment not quite legally built out under the eaves of an old Santa Cruz Victorian. I liked living in what felt like a house, liked having nothing else above me but the sky, liked what climbing the three flights of stairs several times a day did for my calves and my wind. My décor was dominated by my soperas, the beautiful ceramic pots my ochas lived in, and all the exotic and beautiful trinkets I'd bought over the years to make my ochas feel loved and spoiled. Whether they were rocks in pretty pots or living spiritual entities, my ochas were still a commanding presence in my home.

I've heard of people leaving who smash their pots or sell them and throw away the stones. Most of us are less extreme, nostalgic for the sweet certainty and total metaphoric immersion we once experienced. Because the religion is so marginalized, because we so much set ourselves apart when we embrace it, because it is so beautiful and so utterly self-referential, it takes up residence in every atom of its initiates. It colonizes your vocabulary and your world view, redefines the rules of cause and effect. It has an explanation for everything. You live inside it. When logic or disillusionment erodes belief, the pain is almost visceral. In Santa

Cruz, I'd been living differently with my ochas, treating them more as my roommates than my gods. I didn't prostrate myself before them every day, gave my warriors rum and cigar smoke when I felt like it, not because it was Monday and I was obliged. Sometimes for a week or more there were no fresh flowers on my ancestor altar now and I'd started eating apples and wearing my red sweater again. Chango had taken both away in my ita.

Nothing terrible happened. I didn't get sick or lose my job or die. Every time something bad doesn't happen when you break the rules, your shoulders relax a little bit more, your stomach settles, you breathe deeper and swing your arms in longer arcs when you walk. What you recover, slowly and in tiny increments, is your self esteem.

The day so far had been an emotional doubleheader—surfing again and then my encounter with Rosario. Once I closed the door behind me and surrendered to the alert silence in my home, I felt like I'd been run over by a very big truck. In the old days, my pious days, I would have thanked Yemaya for not carrying me off, made her some chocolate pudding as appeasement and thanks. I would have asked her to help Rosario with her problem, which would have absolved me of any further effort on her behalf. Prayers said, case closed. Now, though, it felt as if I might be implicated.

The ringtone on my phone was and still is Lázaro Ros, a famous Cuban, singing the first two phrases of a song to Yemaya. Somebody told me once that the Lucumi words mean, Asesu, why are you crying?

"Where the hell are you?"

That day, at that moment, the caller was Pete from the Clinic.

"An old friend turned up unexpectedly. I'm running a little late."

"Well, it's a madhouse here. Run faster."

"Are you saying two clients at the same time?"

"I'm saying four," Pete said, "and half of them are girls."

"I'm heading for the shower now."

"Jesus."

"Cut me some slack. I *am* a volunteer."

Pete hung up on me. I showered fast. No more than twenty minutes later, I was at the clinic, two flights above the commercial storefronts on Pacific. It had the seedy, hopeful look of an underfunded nonprofit, which it was—odd-lot chairs and dog-eared year-old magazines in the waiting room, a coat of haze on both sides of the window glass, one from years of anxious exhalations, the other sublimed from the elixir of salt and soot that was the local air. Pete was right— the waiting room was in danger of exceeding its capacity to offer isolation to its inhabitants. A fidgety young couple, heterosexual, sat together, a girl of indeterminate preferences, a late adolescent male, obviously gay and kind of cute in a wimpy sort of way.

Pete came round the counter. "That took you long enough," he hissed at me, then adjusted his voice for public discourse. "Tammy Burns," he called. "You'll be talking with Archer first today." Pete handed me her paperwork.

The girl—short bob, grizzled in back, nose stud and a wee rose tat on her neck, stood up and walked toward me. There was nothing shy in her gaze and I wondered how what she saw before her—black, male, most likely gay—would impact her ability to hear what I had to say. "Follow me," I said and led her to one of the interview cubbies in the back where we sat on opposite sides of a battered table. "So, Tammy, what's on your mind?"

"I think I have the plague," she said.

"Uhm, could you be a little more specific?"

"Sure," she said. "I have these nasty hot swollen sores all over my privates. Front and back, inside and out. I also have diarrhea, my body aches all over, and I'm running a fever of a hundred and three plus."

"That plague," I said. "You have herpes. This is the first outbreak, right?" She nodded.

"Always the worst," I said. "And usually much more painful for women."

"Can you make it better?"

"The doctor can prescribe an ointment called acyclovir. It's not cheap and it may not actually help much, but if you want to do something besides wait it out, ask her for a prescription."

"I'm really sick."

"Yeah, I know. So treat it like a bad flu. Lots of rest, good food, fluids, Tylenol for the fever. Take my advice and wear a skirt."

Tammy made a sound somewhere between a deep sigh and a growl. I preached.

"So what your boyfriend should have done, and what you'll have to do from here on out, is not have sex when you have any sores at all, not until they're all healed up and the scabs have fallen off. When in doubt, use condoms. And you never have sex with anybody before you tell them you have herpes."

"That totally sucks," Tammy said.

"Yes, it does. After this first outbreak heals, the virus will live in your central nervous system for the rest of your life. If you get run-down or stressed out, you'll have another outbreak. It probably won't be as bad as this first one. If you get pregnant, make sure your doctor knows you have herpes. If you have an outbreak when you're ready to deliver, you'll need a C-section, for the baby's sake. Otherwise, it could be born blind."

"This is so unfair. It's not like I even had a good time."

"Want to hear the good news?"

"Do I have a choice?"

I shook my head no. "One, herpes will always act as a monitor of how you're treating yourself. If you have an outbreak, it's time to do better. It's an incentive to live healthy. Two, it's not HIV."

Stop whining or I'll bitch-slap you, brat. I kept smiling, but my patience was getting thin. Lucky for her, she just nodded. "The doctor will confirm it, right?"

"That's right," I said, liking her a little better. "And you know what? I'm thinking you might warn the rest of the population about your boyfriend. Maybe something on his Facebook page."

Tammy was really kind of pretty when she smiled. With that, I took her back to an exam room, handed her her disposable no-back nightie and left her to wait for Doc Sam to examine the sores on her genitals and repeat everything I'd just said. When I got back to the waiting room, the couple was gone and only the little boy remained. He had soft brown hair and round deer-eyes that said, *Born to be a victim.* He was a freshman at UCSC, in my old college of political and sexual misfits. I dreaded hearing why he thought he needed to be tested. But he surprised me.

"I've met someone. We've been dating for a while. We both want to have sex."

"Congratulations."

"Yeah. But before we do, I wanted to make sure I know how to have safe sex." He grinned shyly. "I really like him."

I swear to god, he took notes while I explained the basics. Then I gave him a two-week supply of free condoms, courtesy of the California Department of Health. "Remember to have fun," I told him. We shook hands. Not too much later, the young couple burst out of a back office and into the waiting room. She was crying, he was swearing—not an uncommon response to news of a new life on the way. A few minutes later, only the three of us were left, Doc Sam in her rumpled white coat, Pete, doing good to look good on his med school application, and me, Archer.

Why me? When I made ocha, I became a priest.

In Santería, that may be more like a business license than a doctorate of theology, but priest I was. In the Black Baptist church I came up in, the role came with the obligation to be compassionate, to be of service to the suffering. My daddy's father was an itinerant preacher who rarely had a dollar of his own. Grandpa Barron might not have approved of me, but I was sashaying along in his footsteps on the road to redemption, preaching sexual health to all god's children, Pete and Doc Sam my fellow travelers.

They were the kind of friends you make when you're on the road between selves, when just getting up in the morning is both an accomplishment and an adventure, when you don't know where you're headed or who you'll be at journey's end, not chosen for the cautious, canny reasons that start our settled friendships but brought into our lives by proximity and generous accident. We were all in process—Pete almost ready to own what he always knew, that he was gay, Doc Sam still mourning the death of her mother six months before, me losing my religion, a loss that swept up all my losses. We hung out. We held up mirrors for each other, so we could check out what our next selves looked like.

After we locked the front door and put the answering machine on, I told Pete and Sam a little bit about Rosario's visit.

"Rosario and Carlos could sue Michaela," Sam said.

"Because she's not a real doctor, like you?" Pete said.

"Wrongful death is wrongful death, whether you have a medical degree or not."

"Speaking of degrees," Pete said. "You never told us you went to law school, Arch. How come?"

Pete spoke in a bitchy countertenor that undermined his best efforts to talk butch. Most of the time he didn't even know he was doing it. It was fun to flame right back at him, Oh girl, and make him blush but the question about law school got past my defenses. Three years of my life, a catalog of efforts and achievements I was no longer in the habit of remembering, much less owning. The sudden fist of pain at the apex of my rib cage felt physical but probably was not.

"That bad boy is in the closet," I said, but my timing was way off and it sounded lame.

FOUR

I first set eyes on Michaela de Estrella on the middle day of my friend
Benny's ocha. Benny and his partner Lev were my neighbors in San
Francisco. Lev dragged me along to Oakland, mostly for moral support. Michaela's house was in East Oakland, that notorious 'hood, but
even though the local news teams talk about East Oakland as if it were
a monolith of doom and degradation, the fact is, there as everywhere in
the East Bay, elevation is all. Six streets above the flats, the neighborhood
starts greening and the houses have elbow room. Decks, two-car garages,
backyard gardens, the occasional pool for swimming or raising carp. The
houses are newer and flatter, built from the seventies on mostly, some of
them by the black middle class. Maybe I imagined that part, but that's
mostly who lives there now, people with good straight jobs or high rollers
on the cash economy, dealers, gamblers, pimps or the occasional iyalocha like Michaela, who always carries a fat roll of twenties in her pocket
and often reaches in to fondle it.

Lev had made me put on white clothes for the occasion, even though
it was late fall and all my whites then were summer clothes. For warmth
and dignity, I layered. We were supposed to get there early but arrived
late enough that we had to enter through the back and make our way
upstairs. The sound of the drums got louder as we climbed. Of entering
Michaela's living room the first time, my memory holds a photograph
and not a video, taken from the rear of the room with a magical lens, so
that everything is equally in focus—three seated men in white, one black,
one white, one Latin, each furiously slapping an elaborately decorated

drum laid across his lap; a room within a room, three-walled and built of gorgeously draped gold satin, paneled with rectangles of rich fabrics, Benny's room, from the look of it, since he stood in the middle barefoot and wearing what looked like a yellow satin page boy's outfit from the mid-eighteenth-century French court. His face was painted with colored streaks like a cat's whiskers and a coy blue goatee and he stooped under the weight of all the heavy beaded necklaces hung like a noble's sash over one shoulder and under one arm. Benny's longish hair was gone and a bejeweled yellow satin crown sat on his newly bald and lavishly painted head. There's a gaggle of white-clad people in the foreground, a glimpse of vessels topped with what look like bowls of charred meats lined up along one wall. Benny less dances than startles to the drums, which sing in one blended voice, like a well rehearsed trio. His eyes are glassy and a little smile of exaltation flits across his lips. He looks gorgeous.

Now this is drag, I remember thinking. Before that day, I had no idea that dressing up is part of Santería. As we stood there, Lev's hand found mine. The drums found all the secret entries to my body and my soul. I smelled a not-altogether-melodic potpourri of strong incense recently burned, human sweat and old meat. At a certain point, a rush of tears wavered the photograph. I squeezed Lev's hand.

What a day it was. When the music was over, people lined up in front of Benny's golden chamber—his throne, I learned—and prostrated themselves on a rush mat. He in turn prostrated himself to them according to some order I sensed to be present but couldn't quite decode. Then they took a sharp left and threw themselves down on the floor in front of a tall, husky woman wearing a dandy man's tailored white three-piece and a pair of gleaming white bucks. Her Kenta-cloth pillbox hat looked incongruous with the pimp suit. This was Benny's godmother, Michaela. Lev whispered that I didn't have to salute her, could just shake hands, but when I stood in front of Michaela for the first time, it was as if some raw power emanated from her like a burly genie and pushed me down onto my belly at her feet. She lightly brushed my shoulders with her fingertips and told me to stand up. Our relative pecking order was established that day and never really changed.

Because I came with Lev, I had to stay until the ceremony's end, long past November dark, long past the time the spirits came and rode their horses around the room, handing out embraces and advices, delivering urgent messages to the by-then almost one hundred people stuffed into Michaela's daylight basement rec room and dancing to the drums. Lev explained as best he could that the possessed folks were orishas, come to earth to join the party and talk with the partygoers. For most of the evening, I gave them a wide berth and they steered clear of me, too, until the creature who had lately been Michaela and was now devouring the room in thundering giant steps wearing a wine-red sarong over the white suit planted him or herself squarely in front of me, hands on hips and chin out, breathing like a bellows and staring without blinking into my eyes. He—when he shoved me in the center of my chest with the palm of his hand, I decided this was a male entity—grunted with satisfaction—*HUH!*—when I rolled back on my heels. Then he pulled me close. A Spanish-speaking godchild who had been hovering nearby stepped up to translate.

"Aganju says you have the sickness. Ocha can save your life."

Michaela/Aganju strutted around me once, grunted again and moved on without looking back.

One of the first of the second wave, those of us too proud or stupid to learn from the past and thus doomed to repeat it, Benny had already been diagnosed. First among all the reasons he came to be crowned to Ochun was a desire to outwit the virus. The promise that he could.

I was in my second year of law school then, looking good and feeling well. That day, I still believed I would escape forever.

FIVE

It was my mid-week night off the security job and Doc Sam and I had a date. I'd told her about my ladies but she'd never met one. She was curious, especially about Elizabeth, who is no drag queen but an upper-middle-class bitch of the kind who shops at the best department stores and volunteers for all the best causes. Sometimes I think she owns an art gallery. Her makeup is understated, her wig a sleek shoulder-length bob, expensive dishwater blonde. Her wardrobe tends to tailored woolens and cashmere sweaters in a muted palette, silk stockings and plain, elegant pumps. In my imagination, Elizabeth graduated from one of the Seven Sisters with medium high honors. She wears Chanel No. 19 and almost no jewelry. Her racial ambiguity, something suggestively African about her lips and eyes, only adds to her mystique.

I don't become Elizabeth to attract attention. She is my upscale alter ego, a persona I put on to pass where Archer can't. After I described her in some detail, Doc Sam was convinced that if she and Elizabeth met, they'd probably enjoy each other's company. Our date was a goof, girls' night out, daring the world to detect the undetectable—that the graceful well-groomed blonde woman had a substantial hunk of junk under her tweed skirt. We were driving to San Francisco. After dinner, we'd either catch a movie or, if we were feeling more adventurous, go out dancing.

Once we were seated in the restaurant, it was showtime. The waiter was convinced he was serving two women, I think, but if you ask me, we were a little off our marks. In Elizabeth's company, the normally stolid Doc Sam turned giggly and shy. Elizabeth, who never had a girlfriend

24

who was not a boy, felt a little shy herself. Like anybody on a first date Elizabeth took refuge in the menu. "The scampi is tempting," she said. "I love the bruschetta they serve with it."

"I was thinking of ordering the calamari," Sam said. "Would you like to share hors d'oeuvres?"

"Absolutely. Do you like red wine or white? I'm thinking a prosecco might be nice."

We agreed on the bubbly and had just ordered it when Lázaro Ros started singing in my purse. The tune turned heads in the café. I opened my bag to silence it, but Sam said, "Go ahead. Answer."

I'd already pushed the green button by the time I saw the caller ID. Rosario. I wouldn't have recognized her voice because she was crying so hard.

"Easy, girl. Breathe. Breathe deep. There you go." I talked her down to the level of ragged sobs, measured out in slow intervals. Then I asked her what was wrong.

"It's Carlos," she said. "Somebody said he killed his son, and they waited for him and they beat him up bad."

"In jail?"

"Yes. In jail. They took him to the county hospital he's hurt so bad."

"Jesus, Rosario, that's terrible. I'm so sorry. But look, I just sat down to dinner with a friend. Can I call you back?"

Sam was shaking her head, no. "Talk to her now. It's okay."

'We have to bail him out," Rosario said. "They'll kill him if he goes back to that jail."

"Do you have any money? I have a little in savings, but I can't get it until tomorrow...."

Sam reached across the table and put her square-nailed hand on my arm. "I can help with the bond," she said. I started to demur but she shook her head. "It's not a hardship, Elizabeth." Sam smiled, saying the name. "Please tell Rosario we'll take care of bail and meet her at the hospital."

"What about dinner?"

"I'm sure we can find something to eat in Oakland."

We left a generous tip for services not yet rendered and headed out. It hurt to give up a free, legal parking space in San Francisco. On a bad night, it can take thirty minutes or more to find a place to leave your car.

As I drove, Sam googled "bail bonds" on her iPhone. "Who knew?" she said. "The Bail Bond Doctor takes credit cards. I can do this all online." She had to call Rosario in order to fill in all the blanks and swore a lot, trying to type in the information on that tiny digital keyboard, but at last she hit SEND. The tinny acknowledging sound was the bells of Carlos's freedom ringing. The peculiar soundscape of the eastbound level of the Bay Bridge, the abrasion of the roadbed grating on my tires, the car-fart smell that crept inside and the weird yellow light cued memories of other crossings. My body remembered going to Michaela's house and tensed up, my stomach hollowed and my fingers tightened around the steering wheel. And then I caught sight of them, Elizabeth's shapely mauve fingernails. I laughed out loud.

"Share the joke," Doc Sam said.

I drove with my left hand and raised the splayed fingers of my right. "Look," I said.

"Lovely."

"Rosario doesn't know I sometimes dress as a woman."

After a minute, Sam said, "I'm thinking she has bigger things to worry about than your wardrobe."

By this time, I was choking the wheel with both hands. "It's just…"

"What?"

It was hard to explain, even to myself, the sense of being caught in the act or the dread that produced in me. "I compartmentalize," I said. "It's how I cope." It was something I'd known for a long time but not said out loud. It led naturally to the next point: I don't want to be accepted for what I am. I prefer to be an outlaw. It's much more exciting.

From Oakland's bayside flats, we climbed 31st Street until Highland Hospital appeared out of the darkness, a giant wedding cake of a building, a California architect's wet dream of a European cathedral, dreamed in the 1920s and built to serve the county's indigent and traumatized masses. Were they black like me back then or some flavor of just-off-the-boat European? I didn't know. We parked on the street and I called Rosario's cell, but she didn't answer. The entrance to the hospital was through the businesslike new wing, all glass and steel. Visiting hours were just winding down, and the elevators disgorged children and lovers in little spurts, the occasional solitary visitor texting or in tears. The walls displayed schoolkids' art, finger paintings and construction paper mosaics, unframed. My god sister was not in the lobby. I spoke to the receptionist in Elizabeth's standard English. "I believe Carlos Mendoza is a trauma patient. He was brought here from the county jail. I'm supposed to meet his wife here."

"Hold on a minute." The receptionist had winking rhinestones in her glasses and a chest that looked upholstered under her wine-colored blouse. One hung on a black cord upon the other. She placed the glasses on her nose and scanned her terminal. "Okay, I'm going to call upstairs."

Not much later, a uniformed cop, a guy in a gray suit and Rosario emerged from an elevator and made their way toward us. Rosario's eyes were puffy from crying and her tears had washed away every atom of the makeup she usually wore. About six feet out, I saw her see it, the Archer inside Elizabeth. She blinked a couple of times. Then her lips curled slightly, a signal and a smile. Two feet away, she extended her hand. I took it in both of mine.

"Thank you for coming," Rosario said.

"We took care of bail. As soon as Carlos is patched up, you can take him home."

This news did not produce the happy effect I had expected. The police closed ranks around me and Doc Sam. Rosario shook her head.

"How badly is he hurt?" Sam asked.

Rosario's intake of breath broke into a whistling sob. The man in the gray suit—he had a thin gray mustache on his short upper lip—said, "Carlos Mendoza isn't here."

"That was quick," Sam said. "We just filled out the paperwork online, not twenty minutes ago."

"He wasn't released on bail," the man in the gray suit told us.

Rosario peered up at me. "They say Carlos ran away," she said.

"The bastard escaped," the cop in uniform corrected. "Sounds like he should have kept his shirt on." He found this amusing enough to poke his superior officer.

I considered the problem. Whether Carlos was a free man or a fugitive was simply a question of timing. Sam was evidently thinking along the same lines, because she said, "If we paid before he left, Carlos is legitimately out on bail. It doesn't really matter if he knew it or not."

"Until I hear otherwise, from someone whose opinion matters before the law, Carlos Mendoza escaped from custody," the man in the gray suit said, in a voice that invited no further discussion. Would he have been quite so officious if he'd read me as male? It was a stray thought, but provocative. To all appearances, we were three women up against two men. In fact, the uniform was at that very moment ogling my shapely calves.

"Señora Mendoza is free to go," Sam said. "Am I right?"

The men exchanged looks. "We have no reason to believe Mrs. Mendoza was party to her husband's escape," the man in the gray suit said. Then, to Rosario, "You're free to go, for now. But the minute you hear from your husband, give us a call." He handed her a card. When I glanced at it later, I saw his name was Oliver.

Sam took Rosario's arm. "I'm starving. How about you?"

Rosario nodded dumbly. Elizabeth straightened her shoulders, preparing for her exit. The cops watched with unwilling admiration. I tell you, carriage is everything. I took Rosario's other arm and steered us across the lobby, toward the exit doors. The doors anticipated our intention and parted with a whoosh. The night cool seeped in to meet us and knowing the three men were watching, we stepped into it. I was glad for my high heels, my blonde hair, my fake boobs, the gray wool skirt tickling my kneecaps. I was glad for my purse, my carefully curled eyelashes and the feel of real silk underwear against my skin.

Elizabeth was a visitor to Highland Hospital, a wealthy stranger slumming among the hapless uninsured. Archer had nearly died there, back in the day.

Once in the car, we collapsed into silence for a moment, letting the tension dissipate before the questions started.

"Why are you…"

"How bad is…"

"When did they…"

"Why did he…"

They rushed out all at once, our questions, borne on urgency and nervous laughter.

I do drag sometimes. Have for years. Just because.

Carlos has a broken nose, three cracked ribs, a dislocated shoulder. Cuts and bruises all over.

I went to the bathroom. When I got back he was gone. The police were very angry.

Does Carlos have a green card? Is he legal?
No.

We stopped at a taco truck on International, a moveable neighborhood café where black teenagers holding up their pants and jornaleros finally calling it a night stood uneasily on line together looking to redress the indignities of one more day without a job with a couple of pork tacos or a rice and bean burrito. Of the three of us, only Rosario looked at home. She ordered for me and Sam and we took our paper sacks full of dinner back to the car. The corner was noisy and felt explosive, everyone's fuse trimmed short by hard times. My lap covered with an abundance of cheap napkins, I consumed two greasy tacos with unladylike speed. Sam had never tasted tamarindo before and made happy little sounds as she sloshed it around her mouth. Rosario ate methodically, concentrated on her food.

"Where will Carlos go?" Sam asked her between bites.

Rosario dabbed her chin clean of grease and salsa and shook her head. "I don't know for sure, but I'm worried," she said. "Carlos is very angry at Madrina Michaela."

SIX

My first dress was a choir robe. The first boy I had a crush on was Jesus. He was too old for me, true, but more naked than any man I'd ever seen except my father and his expression, encompassing pain and a weird underlying ecstasy, suggested there were subtleties of sensation not dreamed of in Dick and Jane. I was five or six, just learning to read, when I fell in love with the skinny white man on the cross. Because I was born with a sweet high tenor and the innate ability to carry a tune, the choirmaster gobbled me up at an early age and Sundays dressed me in that long brown robe with the starched white collar. Let me blow my own horn; I was adorable. The gospel we sang was soulful, with a big backbeat, and we swayed in rhythmic unison as we sang it, so the music filled our bodies as well as our mouths and produced a kind of quasi-erotic hypnotic trance that amped up our devotion to the Lord.

Music. Religion. Sex. It may be that whoever wired humans deliberately crossed those wires, so the three impulses would be hooked up forever. Among all the flavors of faith I've tasted in my time, this is the common and persistent trinity, a hymn played on the central nervous system, arousing murky longings. My Texas Baptist phase lasted until puberty, when I got caught trading hand jobs with Joey Lopez in the bathroom at Gospel Camp in the middle of the night. If we'd been smoking cigarettes or drinking whiskey, they would have let us off with a warning, but touching penises was a much bigger vice. They called our parents, raised questions about our manliness and sent us home in disgrace.

My crush on Christ didn't survive this incident. Neither did my parents' laissez-faire policies toward their only son. While they didn't exactly demonize same-sex sex play, they made it very clear that they expected me to keep my hands—and my genitals—to myself, at least until I reached legal manhood at age eighteen. The worst part was, news of my shame followed me home and spread like an oil spill across the community, bringing happiness to the hearts of everybody who resented my parents' status as educators and mine as their son, a good boy who always got good grades. The community "knew" I was gay before I knew it myself.

Middle school in East Austin was purgatory but rumors of what happened at church camp turned it into straight-up hell. The third time I came home with torn clothes, snuffing up snot and tears, my parents stayed up most of the night having the longest, loudest fight I ever heard them have. The walls of our house were just thick enough to distort their voices and I couldn't tell who was shouting what, but by the time morning came, they stood shoulder to shoulder. They were enrolling me in the Austin Academy, a small, liberal, Quaker-run school it would be my duty and privilege to integrate for the first time. It boiled down to this: If I was going to be a freak wherever I went, I might as well be a relatively safe freak with a good education. At the Academy, I majored in Tokenism. It cost my parents an arm and a leg.

As a teenager, I flirted with Buddhism, philosophically appealing but lacking in the erotic charge I'd come to crave from religion. Fear and desire were the stuff of life for my adolescent self and I could never quite understand why it would be desirable to have done with them. In my Texas town, for a boy of my proclivities, the two were more or less inseparable.

Then, Santa Cruz. My parents expected I would go to Howard, the site of their courtship and the source of their degrees. Most of my growing up, I imagined myself in Washington, DC, dutifully retracing their footsteps, until one stormy afternoon in the fall of 1985 when I was hanging out in the guidance office as the better alternative to study hall I stumbled on a brochure for UCSC. More to the point, I read about Oakes, that sociopolitical blender of a residential college that not only tolerates but recruits exactly those people most of the dominant culture finds alien, dangerous or unworthy. Black people. Gay people. Latino people. Pissed-off people. People like me.

31

Lucky for me, I was alphabetically (mostly A's), numerically (SATs 1385) and genetically (African American, baby) correct. Not only did I get in, they gave me money to come, a fact that stretched my folks' loyalty to alma mater until it snapped. True, my parents wanted to believe that my homosexuality would magically cure itself just as soon as I met the right girl, but they loved me enough to be glad I would be safe at Oakes in case that miracle failed to take place. I came to Santa Cruz on principle, sight unseen. What I saw when I arrived there changed my life.

Until Santa Cruz, spirit was a hormone, a longing, an idea. In Santa Cruz, I saw it was a planet, too. Wind, river, ocean, garden, mountain, fields and woods, a sky where hawks and eagles soared, a fence post where the red-winged blackbird sang. I saw a world of many sacred energies, whose voices, slowly, I started to be able to hear. The god-shaped hole inside me grew enormous. The scale that teeter-totters between doubt and belief dropped me on my butt on the miraculous hard earth.

That is to say, the seed was planted. The soul cracked open. The possibility of faith, real faith, sprouted inside me, willing to be watered. For the first time, reverence disentangled itself from lust. Lust, too, found itself a place to stand.

Lev, smart, serious, ever-so-girly Lev, was both my next-door neighbor freshman year and my first true love. Our rooms faced the cliffs and the ocean beyond. Extravagant sunsets colored our evenings purple mixed with dusky pink. Storms blew in, slashing the night sky with swords of light. We stopped being ashamed of how we were and did everything to each other we'd dreamed of on our separate smalltown nights, each other's bodies the first and best of the lessons that we learned in Santa Cruz.

SEVEN

Graveyard has one advantage. It's shorter than other shifts. I only had to patrol the grounds, browse the monitors, supply the master key and escort errant coeds back to their rooms for six dim hours at a stretch. And UCSC was peaceful, quiet and safe compared to any other U Cal campus you can name. That meant that while it wasn't taxing, most nights my job was boring.

Sometimes I studied odu in the long valleys between incidents, those numbered snippets of diagnosis and wisdom that make up the currency of the Lucumi diviner. Reading the cowrie shells was the source of Michaela's power and, at sixty dollars a pop, a chunk of her income besides. Mastering it myself was one of two markers of religious adulthood. The other had to do with killing animals, a skill I had no urgent desire to add to my bag of ritual entitlements. I tried to master the lingo of divination the same way I studied other foreign languages, with three-by-five flash cards. My way of losing my religion had some of the earmarks of bulimia, binge, then purge. I was perfectly capable of studying and doubting in two neighboring breaths.

I was not unhappy with my routine, my uneventful nights, my daytime visits to the beach, my healthy diet and the slim list of people I considered friends, but Rosario hit my life like a cue ball. The night that Carlos walked out of the Alameda County Hospital, we swung by their street-level one bedroom on Wentworth to pick up her toothbrush, her cellphone charger and a change of clothes before we headed south. Five minutes at cruising speed and Rosario slid sideways on the backseat, pressed her cheek against the cool window and fell into a deep sleep.

In the rearview mirror, I saw her eyes close. "Poor thing, she's exhausted."

Doc Sam half turned to see. "It's good she feels safe enough to let go." She turned back to me. "How well do you know Carlos?"

That was a tough one. He was a cocky little bastard, barely five feet tall and busting with testosterone and homophobia. If we'd met on the street instead of in Michaela's basement, oil and vinegar would have gone their separate ways. Being part of the same religious family shook up the ingredients until we looked and smelled like salad dressing for a while. "You mean, how clearly can I see him through my prejudices?"

Sam laughed. "Yeah."

"Not well enough to predict what he's going to do. He's got be hurting, though."

"Yeah." Sam glanced over the seat again. "What's their relationship like?"

I examined my memories. "Not demonstrative, maybe, but I think they're pretty close."

"Then he'll be in touch with her," Sam said.

"I expect so." After that, past San Jose, the road rose into the coastal mountains. The higher we climbed the quieter we got. Sam bent her neck onto her shoulder like a shorebird and dropped into a snuffling sleep. I kept myself awake through the descent debating the question: Who has it harder, black queens or Latina queens? Both sides like to claim the honors. Me, I just like to keep my Gemini brain agile by having the conversation with myself. Debate was one of the things I did in high school to pass the time and buy my way into the college of my choice. It may even have something to do with why I went to law school.

We dropped Sam off at her house and circled back to my apartment. Rosario had let so much tension go she walked and mumbled as if she'd been drugged. I propped her against the doorframe while I fumbled for the lock in the dim porch light. Just after I felt the lock tumble, I heard one of the old floor boards creak and spun around to see Carlos behind me, tensed like a tiny action figure and holding a garden trowel.

"Jesus, man, you trying to give me a heart attack?"

"Lo siento," Carlos said. He was about the size I remembered but had an older face, not surprising given what he'd recently been through. His forehead was bandaged, one eye swollen almost shut and all his movements seemed experimental, as if he were weighing the degree of pain something cost versus the reward he would experience for doing it. While I finished unlocking, he put his arm around his wife and gave her a kiss on the cheek. Rosario put her head on his shoulder. Together, we crept up the three flights of stairs that led to my loft, me in an imperfect state of metamorphosis, still dressed like Elizabeth, but carrying my high heels and moving like a man. Even in the dark, I couldn't help noticing that the Mendozas' feet fit neatly on the shallow nineteenth-century treads, whereas mine overhung by inches.

Once we got to my apartment, the first thing my visitors did was look for Yemaya. They wanted to salute her and after her, me. "No really, don't bother, please," I said, and meant it, but they were well trained— everyone is, in Michaela's house—to keep track of the hierarchy and observe it without exception. My ocha had preceded theirs, making me their "elder." What made this more than a little silly was the fact that I was their elder only by a matter of months, a negligible gobbet of time, and I took no great pleasure in seeing people prostrate themselves on the floor at my feet. Though Michaela insisted on strict adherence to her protocols, I'd heard Cuban elders say that orishas don't *like* to see priests on the ground; it looks too much like death. Yemaya tolerated their gestures of respect, though, and I was glad enough to lift them up on her behalf and give them my own blessing, for what it was worth.

After that, I unfolded my futon sofa into a futon double bed and insisted that my guests tuck up, while I took off Elizabeth's wig and her makeup and put on Archer's blue flannel pajamas. While the Mendozas didn't exactly gape at the transformation, they did peek avidly, even though the gender-switch was less dramatic than what often happens at a bembe, during trance possession.

When I was mascara-free and deep-pore cleansed, I took my sleeping bag and blow-up pad down from the closet shelf and made myself a bed on the floor as far from theirs as the space allowed. The Mendozas gazed at each other across the foreign expanse of my bed, not touching and too polite to exchange confidences in Spanish with me around, so that I felt like a very big third wheel. It was that, I think, that made me decide to call Terry Gleason in the middle of the night.

I put on my flip-flops, padded downstairs and called him from my car, not him, really, but his voicemail, where I left what I hoped was a sensible adult message: "Terry, Archer calling. I'm calling because my god brother's been arrested for killing his son. Negligent homicide. I know you'll appreciate this. Michaela convinced them to initiate him instead of having surgery and chemotherapy for his brain cancer. The boy died. Carlos needs a good lawyer and I thought of you. Let's touch base soon."

Had I said too much? Too little? Sounded casual? Did my voice soar into falsetto? My pulse had leapt to fight-or-flight levels during the call, an adrenaline rush triggered by our complicated history. Do not imagine I am talking about sex, or not only about sex, not in the usual tawdry way. Between us fell the devil's ambiguous shadow. Love. And Lance.

Terry was the only lawyer I knew well enough to call.

I deep-breathed my way back to here and now, climbed to my crowded nest and lay down on my pallet at the foot of the bed, feeling not unlike the faithful family dog. Curled away from my visitors, I put my pillow over ears and set sail on a raft of irrational dreams in which I invited assorted of my religious elders to arm wrestle instead of throwing myself at their feet.

When I woke up the next morning, Rosario was alone in my bed. "Dónde va Señor Carlos?" I asked in my rusty high school Spanish.

"No sé," Rosario said.

EIGHT

"No sé," Rosario said.

I wanted to shake her, sad eyes and all, not just for invading my physical space, not just for hijacking my time, though both of those things were mightily annoying. The fact is, I'm pretty sure she knew exactly where her husband was. Somehow Carlos had known where to find us the night before. All of which pointed to the L word. Lies. If you want me to rescue you, don't play me for a fool. If you want me for a friend, respect my solitude. Ever since I was little, I've needed big stretches of time alone, not just to dress up. I am not a morning person.

"No sé," said Rosario and my heart sank. My heart sank and my mind raced, toying with the problem: How can I get her out of here? How can I just say no?

"So, Rosario," I said, "when are you meeting up with Carlos?"

"No sé." She looked at me like I was playing poker with only forty cards.

"You texted him last night," I said. "You had to."

"I should go back to the apartment," Rosario said. "Do you know when the bus leaves?"

I felt reproached. I'm better at bitchy than tough, and besides, my mother taught me that women must be treated well. "Tell you what. I'm going to make us breakfast, and then I'll drive you back to Oakland."

"Oh, no. I don't mind taking the bus."

"And I don't mind driving. I have errands to do."

"I'll give you gas money," Rosario said.

"Okay, sure. I'm going to take a shower now, and then we'll eat, all right?"

Rosario agreed.

When I emerged from my usual long shower, bergamot-scented steam curled out of the bathroom to meet the smell of garlic and ginger simmering in hot oil. The futon had turned back into a sofa, my aging iyawo bedding, grayish by now despite extensive bleaching, was properly stowed. The apartment was even tidier than I insist on keeping it. Rosario stood at the stove, manipulating the contents of the wok with a wooden spoon in one hand while she piled in raw spinach and added a splash of tamari with the other. The woman had moves. I shamed myself in the moment I spent thinking, So this is what it would be like to have a maid.

While Rosario dished up breakfast, I put iTunes on random shuffle, which that morning seemed not random at all but insightfully selected to make Archer squirm. It was bent on serving up orisha songs, lots of orisha songs, maliciously interspersed with ballads about lost love. I finally gave up skipping the hard songs and surrendered to sonically induced melancholia, that feeling that your heart's too big for your body. Rosario kept her eyes down and ate quietly.

"I'll do the dishes later, when I get home," I told Rosario. "Let's just get out of here."

⚊

East Oakland. Taxi drivers won't go there. I mean it, just try to call a cab. It's the land of drug deals and gang shootings, sideshows, high-school-age hookers on East 14th Street, teenage twats barely covered by the tiniest of skirts, simmering tensions between blacks and Latinos that boil over when the weather warms up come spring, bodies fallen on the street and left there too long, the Asian incursion, Chinese family consortia buying up bank repo'ed houses, trapping fat ghetto pigeons and putting them in the chow mein, round-the-block lines at the food banks, two store-front off-brand churches in every block, both sides of the street, and a funeral parlor every other, lineages of feral cats in every neighborhood, the generations identical except for size—one Siamese, two grays, a black, a calico, ubiquitous taquerías, air full of the reek of fried chicken grease, subtly different according to the weather, barbershops where you can spend half a day getting a fade and shooting the shit, a lot fewer nail salons than there used to be two years ago and guess what, it takes three or four nervous white cops, Oakland's finest, to push one skinny black kid in saggy pants to his knees on the street. Hands on your head. Shut your mouth. Ice cream trucks that play "Turkey in the Straw" over and over at a maniacal clip and short guys that look like Aztec gods pulling popsicle wagons up the street, bells tinkling, last decade's lumpy sofa, grandma's stained mattress tossed to the curb months before it's your turn for the Bulky Pickup, what you didn't sell at the yard sale left by the railroad tracks, spilling out of black plastic garbage bags, packs of wild dogs that used to be guard dogs until the price of dog food got so high and the cash got so damn short—all true, but only half the story, which is also about the quiet family blocks, the neat yards with their stiff shrubs and old rose bushes, the etiquette of greeting the folks rooting through your garbage before the city truck comes by, roving bands of Jehovah's Witnesses going door to door in their Sunday clothes all days of the week and never getting shot or mugged, a cacophony of Sunday morning church bells, neighbors chatting by their gates, folks taking refuge inside parked cars for a smoke or a phone call, a moment's privacy, grandkids coming back from the suburbs to visit, cousins coming up from the South to do the same. Hip-hop car bass so basso you feel it instead of hearing it, accordion lilt of Mexican lieder, how kid shrieks escape inflatable party jumpers, the shopping-cart people who live under the freeway, more than one cart being a sign of wealth but also a pain in the ass, the responsibility of having something worth defending, street-corner convocations, barbecue in the parking lot and Raider's black stuff everywhere, the vast sad flea market, the beautiful reclaimed wetlands, forty-two species of shorebird and that many folks who exercise there every day, coming back from calamity—diabetes, stroke, obesity, heart disease or simple lack of romance. The crack grandma who drops her pants on the corner and moons the traffic, hoping against hope somebody will find her skinny ass worth paying enough for she can get high one more time. East Oakland. The heart of our religious community.

Rosario and Carlos lived there, having moved from a slightly tonier neighborhood slightly to the west of mid-East Oakland when the baby came along. Their new apartment, on Wentworth, was bigger, cheaper and closer to Michaela's, at least until she moved uphill. Cynics suggested she'd exhausted the income potential of the 'hood, while the loyal accepted her explanation—that Aganju instructed her to move to higher ground. The Mendozas stayed put. Wentworth was one of those East Oakland surprises, platted on the diagonal for a better view of the sunsets and the hills, a short wide street of mowed lawns and decently kept houses, considering the recession, a street that could have been in Portland or Seattle or Cleveland. Carlos and Rosario moved into the mother-in-law unit of what was a single-family home until the mother-in-law passed on. I remembered helping them clean the house one Saturday before they moved in, smoking it with incense, praying and singing, ringing Obatala's agogo loudly in every room to encourage the mother-in-law and any other lingering spirits to vacate the premises. Me, I tried moving to the East Bay more than once, but it never took for long. San Francisco is my town. Still, their place was cute, cozy, if your taste runs toward velvet paintings and paper flowers. They always put up beautiful thrones on their ocha birthdays and served arroz con pollo to their guests.

Three black and whites were already at the curb when Rosario I pulled up.

"Ay, dios," Rosario said.

"Stay or go?" I asked her.

Rosario sat taller in her seat and surveyed the situation. The door to her apartment stood open. Half-dressed neighbors milled on their porches, watching. I put my window down a couple inches and heard the crackle of the radio dispatcher.

"Stay," she said.

We parked and went inside.

NINE

I saw the uniforms first, which is, I suppose, the point of uniforms. They're meant to override the individual. Three—count 'em—three cops, three nightsticks, three badges, three sets of handcuffs, three holsters, three guns. Three of Oakland's uniformed finest, various in size and shape, all white, were inside Rosario's apartment when we got there, along with one older black man in a rumpled suit. When we appeared in the doorway, all three of those guns came out of their holsters and pointed at us. It was a good-sized one-bedroom apartment, roomier than most, but it could hardly contain the adrenaline. Reflexively, Rosario and I both raised our hands, not over our heads but just high enough to protect our faces.

"This is Rosario Mendoza. She lives here." Friendly, helpful, factual. I tried hard to make sure neither my voice nor my words were loaded. We watched the cops absorb the information.

"Where is Carlos Mendoza?" It was the suit who talked, the one with silver at his temples and brown shoes on his feet. Besides me, the only black man in the room. He introduced himself as Jerry Dixon, detective.

I shook my head.

"No sé," Rosario said.

"When did you last see him?" the cop asked.

"Yesterday," Rosario said. "I saw him at the hospital." As truth goes, it was adequate but not exhaustive. Fortunately, they didn't ask me. They did want to know my name, why I was there.

"Archer Barron. I'm Rosario and Carlos's god brother." I gave them the quick version of responding to Rosario's call, posting bail, taking Rosario to my place for the night. One of the cops recorded my answers in his pocket notebook. When he finished writing, I said, "I'm pretty sure it's not legal for you guys to be here. Unless you have a warrant, of course."

"The door was open when we got here," Dixon said.

"That's what Goldilocks said." Their looks of total incomprehension suggested none of them read aloud to kids or grandkids. "When she let herself into the house of the three bears."

"I know this neighborhood," Dixon said. "My grandma's cousin lived in the next block. Nobody locks their doors."

Of the four, he looked like he might actually live in Oakland, not some redneck suburb.

"The Mendozas do lock theirs. Which should protect them from police invasions." The tallest of the cops took a few menacing steps in my direction. I couldn't tell you if my fallback footwork owed more to Mohammed Ali or Bob Fosse but it was fast and saucy.

Dixon said, "Look, son, this is a homicide investigation."

Rosario slapped her collarbone and gave a little my-world-is-shattering shriek. "Ay, dios. My Carlos."

"I heard there was bad blood between your Carlos and Michael Ann Krawczuk."

"Who?" Rosario and I said it at exactly the same time.

"Can we back this up a little?" I said. "Who's dead?"

"I just told you. Michael Ann Krawczuk."

Another shriek from Rosario, this one expressing joy. "Not Carlos. Thank god. Maferefun Obatala."

Dixon looked suspicious.

"It's another name for God," I told him. And to Rosario, "I think he means Madrina Michaela."

Her cry this time was in a lower register, more like a moan.

To the cops, "Tall, butch woman, mid-forties, lives in the hills?"

"Uses the alias Michaela de Estrella," Dixon said. "That's her."

The news hit me with the force of a sock 'em ball in second-grade gym class, hard enough to take my breath away, hard enough to make me sit down and hope I wouldn't cry. "When?" I said.

"How?" Rosario asked.

"You tell me."

I patted the sofa beside me. Rosario came and sat. She looked as dazed as I felt. I opened my mouth to say something but no words came out. Whatever work I was engaged in, whatever doubt I entertained, whatever self definition I pursued required Michaela's presence in the world. I needed to push against her. She was my perfect adversary. She was my godmother. We were sandbagged, Rosario and me. The cops watched us closely. After what he must have perceived to be a decent interval, Dixon said, "We heard the Mendozas had some issues with Miz Krawczuk."

"We didn't even know her real name," Rosario said with a kind of dumb wonder. I heard the subtext, if the officers did not: So huge a force in our lives, so much we did not know. Madrina Michaela was Polish?

"Would you say that's right, that he had issues?" Dixon asked. I didn't know if he was talking to Rosario or to me because my attention was diverted when my eyes landed on a photograph of Rosario on the shelf just across from where we sat. Extravagantly framed, it was one of those glamour portraits Latina women get taken to commemorate major life milestones—turning fifteen, getting married, being pregnant, even getting ready to pass on. Before the pictures, there's the professional makeup job, the hair stylist, picking out just the right satin gown or the fur stole. Gentle lighting, soft focus. In the photo on the shelf, next to the philodendron, Rosario's chin was slightly lifted, her movie-star eyes looked up and slightly to her right, her slightly parted lips glistened wetly. Jewels dripped into her cleavage and cascaded from her earlobes. Her hair was swept up into a fantastic dark crown. She was grade-A-certified amazing.

The Rosario next to me was small and monochrome. Loss and worry had written on her skin and her loosely braided hair was lusterless, a little frizzy. Just about everything in her life that could go wrong had, but still, she had that picture, a monument to the presence and possibility of beauty to stand against whatever further insults time had up its sleeve. It was bold and transformational, a triumph of artifice over inconvenient reality. I loved Rosario for making herself so gorgeous.

The Rosario next to me on the sofa poked me gently. "The policeman asked you when you last saw Madrina Michaela."

I remembered the event but not the date, a bembe for Ochun. "It's been a while," I said. "Maybe a year. Maybe closer to two."

Dutifully, the writer recorded my response. Dixon turned to Rosario. "And you?"

Rosario looked up, into the corner where the walls and ceiling met. "At the cemetery. When we buried my son." She was silent for a second. Then, "That was the last time."

To a man, the four officers shifted their weight from one foot to the other and looked uncomfortable. After a pause, Dixon said, "Can you tell me when was that?"

"Of course," Rosario said. "It was the twelfth of October."

I was still in my time lapse, viewing clips from that last bembe. What I see is Madrina Michaela on her sofa, guarding the front door, holding court. She fully occupies the sofa. No one would dare to sit beside her. I stand before her in a liminal state, half Archer, halfway to being possessed by Yemaya. The room rocks gently with my mother's presence. An Ochun whose authenticity I have always questioned grips my upper arm and in rapid Spanish catalogs my transgressions, which have to do with my allowing Yemaya to ride me when this has been forbidden. If I were fully Archer, I would argue that it was not my doing, not mine to control whether Yemaya wanted to climb on board, that I was innocent of disobedience. Yemaya, half present, is not amused by the treatment she is receiving. Ochun urges Michaela to punish Archer with a multa, a fine. And Yemaya turns on her, rises up tall as a tidal wave, spits out a fistful of words whose meaning Archer does not understand. Michaela does. Evidently, I have just uttered the Lucumi equivalent of "go fuck yourself." Whether she understands the words or only the tone of Yemaya's voice, my Ochun god sister takes umbrage. Lunges at me, raking acrylic nails down my arm. Archer/Yemaya slaps her, just hard enough to make the point.

"How would you describe your relations with Michael Ann Krawczuk after October twelve?"

"I was very angry," Rosario said.

"If you can't control yourself, Archer, I'll have to forbid you to dance," Madrina Michaela says. "We've talked about this before."

It's a sore point. In Michaela's house, most everyone aspires to be a horse, someone who is possessed by the orisha whose crown they wear, but Michaela reserves the right to refuse trance possession to anyone she chooses. The criteria for her judgments are unspoken and remain unclear. We assume the person in question is not "spiritual enough," is not "ready." We are encouraged to understand things this way. But when Yemaya comes, she whispers in the very center of my brain that Michaela will not allow the presence of a horse unbroken to her will. This has been whispered among the god children: To be allowed to come fully, to be given the right to speak, an ocha must be Michaela's creature, speaking her truth, furthering the business of her house.

"And your husband Carlos, was he very angry, too?"

"Yes."

"Can you tell me why he was angry?"

Yemaya is pissed off, on her own behalf and on behalf of her son, Archer.

She grabs Archer's leather jacket from a nearby chair. I'm going in and out—me, not-me—in such rapid alternation it makes me feel seasick.

"If you leave now, Archer," Madrina Michaela says, "you're going to regret it."

"Do you dare to threaten me?" The voice that came out of my mouth was not my own. It was the sea speaking. My mother. Her voice is contralto, resonant, much bigger than mine.

"Carlos blamed Madrina Michaela for Piri being dead," Rosario said.

Archer plunged through the front door of Michaela's house, slammed it behind him, stood in Michaela's front yard and looked up at the January constellations. I remember Cassiopeia, Orion in the sky. It was cold enough that I could see my breath.

"Motive," one of the four officers said.

The word interrupted my reverie, being both sinister and meaningless. More and more, it seems to me that all crime is meaningless, especially in small bleak cities like Oakland. Got gun. Shoot gun. Don't piss me off. Don't mess with my woman. Don't short me. Don't disrespect me. Motive. Compared to the usual suspects, Carlos and Rosario's motives were complex and nuanced.

"How did Madrina Michaela die? You didn't tell us what happened," I said.

Dixon smirked magnificently. "I'm not going to, either."

"Does that mean you don't know?"

Dixon shrugged. "We'll release that information when we're ready."

When I stood up, the three white cops tensed up. *Not just black. Tall and black.* I could see Rosario's and Carlos's soperas around the room and feel the energy they emitted.

"So, do you guys have everything you need? Because I think you're trespassing on Mrs. Mendoza's hospitality if not actually violating her civil rights." I was practically purring, my voice was so level and warm.

"Mrs. Mendoza is a person of interest in this case," Dixon said. "So are you." He looked me up and down in a way that was both speculative and less than friendly. "Is Archer Barron your real name?"

I took a step toward him, reached out my hand and stroked his cheek with my forefinger. "Every bit as real as yours is, honey," I said in Darla's voice. There are threats and threats. That one took.

"Let's get out of here, boys," Dixon said. "Barron, Mrs. Mendoza, don't leave the area." The cops moved as one eight-legged animal. I followed them. Once they were outside, I struck a pose in the doorframe. "Bye bye, boys," I said and gave a little wave, to send them on their way.

TEN

Life's a performance. Every time I go out the door, I'm on. I'm making it up. All I've got to go on is a set of premises, some backstory and a feedback loop. The world's a mirror and I see everything in it, not just me but how the world sees me and how I would see myself if I were the world. It's an orderly kind of splintered vision, each reflection on a separate plane, and all the planes set up just so in order that every one reflects every other one. Put that in real time and it's absolutely exhausting.

Archer is the hardest character. He's the one that's on most often but it is freaking hard to know how that still-sort-of-attractive almost-middle-aged look-at-those-flat-abs light-skinned black man is supposed to behave. More and more, I let anybody else who's around bleed through, so just when a cop thinks he knows who he's talking to, Darla will take over, or Elizabeth or some other femme demon I don't even have a name and a wardrobe for. Then we're off to the races and hold on tight. It's not that I improvise so much, more like, I am improvisation. Or put it another way—identity's a keyboard and every encounter is a tune I play. "Late Morning at Rosario's" was sad and complicated jazz. By the time I got back to Santa Cruz, I was wiped out.

It had been months since I'd taken a white bath, but it was the only thing I could think of that would clean me up enough to make it through the night. I said my mojuba—a special prayer—over a jug of cool water to sanctify it, then added powdered eggshell and Florida Water, an old fashioned spice and citrus cologne, cheap and ubiquitous enough that almost everybody can afford it when they need a spiritual pick me up.

The smell is one that every Santero and Santera holds up against bad luck and evil spirits, that washes them away. If I'd had any around, I would have added white flower petals, goats' milk and a little honey, but in the process of losing my religion, I'd let my supplies run short. After my shower, I took a deep breath and poured the white bath over my body. It felt like a cold breeze, like liquid light, and I shivered inside it and felt cleansed. Old habit or real magic? If something works, I'm not convinced it matters why. I smelled fresh and felt better.

I tucked my MacBook in my backpack when I went to work. In the middle of the night when the campus is quiet, my browser's the window I sneak out of. Once every five minutes I scan the monitors. That takes about thirty seconds, leaving four and half minutes, plus or minus, when I can pursue my own enthusiasms. Since I use my own computer, the university has no record where I've been when I slip away, whether my adventures are intellectual or social or carnal. In the course of a full shift, I usually get around to all three.

The campus was quiet, the only figures in motion had student baggage and student moves, hustle home or lost in thought. The Student Handbook says don't wear earphones if you're out alone at night but no one reads it. Everybody out there has a voice in his ear, somebody else's music playing inside his head. If I'm really bored sometimes I try to guess what people are listening to by the rhythms that show in their walk. It would be easy to mug most of these kids but nobody does.

News of the day. I read *Huffington Post*, the *Guardian*, the *NY Times*. Let me start again. I scanned, them and the blogs I subscribe to. I was shocked to learn the recession had not ended since yesterday, all the world's wars were still going on, Tiger Woods had more mistresses than fingers and toes, the disappointed nation was turning on him and the black man it had elected president. Things were still fucked up. My favorite porn sites still had the power to arouse me, at least a little.

Monitors. The last of the janitors called it a night. With all the layoffs, it takes twice the time to get the university half as clean. Facebook. Snarly snippets from my favorite queens. YouTube links. Angelina Divine poked me. I poked her back. It used to be I had as many Santería friends as gay ones but not anymore. When I started acting up, Madrina Michaela and all her obedient godchildren unfriended me. My heart fluttered a little when Robbie popped up in the chat window. Of course I'd like to get together for a drink sometime soon. Make mine carrot juice. We haven't had the HIV conversation yet but I think it might be coming soon. Physiologically speaking, anticipation of real action trumps pornography.

Monitors. Damn it's dark out there. I think it started to rain.

My heart sank when I pictured my godmother dead and buried in the cold wet earth.

There it was, the lurking elephant come inside, the thing I had all day long deliberately not thought about, not felt. It was so big in a small room it hardly left me any oxygen to breathe. When my Grandma Barron died, I was sure I'd killed her by shoplifting at the corner store. Clearly my father died because I was a gay pagan. Lance died because I loved him. (Yep, Archer and Lance, but that's another story.) Guilt was my fellow traveller and always had been, a life sentence and a soulmate all in one, my dark familiar. If Michaela was dead, then I had killed her. My doubt was the knife at her throat. My anger was the poison, my bitchy behind-the-back smack talk the bludgeon that cracked her skull. I drowned her in the bathtub, I hanged her from the rafters, I shot her in cold blood and beat her with my fists until she died. I choked her with my beautiful, long strong fingers, I burned the house down, I was lightning and I struck, all I had to do was wish it and she died.

I had no idea how Madrina Michaela met her end, the policeman wouldn't say, but I knew it was my fault. I've known I was guilty since I knew was gay, a very long time. Eve ate the apple, but I wanted Adam.

Monitors. I expected peaceful screens and found them, except for the last one in the third row. I don't know how he found the security camera by the bookstore, but Carlos Mendoza had planted himself in front of it, close enough that his face on the screen was bigger than mine in real life. I had the unsettling feeling that he could see me as clearly as I saw him. It was stupid to get himself photographed on the surveillance tapes, that was my first thought, before I realized that showing up was probably less risky than calling my cell.

In the logbook I noted that I was going over to the Merrill dorm with the master key and headed off in the opposite direction to meet my god brother.

The last thing I wanted was to be involved but somehow, clearly, I was.

ELEVEN

The UCSC bookstore is strictly American primitive, rough hewn and hidden in the trees. When the campus was laid out in the late sixties, it was designed to defuse dissent. There is no quad, no square, no student union, no one rallying place where a dissident population—or even a frivolous one—can come together in numbers large enough to cause trouble. What seems bucolic now was counter revolutionary back in the day. The bookstore is no great center of commerce, but since everybody needs to buy books, it merits signage and because it's the place the electronics live, the iPhones and the iPods, the MacBooks and the Dells, the Canons and the Nikons, it's worth a security camera of its own. Carlos was tucked up under the eaves, out of the rain, when I got there.

I came on foot, in spite of the weather. Whenever I have a chance to go outside during a work night, I feel like I'm getting away with something, even if I get wet. Our Lucumi greeting melted into a long hug. With my arms around Carlos, I could feel how small he was, how wilted by his misfortunes. Otherwise, I doubt he would have hugged me at all.

"What's up, my man?" I asked him. "Have you talked to Rosario?"

Raindrops shone like diamond dust on his thick black hair, a fairy hairnet above his scarred face. Carlos shook his head. "I saw on TV they're looking for me."

"I missed that."

"The police think I killed Madrina."

"They think you had a motive."

"In my dreams I killed her. Not in real life."

50

"I understand. Me, too."

"I don't know what to do," Carlos said.

"You need a lawyer, man."

"I don't know any lawyers except Virginia and she does taxes."

"There's a guy I went to law school with. I haven't talked to him in four, five years but he became a lawyer for the right reasons, you know? I left a call for him last night. I think he might be willing to help you."

"I don't have much money," Carlos said.

"I don't think Terry cares that much about money."

"I could take care of his lawn," Carlos said. "I could paint his house. Rosario is good with kids." He said it, heard his own words and almost lost it. "I'm a good worker," Carlos said.

"I know. I'll call Terry again tomorrow. You better stay out of sight until we know what he says."

"How?" Carlos said.

It was a good question. If he went home, the cops would be sure to know. If he came to my place, maybe. Turning himself in before he had a lawyer on his side seemed stupid in the extreme. Then I had an inspiration. The clinic. Nobody would look for him there. We parked his truck behind the bookstore and walked back to the Administration building. I signed back in, checked the monitors, then took my three-AM lunch hour. It's only a half hour, really, but it was long enough to run him downtown and let him in, find the threadbare blankets Doc Sam uses to keep her patients warm from the waist down, and show him where the toilet was.

"You can sleep on one of the examining tables. It's not fancy but you should be safe here."

Gratitude, relief, distaste for queers. Warring emotions distorted Carlos's face and the spectacle of it slammed up against something hard inside me, reminding me how tired I am of trying to make the world safe for heterosexuals. The me that is ever so angry, ever so tired of making nice yelled, *Fuck it,* tossed down a mime grenade of rage. *Why are you my problem, little man?* Welcome to the caustic renegade self, the queen without patience for the breeders, the preachers, the makers of false promises, the swinish healthy and their cautious little lives.

I took a deep breath, the way I always do. On the exhalation, gently closed the door to the examination room and Carlos's ambivalent thanks, called out to Yemaya-who-lives-in-my-head for a dose of cooling down and seconds later felt the tension in my body wash away, her usual answer. The backwash of anger is compassion, a few moments' sloppy wading in the shoes of the other, whether I want to or not. I was alone in the clinic waiting room, scarred chairs half revealed by the streetlight through grimy window glass and suddenly not-alone, either, since the room still held the emotional residue of the passions and desires that drove people to behave in ways that brought them here, needing diagnoses, medicine, protection, advice, forgiveness, a change of fate, an irresistible tsunami of lust, lust so powerful it washes away all niceties of gender and taboo and leaves us bobbing in the common human soup.

I let myself out. Returned to work. I left a message on Doc Sam's cell phone so she wouldn't be surprised when she found Carlos the next morning.

The rest of the night was uneventful.

"Archer Barron, oh my god."

Real enthusiasm, no detectable hard feelings. Hearing Terry's voice relieved my apprehension. "It's been a while," I said.

"April twenty-third, two thousand five," Terry said.

"Damn."

"I have an embarrassingly good memory for dates," Terry said.

"Is this a good time to talk?"

"I'm eating a corn-beef sandwich at my desk." Okay, I thought I could hear him chewing. "You taken the bar exam yet?" he asked.

"I haven't, " I said. Then, "I've been thinking about it, though."

"Good."

"Yeah, maybe." I spent a few seconds trying to convince myself to be mysterious, abstemious of gossip, before I said, "I'm reconsidering my spiritual direction."

"High time," Terry said.

"So, are you still a public defender?"

"I'm off the government payroll. Still a defense attorney. I got your message, by the way. Sounds like your friend is in deep shit."

"God brother," I corrected. "And the shit's much deeper now. Madrina Michaela is dead."

"Wow," Terry said. "Tell me everything."

In the telling, some of my law-school skills stood up, dusted themselves off, got to work. I gave Terry what I thought was a pretty succinct account of the facts and the issues in play, and he rewarded me with a "nicely done." Then he asked me, "Did he do it?"

Funny, but I'd never seriously considered the possibility that Carlos was guilty. I took off my god-brother-right-or-wrong glasses and had another look at the facts. "Damned if I know."

"I got a monster off a couple of years back. It left a bad taste in my mouth," Terry said. "I'd rather not go there again."

"I understand. On the other hand, if Carlos did it, you could make a hell of a case for justifiable homicide."

"Just like the government sells us righteous wars."

Right. Terry was beyond liberal, practically a red diaper baby. It was all starting to come back. I found myself feeling two things at once, slightly uncomfortable, slightly aroused. "I was just saying."

"I was just teasing. When and where can I meet with the client?"

I explained that I was living in Santa Cruz. Terry professed to like Santa Cruz. No, no, the drive didn't bother him, and better to keep Carlos out of sight until we had a plan. Finally, we agreed to meet on the Boardwalk, at the Arcade, by the skeeball machines. I was supposed to work that night, but if we weren't done in time, I could always call in sick.

"Eight o'clock," Terry said. "I'll see you then."

"Till then," I said and disconnected.

TWELVE

By the time I finished the last question on the Criminal Procedure final, I thought I was going to wet my pants. I just made it to the men's room, unzipped and let fly—a piss so urgent it felt orgasmic. Did I make some noise of animal contentment? Maybe so. Anyhow, once things slowed down a little and my consciousness climbed out of my urethra, I noticed Cute Boy was right beside me, hosing down the neighboring urinal. And, ever so casually, did I let my eyes rove in the direction of his equipment? Of course, though I didn't see much because quite unexpectedly, Cute Boy talked to me for the first time all year.

"Going to the dance tonight?" he asked.

It was June, Pride time, and we'd just finished our last final of our second semester of law school. We'd identified each other as fellow queers by the second day of class, at least I'd nailed him, but all year we'd behaved like a pair of those magnetized Scottie dogs, whose opposite charges always make them spin away from each other. He was smart, came to class prepared, stood up well under professorial interrogation and made no effort I could discern to appear an eyelash more butch than he was. That is to say, not at all. Next to Cute Boy, I was Clint Eastwood, Denzel Washington, John Fucking Wayne.

In my undergraduate days, I lived for Friday night at Pride, that rainbow meet-and-greet extravaganza in the queerest city on earth. Anybody who could go and not get hooked up was autistic, a recluse, a castrato, a piece of driftwood slowly drying on the beach of life. Now that I was older, now that I was in law school and the alumnus of several almost satisfactory amorous relationships, I found myself moving into the camp that saw the annual Pride festivities as, well, kind of jejune, which was one of my favorite words that year.

I zipped my fly. "Oh, right. It's tonight, isn't it?"

By this time, we'd moved on to the row of sinks to wash our hands. Our eyes met in the mirrors. Damn, I didn't call him Cute Boy for nothing, that alabaster skin, the blue eyes, the wing of soft blond hair that tumbled into his eyes, his scruff of beard a different color, tinged with red. Standing this close, I realized he was bigger than I'd imagined from seeing him across lecture halls and at the end of long corridors, not that much shorter than I am, though slighter. He had beautiful hands. After he dried them on a paper towel, he held one out to me. I pumped it, collegially.

"I'm Terry Gleason," Cute Boy said.

"I know. I'm Archer Barron."

"I know," he said. "I'm glad I finally got up enough nerve to introduce myself."

"Damn, girl," I said. "I was afraid to talk to you."

Laughter broke our year-long shyness. It also opened his mouth up far enough that I could see his teeth for the first time, very white but charmingly crooked.

"So, what time are you going?" I asked him.

Cute Boy sniffed his armpit, cutely. "I stink," he said. "Nerves." And then, "I need to go home and change and meet up with my friend." It was back in the day people still wore watches. He looked at his. "Not before seven, seven thirty. How about you? You want to meet us there?"

Until that moment, Archer wasn't planning to go downtown. If anybody was going, Darla was. She was brand new then, still finding her shape, her tics, her voice and her backstory. Backstory is important, even if you never share it with another soul. She'd had a solitary small-town childhood, a cloistered puberty. A strict and overprotective father kept her away from suitors and predators, made her wear androgynous clothes, jeans, sweatshirts and sneakers that kept her burgeoning sexuality of sight. Darla never went out on a date until she was eighteen years old, and that was movie and Cokes only with a curfew worthy of Cinderella, midnight being the hour of dangerous, deal-breaking transformations. At eighteen, Darla was modest and pious, obedient to the wishes of the patriarch. At nineteen, so my fairy tale went, she met Archer and went wild.

Young Darla was not a caricature, not a clown but an exquisite creature, all the feminine in me exalted, exaggerated, enshrined. She reserved the right to age her own way, to grow thick and coarse and comic over time, but in her debutante season, she really meant to be Cinderella, the mysterious beauty who turns up at the ball, then disappears, leaving tongues wagging, hearts aching.

Why didn't Darla go to the street dance that night? For one thing, Archer was flattered and intrigued by Cute Boy's invitation. Law school had crippled if not completely killed my social life. I was studying my butt off. After the thirty-seventh time I said no, my old friends stopped inviting me to go places and do things with them. Can we say lonely? That was only part of it, though. By the time I finished all my finals, I had huge gray bags under my eyes, lots of small zits on my forehead and a big one on my chin. I'd eaten so much shit food it felt like I was packing an extra five or six pounds around my waist. Then there was the matter of facial and body hair. I had too much of it, everywhere. To transform that greasy bristly exhausted student man into a credible contestant for Miss California would have taken all night if not all weekend.

Let me note here what I admired and envied about Cute Boy then, Terry later—his personal style, a way of being girlishly boyishly fey every moment, the degree on a sliding scale, appropriate to the occasion, so he was never inauthentic and never disguised, just variably fragile and swishy. It made me absolutely trust his integrity, much more, I might add, than my own.

We agreed on a venue and a time to meet—a Mediterranean place in the Mission we both knew and liked at eight PM, far enough away from the action that we could talk and get something in our bellies before we joined the celebration in progress and our own wild rumpus began. That gave me enough time for a long bath with slices of cucumber on my closed eyes, for some wardrobe trial and error, some ironing, some attention to my hair and nails, which had been sorely neglected in the run-up to finals. I had a glass of white wine while grooming, chose my look and my cologne with care. By the time I headed for BART that night, I was stylish but understated, just slightly to the masculine side of the gender tao, and I felt detached, a little superior in a car full of giggling gay boys from the exurbs in their short shorts and hot-pink boas, their rainbow Afro wigs and wash-off tattoos.

Cute Boy and his date were already at the café when I got there, perched on stools and drinking beer, and I will always remember a sublimely fractured instant when I saw my own reflection both in the mirrored wall behind them and in their eyes. Hello, there, Archer, looking good.

Cute Boy put his arm lightly around my shoulders and drew me into their space. "It wasn't easy but we saved you a stool. We already ordered. You better catch up." He nodded toward the pretty Filipino by his side. "Lance, this is Archer Barron, the only other queer boy in my class. Archer Barron, meet my friend Lance."

THIRTEEN

When his ball jumped the track for the third time running without logging him a single point, Carlos grabbed the next ball and lobbed it straight at the scoreboard. The hard plastic cover cracked and the inner lights went out. I expected sirens but none came. I'd picked the skeeball machines as a meeting place because I love skeeball. Carlos hated it. As it turns out, short arms and legs are a serious skeeball handicap.

"Fuck." The quintessential syllable.

I put my hand on his shoulder and steered him gently away from the skeeball area to the nearest bank of pinball machines, where we could keep an eye out for Terry without being fingered as vandals. It was a tense fifteen minutes or so, Carlos silent, me queasy with nerves about seeing Terry again.

"You want to play pinball?"

"No."

"You want a beer? How about some popcorn?"

"No."

"Hey, look they've got those driving games, where you…"

"No," Carlos said.

He was like a black hole, wanting nothing that hadn't already been taken away from him. I left him alone and concentrated on my own malaise. Eventually, Terry showed up. Five years older, his face leaner, hair shorter and darker blond. Not so much cute anymore as…I searched for the right word without finding it. Hardened, maybe, the way steel gets, a kind of refinement. As they get older, a lot of men look softer, round where they used to be flat, but Terry was pointier somehow, with sharper edges. He looked tired. I studied him for a minute before I stepped forward. Pain, shock, pleasure and so on into a deeply brotherly embrace. I felt his boniness and knew I'd missed him. Carlos, being no fool, could sense some history between us. Our camaraderie intensified his gloom, at least until Terry gave him his full attention, which, it seemed, still had some of the beneficent properties of sunlight. Carlos straightened and brightened inside it.

"How about we find someplace quieter to talk?" Terry suggested. "I could use something to eat." We left the arcade for a battered tavern along the palisade. Terry ordered a hamburger and fries, I managed not to comment on his nutritional sins, and Carlos dove into a Corona.

"Correct me if I'm missing something," Terry said, "but you've been charged with negligent homicide in the death of your son. You haven't yet been charged with any other crime."

"They might be mad that I left the hospital." Carlos shrugged. "When I left I didn't know I made bail."

"We can deal with that," Terry said. "What I'm really concerned about is the twenty-four hours between when you left Archer's apartment in Santa Cruz and when you turned up at the bookstore. Where were you?"

Carlos stared at Terry for a long time, long enough to make me remember the word in Michaela's house that Carlos had some serious powers, that his spirits were strong. Evidently they told him to come clean with Terry.

"I needed to think," Carlos said. "That's why I left. It was maybe four in the morning. I drove back to Berkeley and stood on the corner down at 4th Street, by the lumberyard, hoping I could get some day work. They only picked up a few guys, though, not me. I got a cup of coffee and a donut and I went to the cemetery. I sat by Piri's grave for a long time. I talked to him." He paused, looked at Terry. "The dead, after they die, they're wise. It doesn't matter if they were only children when they were alive."

"I understand," Terry said.

"I think I fell asleep for a while. It was a pretty nice day. I hadn't slept for a long time."

Terry nodded. "And after that?"

"After that I went to Madrina Michaela's house."

We stared at him.

"Piri told me I had to talk to her," Carlos said. "He said I needed to tell her everything I felt, so it wouldn't eat me up inside."

When did Terry learn to keep a poker face? When I knew him, he was the most transparent of men, his expression and his body language a magic lantern show, every thought and emotion projected for the world to see. "And did you talk to her?"

Carlos shook his head. "Her truck was there but she didn't answer the door."

"Do you know what time that was?" Terry asked. His voice was beautifully neutral.

At first Carlos said no. Then he pulled out his cell phone. "I called her before I left the cemetery. It probably took me half an hour, forty minutes to get to her house."

"Did you talk to her?"

"I left a message."

"Okay," Terry said. "That's okay. You wouldn't have done that if you were planning to do her harm."

"Piri said if I could tell her how I feel I could stop hating her. I was going to hurt her with words." Carlos opened his call log. "It was nine thirty-three when I called Madrina," he said.

Terry looked at me. "Do we know time of death?"

I reviewed our encounter with the cops. "I don't think so. Only that the police told us she was dead around one."

It was the first time I'd said it out loud, that my madrina was dead, and it left me feeling hollow, bereft. Across the table, Carlos's face had darkened, gone into a mourning that mirrored mine.

Knowing what you know, does that sound crazy?

Before I take another breath, I must say this. No one comes to Santería who has not thought he was crazy because he routinely experiences improbable things. We are the people who see things that other people don't, hear things when no human voice has spoken, know things before they are knowable, who speak to clouds or rivers or trees and are heard, our granted wishes the proof.

We are superstitious, yes, and the religion makes us more so, we are gullible and so are gulled, but we are something else besides, possessed of a childlike incandescent faith in a realm of spiritual connections and transactions that for a little while or a long time we inhabit in company with others who are more like us than they are like most people in this world. Even those who come in desperation, as a last resort, come because they are able to embrace the improbable.

Carlos and I shared the same sense of bereavement, however improbable it was. The pain in Terry's eyes had a different source. "I can't imagine you were the only person who wanted to hurt Michaela with words," he said.

My god brother and I laughed uneasily in near unison.

Terry rubbed his beautiful hands together. "Look, from the police point of view, Carlos is low-hanging fruit. He had motive and opportunity and he left tracks. I wouldn't want to go to court without an plausible alternative or two." We were all silent for a moment. Then Terry said, "Especially since the best way of defending the first charge sounds like an admission of guilt on the second, more serious allegation." He sighed. I was impressed with his grasp of the situation, his professional demeanor, the fact that I was wholly unable to read his thoughts until he spoke them out loud. "The first thing we have to do is make sure Carlos is safe. The second thing we have to do is prove that he didn't kill anybody."

"I am responsible for my son's death," Carlos said. "Piri forgives me. But I trusted Madrina Michaela. I made a mistake."

"That's the last time I want to hear you say that out loud, okay?" Terry said.

Carlos dropped his chin toward his chest and mumbled something about money. Not having any.

"The firm I work for lets me take three pro-bono cases every year," Terry said. "I have one left. What I don't have is money to hire an investigator. Archer?"

"Yes?"

"If you want me to work on this, you need to help me build a beautiful castle of reasonable doubts. Can you do that?"

Against my better judgment, I said yes. I said yes because any excuse I might have given for saying no made me sound like a selfish asshole.

Terry headed back to San Francisco then. I took Carlos back to the clinic for a second night in hiding. Alone in my attic at last, I told my ochas that Michaela de Estrella was dead, though I imagine they already knew.

FOURTEEN

⚡

"**L**ance does theatre."

"What kind of theatre?"

"I study part time and work part time."

"What do you do for work?"

"I act."

"He's being modest. Lance is in a play right now."

"What play?"

"*Who's Afraid of Virginia Woolf.*"

"Oooh, I love that one. I love all of Edward Albee, but that one's amazing."

"Lance is amazing."

"Let me guess, you must play Nick."

"Honey, I play Honey."

"It's an all-male production."

"Oh my god. That's brilliant."

"Lance is awesome."

"Do you do it like…is it like, drag, or do you do it straight?"

"Honey, the play is drag. Psychic drag. It's just, nobody plays it that way."

"Lance has this blonde pageboy wig, just like Sandy Dennis."

"We're pushing Mr. Albee out of the closet."

"I love it. You know, I'm working on this character…."

"I knew it!"

"Really?"

"You move like a queen."

"I do?"

"Only sometimes."

"Her name is Darla. She was going to come tonight, but then Terry invited me to hook up with you."

"Tell me about Darla."

"I don't...what I mean is, she's a work in progress."

"Would you like me to help you with your makeup?"

"Oh god. Would you really?"

"You're actually lighter than I am, but I think most of my stuff would work well on you."

"I've picked up some things...."

"MAC? I love MAC."

"Some, yeah. A lot of drugstore stuff. I get embarrassed in department stores. I always pretend I'm shopping for my sister."

"Ha ha. We're all shopping for our sister. Do you have a sister?"

"I'm an only child."

"I have three older sisters. They used to dress me up."

"Ooooh, fun. Do you make Terry up?"

"He doesn't like to wear makeup."

"I break out easily."

"He's worried about the bar."

"Oh, that. I suppose I should be too."

"Don't you dare. When do you want to get together?"

"Hey, whatever works for you...."

"How about Sunday?"

"Well, sure. Sunday works for me."

That's how it started. Over eyebrow wax, foundation stick, false eyelashes, matte powder and lots and lots of lip gloss. Lance liked the flavored ones. I never did.

Funny how I remember every word.

FIFTEEN

For whatever reason, my god brothers and sisters were suddenly ready to be in touch with me again, sending emails and text messages. Re-friending me on Facebook. A couple even left voicemail. All it took was a death in the family.

Bendición, Archer.

I don't know if you already heard but Madrina Michaela passed on Tuesday. We are collecting $$$ for her itutu & her funeral & her coffin & cemetery plot. This stuff is not cheap. We are saying prayers for her every night. If you can't come, pray at your own table for 9 nights. Also, you have to put your ochas on the floor and cover them with a sheet. Do you know if Madrina had a will? Do you know anything about her family or how to get in touch with them?

Alafia,

Ibu Toke (Ernesto)

Reading between the lines, I felt that my god kin were forced to recognize both my relative seniority in the house and my common sense. Too bad I didn't really care anymore. What I did care about was finding out what happened. The police made a small and cagey announcement of Michaela's death without elaborating on the details. The local TV news and the *Oakland Tribune* picked it up. There was a lot of back and forth on Facebook, but very few facts. I didn't post directly but added questions and comments to things other folks wrote:

Does anybody know how she died?

Who found her?

I sure hope she didn't suffer.

Will the service be open casket?
Who saw her last?
Who would do such a thing?
And my favorite, *Do you suppose it was brujería?* That's witchcraft. Black magic.

None of these pokings and proddings shook loose much information, though folks seemed more than willing to believe there was a supernatural dimension to the event.

You know how Madrina always said her enemies were working her so maybe so.
People were jealous of Madrina's success I think they wanted to see her fail.
Scary!!!!!!

I slipped right back into the digital village. Every time a friend of a friend in the ocha community posted something on a friend's page, I sent them a friend request. The number of my friends doubled in short order, and doubled again and yet again as I cast my net in wider and wider circles, until I was seeing not just the platitudes and the condolences but the rumors and the grisly jokes as they spread through concentric communities: Michaela's house, the houses of her god kids who had god kids, other people's ocha houses, ocha dancers, ocha drummers, oriates, obas, espíritistas, Babalawos, botánica owners, ocha artists, Paleros, mambos, Haitian dancers, Cubans, Brazilians, salsa dancers, witches, lesbians, diviners, herbalists, folklorists and so on, until I'd reached across the country and around the world.

Butch bitch. Carpetbagger. Culture vulture. Greedy. Mean.
Ambitious.
Homophobic.

Of course, Madrina's fans had a different list. According to them, Michaela was powerful, brilliant, studious, strict, knowledgeable and demanding. I was struck by the things no one said, the virtues that failed to appear when her attributes were enumerated: kind, generous, loyal, humble, loving, wise.

I heard they put Carlos in jail for killing Piri but he escaped—I bet he was really pissed off at Madrina.
Do they think he kill her?
Poor Rosario.
Has anybody see them?
Anybody else pissed off at madrina? I posted that myself.

Haha.

Do the police read Facebook? That was me again, pretending not to be. If I could work it, I'm sure the cops did too.

Haha.

The night was long and the campus was quiet. My eyes burned from staring at my laptop screen and my brain buzzed from eavesdropping on so many digital conversations. Is there a hormone that triggers philosophical musing? If so, loss and lack of sleep had released it in me, so that by around four AM, I was obsessed by the shortness of life, the impermanence of achievement, and, truth be told, how horny I was. A reminder to die and another to wear a condom. I knew how to say one in Latin but not the other. It didn't occur to me until I was too tired and too close to the end of my shift to pursue it that I could have spent the night chasing down Krawczuks, seeing where that took me. I resolved that after I got some sleep, after I caught up with Terry on Skype, I would take on the K's of the world.

Driving home just before dawn, an even grimmer realization: I might have moved away, I might have turned away, I might have tried to recapture my sense of self worth and intellectual integrity and take back my time, but like it or not, Madrina Michaela was still right there and using me.

Doc Sam excused me from my volunteer job at the clinic so I could do my other volunteer job. Archer Barron, private investigator, Terry's dusky-skinned Paul Drake. Early that morning, Sam had taken Carlos to her own house to keep him off the street and out of sight. Before I got on Skype video, I showered and shaved and put on a nice shirt. Even though Terry wouldn't smell me, I splashed myself with cologne. Who says computers save time?

"Damn, you're telegenic," I said when Terry appeared on my screen.

"You might want to move back from the camera and set the laptop on something higher. Right now, your nose looks as big as Idaho," Terry said.

"Thanks."

"Seriously, Archer, you do look good. I don't know how or why."

"Thanks."

"What did you find out?"

"People disliked Michaela. People are speculating about Carlos. Nothing we didn't already know. How about you?"

"I've invited the DA to sort out where Carlos stands on the bail issue. If they want him in custody, I'll tell them there are conditions. He's kept apart from the other prisoners. I'll try to get a promise to expedite the trial and, if he's convicted, get him credit for time already served. An Oregon jury just let a faith-healer father off with a wrist slap in a similar case."

"I'm betting he didn't kill goats."

Terry grinned, showing his still unstraightened teeth. "Nope. A Christer through and through."

"So, can you find out what the police know?"

"Archer, please. You're just one test short of the bar."

"No client, no charge, no right of discovery."

"Bingo."

"So we have to sacrifice a pawn."

Terry sighed. "I'm afraid so. We can set it up so he has a chance to see his wife first. How about your place?"

"It's a studio."

"They can have the apartment. We'll get a room."

Thank god the camera was trained on my face. Was he laughing at me?

"Set things up with the wife. Explain to Carlos that he's going to give himself up tomorrow. Make them understand why," Terry said.

"You're asking them to have a lot of faith in the system."

"I'm asking them to have a lot of faith in me," Terry said. "Do you still prefer white wine?"

"I don't drink anymore," I told him. "Bring chocolate instead."

SIXTEEN

I hadn't remembered about lágrimas—tears—or maybe I'd never really known. Much as Madrina Michaela encouraged us to believe we were practicing an ancient tradition, practicing it properly, the truth is we were all newbies in a new world. It takes a couple of generations for a community to move through the birth-to-death cycle a time or two, to become ritually competent in marking the big passages. Michaela had crowned her first godchild a dozen years before, the house had celebrated three weddings and two births and, counting Piri, three deaths in that time. I admired her hunger for knowledge and her acumen in digging it out and putting it to use, but really, our godmother was like the student teacher who manages to stay a chapter ahead of the class.

I remembered hearing that when a godparent passes, the ochas they birthed for you spend a whole year disabled by grief. You don't work them, you don't feed them, you just put them down on the floor like newborns and leave them alone, covered by a white sheet. I'd heard too that when the year was over, only a Babalawo could dry their tears and lift them up again, this for a hefty fee. Compared to, say, my father's Baptist passing, a Lucumi death is seriously expensive. Think every godchild of Michaela's house times fifteen hundred dollars and it's easy to see that for the Babalawo who does the ceremonies, death is a killing.

After I'd talked to Terry, after I called Rosario and went to Doc Sam's in person to let Carlos know what his new lawyer advised, after I called my boss Don at the university and told him I had a bad sore throat, I went home and sat cross-legged on the floor. My ochas were deployed around the room, their soperas the most beautiful and expensive things I owned and, truth told, I was used to living at the heart of that circle, taking comfort and strength from the balance of their energies surrounding me. Yes, I had been flirting with disbelief, trying to demote them to the status of mere things, but agnosticism and I, we had not yet consummated our relationship. Not quite. The world is full of people who are half in, half out, the lapsed Catholics and the Jack Mormons, the Baptists who dance and tipple, the secular Jews, people who observe that which is convenient, take comfort from the familiar and dismiss what's too hard to do and too hard to swallow as quaintly orthodox. Why couldn't I be one of those?

I'd heard that in Cuba, lots of people go to Mass on Sunday and to the botánica on Monday morning, a both/and proposition that made perfect sense to me. Now, just as I was edging toward equilibrium, I had to give my ochas a year's sabbatical. The forty seconds in which I considered not doing it passed heavily. Michaela had birthed them, I had to believe she'd done it to the best of her ability and whatever happened between us subsequently, she deserved that respect.

The wall under the windows was the least trafficked part of the room. I spread my biggest mat there and set my ochas one by one upon it: Elegua, keeper of the crossroads, carrier of prayers; Ogun the tireless in his three-legged iron pot; ever watchful Osun, the rooster, who warns of calamity approaching; Ochosi the hunter, most elegant of warriors; Ochun the youngest, the sexiest, all gold and honey, saver of lives and kicker of asses; Obatala, king of the white cloth, my father and the world's; Chango, dancer, king, son of my mother and his companion Oggue, the ox horns; Ibeji, the young/old twins, bringers of improbable blessings, outwitters of death, Aganju the volcano, from whom my stones were born. Heavy and beautiful, our lady of molasses, the ocean's boundless energy, its endless plenty, my mother Yemaya. That was my basic starter set, Ochosi a personal enhancement, maybe because he is a bow hunter and I am Archer. Then I moved on to the adimus, the extras—Ideu, lost brother of the twins, Olokun who lives at the bottom of the sea with his nine wives and owns its treasures. I felt their weight, my wealth in possessing them.

Two pots, two sets of rocks remained. No one had told me so, but I assumed that they should join the mourners on their mat. Ochun Ibu

Kole in her pot of gold, Oya the wind, first breath and last, who rules the cemetery and the marketplace. When a Santero dies, his ochas are given a choice: be decommissioned, the pots broken, stones surrendered to the ocean, or choose to stay among the living, designating a new caretaker. It was in that latter way these two had come into my household. Lance's Ochun, his Oya had chosen to come to live with me.

At faith's full tide, I would have carried on a kind of ritual discourse with the spirits in my pots, addressing them as if they were family and royalty both, telling them what was happening and what was in my heart. I would have spoken in a stage whisper to each in the space between *Dide* (rise up) and *Dide ma* (sit down), confident that this was my job, that they needed to hear what I had to say. That day, I couldn't. I moved them mutely, inside a great silence. When they were all arrayed on their mat on the floor, more thing-like than they had seemed for years, I shook out my biggest and cleanest white sheet, in fact, got fascinated by the soft breeze the shaking made and did it many more times than was strictly necessary for the pure joy of the wafting, then finally let it settle over them.

For a moment, everything was white, as if I too were covered by a sheet of tears. Then I grinned, realizing that with my ochas covered, it was no longer off-limits to have sex in my apartment. If Carlos and Rosario wanted to get up to some conjugal high jinks, there was nothing to hold them back.

Maybe a year off was exactly what I needed.

Later the apartment was full of living humans—me, Terry, Rosario, and Doc Sam, who brought Carlos with her, an unprecedented crowd. The Mendozas stood side by side, touching lightly along the length of their bodies, two parallel lines. Terry and I were still negatively charged, engaged in dancing away. Doc Sam was stalwart, our calm center. As soon as she arrived, she enfolded Rosario in a consoling hug.

When they separated, Rosario said, "I can't stop thinking about those poor folks in Haiti. I wish I had more money so I could send them some."

"Money hardly seems like enough," Doc Sam said. "I've been thinking I might volunteer to go there for a few weeks."

"Our office helped pack supplies last weekend," Terry said. "We're going to do it again."

Frankly, I found it stunning that folks with so much on their minds could find the bandwidth for compassion. The extent of my philanthropy was to order two large pizzas, one with meat, one without. When the buzzer rang, I went downstairs to fetch and pay. Because I'd forgotten to order drinks, we had to take tap water with our pizza, which made the occasion less festive than I'd intended, more pointedly a last supper. Still, five was a number big enough to approximate community and it felt good. We were slow to say goodnight. Doc Sam hugged both Mendozas warmly, wishing them luck and offering her continuing support. I sometimes suspected that her mom's death left her with too much love on her hands.

It was weird to leave my apartment in Carlos' and Rosario's custody while I headed out with Terry, too much like going on a date. We were stiff and giggly. "Adieu. Sweet dreams! You two be good." To postpone the awkwardness of checking in at the Holiday Inn, we went for a stroll along the pier. I remembered being there with Lance. Because he didn't say much, I don't know what was going on in Terry's mind. Finally, a light rain started to fall and drove us inside.

In the heartland, it might have been plastic-coated haystacks or water lilies on the walls. In Santa Cruz, we had seascapes. Apart from that small nod to regionalism, our room looked and smelled generic, the wallpaper pinstriped like a salesman's shirt. We shut off our smartphones and set them side by side on the round table near the door, sat opposite each other in matching upholstered side chairs and took each other's measure. Hard work ahead. April 23, 2005, the day we'd last seen each other, was the day they buried Lance.

I broke the silence first. "Terry, I'm sorry."

"About which part?"

"All of it."

"You don't have to go that far. Some of it was his fault." A wan grin. "Some may have been mine."

"True."

"I have been so fucking angry at you, Archer."

"Ditto."

"At me or at yourself?"

"Both."

"That's fair."

"I'm fucking angry at him," I said. "At Lance. Prick up and died."

"Suffered and died."

"Horribly."

"Shit, it was horrible."

"He was so beautiful."

"Yeah, I try to remember him that way."

We were quiet for a moment but still we didn't blink. You blink, you lose. Finally, Terry said, "It was his choice to leave me for you."

"Whose choice was it not to wear a rubber?" Simple and ugly. Wanting someone to blame.

"Christ, Archer, I'm sorry. I really didn't know."

"I hope you behave better now that you do." It was a cheap shot, but I couldn't help it. I volunteered in the clinic, after all, preaching sex ethics, forewarning kids about the consequences of their actions.

Terry dropped his eyes. I won the staring contest but the victory was hollow. I stole his lover, but he stole my health. Terry was that rare thing, an asymptomatic carrier. That was the short personal chain of blame. Of course we both knew the string of causation was decades longer, our own links petty and small. A fucked B fucked C and so on down to fucking Z, in every alphabet on earth. Neither of us mentioned the fact that Lance and I had barebacked, too.

"I hate Michaela de Estrella," Terry said. "I hated her."

"I know."

"I'm not sorry she's dead."

"It doesn't matter."

I meant, none of it matters. We still stared at each other, but it was different now.

"You seeing anybody?" Terry said.

"Not right now. You?"

He shook his head, then took a deep breath. "I was wondering, Archer. Do you suppose we could just—"

"Hold each other."

"Yeah."

We did.

PART TWO

Well, you want my money baby, you want me to spend it on you.

Well you want my money, baby, you want the Wolf to spend it on you.

Just as soon as you get my fortune

She said, What in the world I want with you?

Howlin' Wolf

SEVENTEEN

⌒══╪══⌒

My butt was numb from sitting on the floor. A cloud rose above my god brothers and sisters, not visible but smellable as the blend of too many bodies' odors trapped in a too-small space. It was not a perfume I'd ever want to wear. People were friendlier than I expected, but we all reeked of anxiety. Part of mine was due to Madrina's death. The other part was about how much money the godkids were about to extort for her funeral expenses. How many of us were still paying off the loans we took out to make ocha?

Looking around, I saw a lot of strangers, people who hooked up with the house after I left. Of almost thirty of us trying to get comfortable on Madrina Michaela's floor, I was one of the eldest priests. As I may have mentioned before, I don't believe that the number of hours, days and years put in automatically confers either esoteric knowledge or good character. Some of my god brothers and sisters—straight guys and dykes—had worked it, kissing Michaela's ass and studying her every move like true disciples. That wasn't me. My status was more like the straight women who cleaned her toilets, folded her laundry and threw away the spoiled food in the fridge once a month—lower, really, since I didn't have any kids Michaela could crown at 10K a pop when she wanted to buy a new car. The disciples took on the important ritual responsibilities, while the rest of us proved our loyalty through grunt work. From my spot on the floor, I had a panoramic view of the outsize flat-screen HDTV and game console, the fat fake suede sofa and love seat, the matching footstool that looked like a big square mutant mushroom on casters—things that, along with the pearlescent red Escalade SUV, defined Michaela's idea of abundance and her vision of class.

Finally Ernesto, Madrina's latest lieutenant, stood up, elbowing the wall as if his stout body was a bothersome accessory he didn't quite know how to wear. He thanked us all for coming. I expected the Cemetery Pledge Drive to start right up. Instead, the house lights went down and after a minute or more of silent dark, a square of white light blazed on the blank wall across from the TV. Four man-shaped shadows came out of the kitchen and posted themselves by every doorway, sealing off any route of escape. The first picture appeared on the wall.

What was it? It looked like somebody had spilled a couple of gallons of a bad shade of red paint on the floor of...was it Michaela's garage? The paint had thickened and halfway dried, was starting to look like nasty pudding. Murmurs of distress rose from our seated mass as we decoded the image, serially not simultaneously *got it* that the pudding-coated shape in the bottom left corner was Michaela's hand, let our eyes follow arm to shoulder, shoulder to chest. The slide changed. So did the placement of the camera. Now we could see the whole body slimed in gore. The rate of oxidation wasn't uniform, so that some of the blood had darkened, was no longer the bright fluid that flows from a fresh cut but a shit matte brown, while here and there dashes of living crimson still showed.

It was sickening and fascinating at the same time. Like animals, we filled the dark with noises that had no meaning but distress.

Where was Madrina's head?

We missed it in near unison as our eyes found and understood the broken stem of neck. The gash. The desecration. I wanted to throw up.

Maybe because it was all I knew of death, I pictured Lance, dead.

Click.

Madrina's head sat on Aganju's lebrillo as if it were her neck, her square chin resting on the lip of the pot, eyes closed, her tongue protruding. In the picture, her skin was the color of old fish. A thin string of drool dribbled from the corner of her mouth and down her chin.

And then the lights came on, making the private public. The four cops watched us closely, keeping their faces blank while they read ours. We blinked, we wept, we stared, we coughed. My god sister Betty said she had to go the bathroom. One of the uniforms escorted her. I remember wondering what I looked like then, wishing I had my sunglasses, that I could seek asylum inside one of my characters.

The black detective we'd encountered at Rosario's stepped forward. For a minute, before somebody turned the machine off, Madrina's severed head was projected on him, ghostly everywhere but against the slice of white shirt that showed under his jacket. "I'm Jerry Dixon, detective with the OPD. I'm leading the investigation into the death of Michael Ann Krawczuk. Before we let you go, we need to talk to every one of you."

The detective smiled grimly. "There's some basic information we need to collect. Two interview teams will talk to three of you at a time. It should go pretty fast that way. Just answer as completely as you can," he said. "Team One will be in the kitchen. Team Two will meet down the hall, in that room with all the statues."

They sorted us out—one, two, three, one, two, three and then sorted again, these for the kitchen, these down-the-hall. We lined up. I felt like a third grader or a cow. Donna, zaftig, chocolate brown and bleached blonde, crowned to Ochun, and Luisa, small and Puerto Rican, a dancer made to Obatala, were in my group.

"I don't believe it," Luisa said. "Who would do such a thing?"

Donna said, "Somebody has one sick sense of humor. Archer, I haven't seen you for ages. Where you been?"

"I moved to Santa Cruz."

"What for?"

"Work. Weather. Surfing."

"Did you leave the house?"

"Not officially."

"What does that mean?"

"I'm taking a break."

Donna laughed. "That's code for See ya, suckers."

"Hmmm. How about you, Luisa? Last time I saw you, you were applying to cooking school. Did you get in?"

"Just in time for the economy to fall apart," she said. "Now I can cook like crazy but nobody's eating out anymore."

"I like the new glasses," I said. "They bring out the color of your eyes."

We were the second group called into the eggun room, where Madrina staged misas at her ancestor altar. The two cops sat with their backs to the table, a tall, mournful San Lázaro with ecumenically gray skin peering between their shoulders. Pictures of assorted ancestors, some Michaela's, some from her lineage of ocha priests, looked down sternly from the wall. Back in the olden days, nobody smiled when they got their picture taken.

Name. Address. Phone number.

How long have you known Michael Ann Krawczuk? When did you last see her alive?

Where were you on Tuesday night?

Luisa was at home with her two young kids. Donna was salsa dancing. I had a date in San Francisco.

We all had alibis. We were as innocent as rain. The policemen took names and times. Then they asked their last question: How would you describe your relationship with her? My god sisters went first and talked about R-E-S-P-E-C-T. Then it was my turn.

"It was always prickly," I said. "Madrina didn't much like smart people or gay men. I'm both. When I wouldn't give her my balls, she kicked my butt. We were having a time out."

That shocked a big laugh out of Donna. "I don't believe you said that, Archer."

"Come on, Donna. I don't believe that 'Oh, we were on really good terms' bullshit. Everybody had their issues with Michaela."

Donna swallowed the back end of her laugh. The policeman's eyebrows stood on alert.

"Besides," I said, "in my ita, Yemaya told me to always tell the truth. If I do that, she promised always to help me out."

I've always been able to read upside down. Scanning the cop's notes, I noticed a grave misspelling. "Officer, that's Y-E-M-A-Y-A," I said.

Slowly, he made the change.

We were free to mingle while we waited for all the interviews to be done. Michaela's godchildren wandered about, bumped into each other, exchanged snippets of language no longer or more meaningful than fortune cookie homilies.

No new boyfriend. How about you?

In time of loss, keep busy.

Who needs money when you have ocha?

Finally, Dixon clapped his hands to silence us. He told us not to leave town. To be in touch if we learned or remembered anything that might be significant. Did we have any questions?

I wanted to ask how long they were going to hold Carlos, but I wanted to go home more. After Dixon thanked us and dismissed us, people traded speed hugs and air kisses, then beat feet. As the house emptied, I stood on line for the bathroom. I knew I'd never make it back to Santa Cruz without a pit stop. I was standing on one foot, then the other, trying to take my mind off my bladder, when I realized Jerry Dixon was looking at me from across the room. I met his hard gaze, grinned and waved but got no response except more speculative stare.

I know when somebody's coming on to me and he was not.

EIGHTEEN

c=—✦—o

Madrina Michaela read me first, then Lance. Each of us took notes for the other, notes that included the numbers of the odus that fell, and their orientation—*ire*, good fortune, *osogbo*, bad luck, but none of the attending theology. That was standard practice with the uninitiated, an assumption that you'd come to get your fortune told. Only as you moved toward ocha did you learn the names of the odus, what they meant in the cosmic scheme of things. Part of the job of the shells, of course, was to move you along the road toward initiation.

"Sit at the table with us, Archer," Michaela said. She patted the empty space next to Lance, across from her. I closed my notebook and bellied up to the table. Both of us, Lance and I, were awed into wide-eyed silence. The shells had told us just enough of our own deepest secrets that we were hooked. It is the genius of the dillogun that it knows humanity's secrets and invites the client to particularize. In the hands of the shrewd and intuitive diviner, the reading holds up a mirror of the soul, the generic wisdoms of the odu cast as personal messages spoken directly from god's mouth into the client's ear.

That's the cynical view. Suspend disbelief and the shells truly *are* the mouths of orishas and the reading *is* unique, unsullied by the designs of the reader. It defies statistical probability and laughs at random chance. Interpreted most mystically, the orisha whose shells are being read, most often Eleggua, whispers in the center of the diviner's brain, imparting information of the utmost urgency to the person who sits before her. What is told and foretold is absolutely true in the present moment and absolutely subject to alteration by ebo. Ebo is a gift, a sacrifice, a propitiatory behavior that can turn a sour future sweet or a neutral one triumphant. Before she began the reading, Michaela had recited a long prayer, calling on all the living and dead priests of her lineage to add their energy to hers. Whether it succeeded in gathering the living and dead around us, Madrina's incantation put us, and her, into the zone.

She consulted her notes, then looked up, studied us separately and then together. "Eleggua says your destinies are entwined, with each other and with the religion."

She paused long enough to let us exchange a joyous look.

"He says that one day the two of you could have a house of your own and help many people."

Again, our eyes met. Under the table, Lance reached out and put his hand in mine.

"But you're in danger, both of you. Grave danger. Your health hangs in the balance. You know what I'm saying, right?"

Lance's grip tightened on my hand. I took a deep breath.

"Eleggua says he can save you, he can give you long life. He wants to make you healthy. But he can only do it if you both make ocha."

"When?" Lance was almost whispering.

"As soon as possible," Michaela said. "Eleggua says the situation is very serious. He says there is no time to waste."

"But isn't ocha expensive?" Lance said.

"Eleggua says hospitals are expensive. Drugs are expensive. Death is expensive." Madrina's eyes were hypnotic, large and round, with irises almost as dark as the pupils. Her lashes were sparse and she often had purplish blue smudges from the place the inner corner of her eye met the bridge of her nose to the outermost corner, at her temples. Her skin was rather sallow and she never wore makeup. All these things together gave the eyes themselves a spooky prominence. She turned them on us now and did not blink.

"How much would it cost?" I asked her.

Muttering to herself, Michaela scratched some figures on her paper, added them up, stroked her chin. "Depending on which orishas claimed your heads, separate ceremonies would run ten thousand apiece, give or take. Depending on what I had to pay for the animals, I might be able to include ebo meta in that." A thoughtful pause, then, "And you know,

I have to ask Aganju if it's all right. If he wants me to make you. Otherwise, we'll have to find you another god parent."

None of this made sense to us then, but it sounded important.

Michaela looked up from her calculations. "Of course, if one of you has to be made to a warrior, the price goes up." Her spooky eyes assessed us. "I don't think that will happen, but...."

"We don't have that kind of money," I said.

Madrina smiled, one of her dawn of time smiles, packed with knowingness. "Nobody does." She shrugged. "Until they make up their mind to." A few beats of silence, then, "If you're serious, you should each buy a white sopera for Obatala and start putting money in it. As soon as Obatala knows you're serious, he'll make sure that money comes your way."

"I've heard of that," I said. "That's what Lev did."

Michaela nodded. "It works. If you're serious."

I looked at Lance. "We could race."

"Yeah, right."

I was running numbers through my brain, the sum of my student loans, my income expectations once I passed the bar. How much it cost to keep me in food, booze and pantyhose each month. How much I could save. Ten thousand dollars, twenty for the two of us, seemed insurmountable.

"If I made you together, as twins, there would be economies of scale," Madrina said, as if the idea had just occurred to her. Maybe it had. "Say, sixteen total." Back to scratching. "Of course, the oba would have to agree. But that's only one bembe. At ebo meta, your ochas could eat together, so it's half the animals. One set of derechos for the priests. Half the food." Slowly her thin lips curled into a grin. "As long as neither of you is a warrior, I could do it for sixteen."

It was a negotiation, of course, Madrina's house and car payments versus our lives, even though Lance and I didn't see it that way at the time.

Madrina folded up the paper and put it in her pocket. She collected her cowries, her bones and stones and tucked them back in their bag. "This is a serious decision," she said. "You should take some time and think it over." She pushed her chair back from the table, a disengagement.

"Wait," I said. "What happens if we want to go ahead?"

Michaela settled back in her chair. "When you have half the money saved, four thousand apiece, you bring your soperas to Aganju. Then he knows you're serious. We mark your heads then and put you in pressa." She smiled. "At that point, we can start talking about a date."

I can only describe it as thrilling, that sense of a bright future, a new road opening. The orishas wanted us. They were going to save our lives. Hands joined under the table, Lance and I looked for a moment into one another's eyes and saw the flicker of complicity. It was a highly charged moment, deeply spiritual and oddly erotic. Michaela stood up, and we did too. Shoulder to shoulder, hands joined, we faced her.

"We want to," Lance said.

"The answer is yes," I said. "Count us in."

Across the table, our madrina nodded her approval. "You won't regret it," she said.

NINETEEN

Whenever I've seen or imagined I saw Iku, death, he is taller than any human being and thin as a scythe, a vertical black line slashing the canvas of everyday reality. If you were to poke or pick at the edges of the slash, it would pull apart, making an opening between the worlds. Whenever I've seen or imagined I saw Iku, it's knocked me off-center, stolen my balance and clouded my vision, left me sweaty and afraid. It is almost as if, in an instant, I passed through the slash and then fought my way back to this world. Metaphor, hallucination, reality—as anyone who lives with HIV will tell you, this is all three.

The night the Oakland cops shared their images of Madrina Michaela with the rest of us, I dreamed a dark figure that mashed up skinny Iku and massive Darth Vader into one formidable, light-eating being. I come into his presence much as Luke does in the movie, in a setting bare of props or places to hide. Unlike Luke, I have no weapon on me.

For a long time, Darth/Death does nothing, just stands in the center of my dream, and I'm paralyzed by his presence, too scared even to piss my pants. After a slow while, though, I calm down enough to counsel myself to breathe, breathe slowly and mindfully, the best defense I know against both terror and despair. In, out. In, out. My body starts to feel denser and more compact. Light gathers at my core. I lift up my chin and look my adversary square in the eye slits. It's a long way up.

For the first time, Darth/Death moves, lifts his impossibly long arms and takes off his Star Wars helmet. Pale as a mushroom, drooling a string of blood, Michaela's severed head sprouts from his shoulders. When she opens her eyes and stares at me, I scream.

Archer, I am your father, the apparition says.

⁓

"The DA decided that Carlos left the county hospital legitimately, after making bail," Terry said. "They're not ready to charge him with Michaela's murder. He's still a person of interest."

"Why didn't you tell me?"

"They made me promise not to."

"A warning would have been nice."

"Archer, honey, I have to stay on the good side of the police." On screen, Terry batted his pale eyelashes at me. "What happened at the meeting?"

"They made us promise not to tell." I said it to be bitchy.

"I deserved that."

"Uh huh."

"Archer?"

"Uh huh?"

"Let's go out sometime. Soon."

"Come on down to Santa Cruz. I'll make you dinner."

"I want to go *out* out," Terry said.

"Sounds expensive."

"I miss Darla," Terry said.

My first thought was, Hassle. My second thought was, Trouble. My third thought, I spoke out loud. "Me, too," I said. Then, "Who are the cops looking at besides Carlos?"

If Terry knew, he wasn't saying.

⁓

"Well if it isn't Archer," Pete said. "So glad you could stop by."

"Go ahead, dock my pay."

"Very funny. You know it takes both of us to make this place work."

"Actually, it takes Doc Sam. You and I are expendable."

"It's your turn to give the abortion speech," Pete said, jerking his head toward the tense young couple sitting in the waiting room, not talking and not touching.

"They look happy."

Pete handed me their paperwork. We went into one of the counseling cubicles. First I asked questions, then I answered theirs. I swear I will never understand how kids bright enough to get into college think they can outsmart biology, especially with fuzzy math. "It was only thirteen days since my last period."

"Started or ended?"

Uh oh. She looked confounded.

He said, "You told me—"

I said, "Shut up, Bruce. It was your penis."

Once things were back on track, I explained what a DNC is, what it would cost, how long it would take to recover physically.

"Will I still be able to get pregnant, after?"

"If you're asking if you'll still need to use birth control, the answer is yes."

"I want to have children someday," the girl said earnestly. "Just not right now."

"When it's more convenient. I understand."

"Why are you being so judgmental?" the guy said. "I thought this place was supposed to be progressive."

"Progressive and amoral are not synonymous." Damn, I was snappy. I bit down on the impulse to apologize. "Why don't you think it over and give us a call if you decide to go ahead. We can schedule you within three to five days."

I shooed them out, then went to the window to watch them leave. About one time out of ten, things get violent. These two were using their words. I turned away from the window to find Doc Sam, unbuttoning her lab coat.

"Archer, go home."

"I'm fine."

"It's a short day. I have a meeting in San Francisco."

I turned back to the window and squinted out into the afternoon, trying to assess the probability of surf worth riding. A veiled sun yellowed the clouds. None of the leaves seemed to be moving. I startled when Doc Sam touched my shoulder.

"You need to take care of yourself," she said. "This is not an easy time."

Even as she attempted to mother me, Doc Sam was slipping out of her lab coat, slipping into her cinnamon high heels. She wore her brown suit, a white sweater with just a dash of décolleté.

"You're raising money again."

Doc Sam laughed. "You know all my tricks." She stepped into a fine spritz of Je Reviens, fluffed her hair and punched me on the arm. "Go home and take a nap." Then she was gone, in search of cash.

~~

I didn't want to be at home. Grief steamed off my ochas on their mourners' mat and filled the apartment with sadness. And yeah, Doc Sam was right. I did need mothering. If I couldn't talk to Yemaya in her pot, then I would have to address the whole great sweep of her. I grabbed my wetsuit, just in case, and strapped my board to the roof of the car, then drove north out of town to Dickinson's Landing, a pocket beach that scared me less than the high cliffs and high surf of Santa Cruz. It was going to take a while to get my nerve back. The waves were tame but a few newbies paddled around hopefully, waiting for a big one to roll in. Worth getting wet? The horizon, flat and silver, drew my eyes and I felt my gaze widen to take it in. Rain started to fall, hard enough to pimple the wave tops and darken the sand. I rolled down my window just enough to hear the ocean whispering.

A tapping on the window woke me up, I don't know how much later. What I saw was so incongruous I assumed I was caught in a dream that wasn't quite ready to let me go: The cop Jerry Dixon, wearing a red windbreaker and hiking boots with his gray suit, sucking on a cigarette and staring down at me. Rain was still falling briskly.

"Hey, Barron, let me in."

I unlocked the passenger door. "No cigarettes in my car."

He tossed the butt away before he climbed in, trailing the stink of smoke. I rolled his window down a little.

"I've got some questions," he said. Reflexively, he reached for the pack of Camel Filters in his shirt pocket. I scowled. He aborted the light-up and folded his hands in his lap.

I decided to be proactive. "So do I." I plucked one out of the stale air. "Have you found her family?"

Dixon flexed his fingers for something to do with smoke-free hands. Two of the nails on his right hand were stained a deep, disgusting yellow-brown. "What's left of it," he said. "A sister and an uncle."

My scalp tingled, I swear. "Please, tell me."

"Polish family. Came here at the end of the war. Mom left dad. Grandma, dad's mom, raised the girls. The rest of her family died in Majdanek, a concentration camp, but grandma survived. Which according to the sister, Esther Ann, made her crazy. Survivor's guilt. Dad shot himself. Michael Ann ran away."

"From where?"

"Just outside Pittsburgh."

For a minute, my head swam, filled with Michaela's suffering ancestors. I said a swift and silent Hail Mary and an Our Father for good measure, then almost immediately was embarrassed by my reflexive nod to superstition.

"Polish Catholics," Dixon said. "I don't think it's a family thing, though." Again, he reached for a cigarette and aborted the gesture. "I'm thinking this is purely local business."

"You're looking to get promoted, aren't you?" The thought came powerfully into my mind and I didn't stop it from coming out of my mouth.

"One more time and the pension looks pretty good." Then, in the next breath, "How angry were you at your godmother?"

It was a smart question. As soon as I looked for an answer, my grievances filled up my chest until I thought it might bust open. "On a scale of one to ten, I'd give it a ten." I don't think Dixon expected that. He shifted in the seat so he could see me better. It's hard to explain, but I felt like I was surfing, too skilled to fall. "You've got to understand, I'm just as angry at myself." And then I hastened to explain. "The masochist finds the sadist. Only the dupable get duped."

It was like talking to my father. Dixon had the same cheek-creasing eye lines, the same look of strained credulity.

When he spoke, it was to say, "Barron, I'm going to have to ask you to come with me. We'll take my car."

He let me move mine to the most sheltered spot in the little beachside lot. Since we were riding in his car, Dixon got to smoke. On the long drive to Oakland, he must have gone through half a pack. Every time he asked me a question, I asked one back.

How did I hook up with Michael Ann Krawczuk?

Just lucky, I guess.

How come he became a cop?

For the pussy.

Had I ever gone to see a therapist?

Not lately.

How many murders does Oakland have a year?

Number 6 in the US. Dropping faster than the national average.

You political, Barron?

Registered Democrat. Radically queer.

You like your job?

Same old, same old. Drugs, gangs and domestic violence.

How come you never took the bar exam?

How about you mind your own business?

Then I asked him if he really thought I killed Madrina Michaela.

Somebody thinks so. We got a phone call.

He wouldn't tell me who, or when, or what they said.

I slid down in the seat, folded my hands across my stomach and closed my eyes. By the time we got to Oakland, my eyes were puffy and I smelled like an ashtray. I had to share the holding cell with seven other guys.

TWENTY

In the U.S., most people who receive Ibeji, the twins, head round to Toys "R" Us and pick up a set of identical plastic baby dolls to represent them. Good luck if you want them in something other than pink. Take the twins back to Africa, to Yoruba-land, and you're looking at a couple of grave-faced coneheads who should be running companies or countries. In any case, Taiwo (first born) and Kehinde (last) are magical beings who achieve improbably good results for their devotees. They're little kids and ancient wizards at the same time, with the power to lure death out of your house.

Ochun gave birth to the Ibeji, so the stories say, then passed them on to Yemaya to raise. Priests initiated to Yemaya receive Ibeji automatically, as part of their initiation. If two new priests get initiated together, they're "made as twins." To be "real" twins, one should be made to Yemaya, one to Chango. When they marked our heads, that's how Lance and I turned out, the genuine article, and Madrina, who liked to be and to do things first, especially if there was cash or status involved, really got into it. She also said it "took a lot out of her," which it probably did. I don't know about giving birth to ochas, never having done it myself, but organizing the days of ceremonies involved to make even one person is enough to kick your ass. There's an avalanche of details involved.

For me and Lance, it was a good time. We were young. We were in love. Lest this start to sound like a cheesy pop song, let me add the kicker. We were healthy, positive but not yet afflicted, and oh so beautiful. Remember this, dear reader, that no matter how he dressed, in a tuxedo or an evening gown, Archer Barron was once one stunning man. And Lance. Lance was one of the prettiest boys I've ever known, big eyed, lush lipped, well made, with skin the color of some exotic hardwood and lashes so extravagantly long you could have used them for a makeup brush. Our misas were full of drama, the espíritistas of the house readily possessed and seeming to compete in the extravagance of their visions. The river made my willy shrink, we came back shivering and passed the evening before our initiation in a long limbo, sitting on Madrina's couch while our god sisters and brothers bustled purposefully around us, occasionally stopping long enough to ask if we were hungry or thirsty or wanted to go to bed. That night we slept in our clothes on the floor of the eggun room, whispering like little kids whenever no elder was close by enough to shush us.

The next day was monumental, for the length of the waiting, the suddenness of action, when it came, the surrender, eyes closed, to the ritual befalling, voices whispering in our ears, lifting in song around us, the prayers and cleansings, the tapestry of new smells and indecipherable sensations, the final mystical transport to a place that was not Madrina's house, was not California, maybe was not even of this world or time. Lance's finale was different from mine, as different as the orishas seated on our heads, but we both experienced something profound and inexplicable.

We ate a salty soup on our throne, and then our newborn ochas ate, too, the blood of many birds and animals.

While our god brothers and sisters worked long into the night on our behalf, Lance and I with our newly bald heads, our painted faces and our all-white clothes curled up on our white comforters on the floor of our double-wide throne and swooned into dreams. We slept chastely, head to head. One of the things we would give up for our year as iyawos was sex. Other big ones included being out after dark, wearing colored clothing, drinking alcohol, putting on cologne, and on and on. For the first three months, sleeping on a bed, eating at a table, getting a hair cut or looking in the mirror were all off limits. The more stringent the initiation, the more likely it is to stick. That night, nobody the wiser, we managed to hold hands as we fell asleep.

The next day, the second of three, got off to a crotchety start, with sleep-deprived priests bringing us tepid scrambled eggs and scorched toast that we had to eat in silence, sitting on the floor. Lance did his best to ask for butter in sign language but no one was really listening. Then came the morning rituals. Our eyes stayed closed while we were stripped naked and bathed and our heads were painted red, white, blue and yellow. Finally, finally it was time to get dressed for our party. Madrina shooed everyone from the room while she and Ochun Bi dressed us in our satin suits—Lance's red and white, mine blue with silver trim. Our tops were the length of morning coats, the pants snug and fitted to just below the knee. A double-headed axe was appliqued on Lance's jacket, a rolling ocean wave on mine. On our heads, fantastic crowns. Madrina painted sandals on our feet and little goatees on our chins and hung heavy beaded necklaces across our chests. We couldn't see ourselves but we could see each other.

I don't know what iyawos wear in Africa, but in the New World on the middle day they dress like courtiers in a kingdom of the imagination. The queen in me and the lefty both found my outfit silly, but as the day wore on and I dove deeper and deeper into its ritual context, as the drummers drummed for us, as priests saluted us and visiting ochas scampered to our throne to bring us messages, as we ate tasty bits, lovingly prepared, from the animals sacrificed in our ceremony, I surrendered both to the event and to the costume. Lance looked adorable. I decided to believe that I did too.

My parents came, god bless them, and sat next to Madrina Michaela beside the throne. She mothballed her gangster-rapper ways and rose to the occasion, behaving for all the world like a mature spiritual leader. My parents seemed favorably impressed, and it looked to me like Madrina was enjoying herself, proud of the new priests she'd made. I had a twenty-four hour fantasy of becoming one of her favorites.

It ended the next day.

TWENTY-ONE

Never underestimate the power of venue.

The interrogation room at Oakland police headquarters was déclassé in the extreme. Low ceiling. Dirty walls. Scuffed linoleum with grooves so deep my chair legs wobbled. The narrow table that separated me from Jerry Dixon appeared to have been custom-coated with some sticky substance that might have been human in origin. I was sure that touching it would turn me ugly and make me sick. The lights were weirdly dim, as if the OPD was saving money on electricity. Taken all in all, the room felt like a state of mind, just an inch or two short of pure despair. Even in the police car, I had felt a kind of parity between me and Dixon but here that no longer applied. He had the key.

"You lied," Dixon said.

"There's a difference between lying and failing to make full disclosure." I tried to sound snappy but the room was sucking up my snap. "Besides, I still don't know when Madrina was murdered."

"Let's roll it back to Monday night."

"I went out to dinner with a friend."

"The waiter remembers your friend, not you. He says she was with another woman."

"Elizabeth."

"You want to revise your statement?"

"I am Elizabeth. Elizabeth is me."

"Right. And I'm Kermit the Frog."

"Do you ever dress up as Kermit the Frog?"

Dixon shook his head. Negative.

"I dress up as women sometimes."

Dixon's sigh started out in mid-belly and fluttered his lips on the way out of his mouth. He stared at me.

"It's not illegal," I said.

"Just unnatural."

"Liberating," I said. "You should try it sometime."

He looked at his notes. "So, you and your doctor friend left the restaurant without eating. You went to Highland Hospital."

"That's right."

"The officers say they met two women."

I nodded. "Me and Doc Sam."

"What was your intention?"

"We'd posted bail for Carlos Mendoza. His wife was afraid he'd get killed if he went back to jail. When we got there, Carlos was gone."

"The officers you say you met there don't buy the crossdresser thing, Barron."

"I'm good," I said. I pushed my voice up gently, into Elizabeth range. "Those policemen couldn't get enough of my legs."

"So you three women left Highland Hospital at ten past nine. What then?"

"I am aware that I don't have to answer your questions right now."

"Are you aware that you have no alibi for the time of your godmother's death?"

I needed to think clearly, but the interrogation room was making me feel like I had a bad hangover, my brain on sludge. Did they know I'd taken Rosario home with me? Did they know the Mendozas spent the night? If I saved my ass, would I be putting theirs on the line? "I'm not aware of that, officer," Elizabeth purred. It was a stalling tactic but it took him by surprise. I liked the look on his face. Elizabeth liked it.

Dixon was interested in spite of himself. "So, let me get this straight," he said.

Elizabeth interrupted. "There's nothing straight about it, I'm afraid."

"What are you?"

"A human being," Elizabeth said.

"You know what I mean. Are you a trans—" He stopped there, not sure what syllables came next.

Elizabeth said, "Archer Barron is a gay man who sometimes passes women."

"He passes as a woman?"

"Those policemen seemed to think he passed. But I mean *passed* more like *possessed by*, if you know what I mean."

Dixon shook his head. Inside Elizabeth, Archer liked him for not judging, for not saying crude things about what he didn't understand. Together, we tried to help. "Like Santería priests do sometimes. It's not about sex. At least not entirely."

"Okay," he said.

"Thank you," Elizabeth said.

"Where is Carlos Mendoza now?" Archer asked Dixon.

"Where were you that Thursday morning?" Dixon asked. "Who were you?"

"Archer," Archer said. "If I don't take off my makeup at night, my skin breaks out."

"Archer, someone called the department and said they saw you at Michael Ann Krawczuk's home that Thursday morning, around ten."

"Not true. I was driving to Oakland from Santa Cruz."

"Can you prove that?"

I swallowed. I leaped into the truth. "I was with Rosario Mendoza," I said. "She spent the night at my house. I was taking her home." It felt like bottom was a long way down.

"Rosario Mendoza hasn't confirmed that," Jerry Dixon said. For a fleeting moment, I wanted him to father me. I wanted someone to take care of me.

"I'd like to call my lawyer now," I said. I assumed that Terry would agree to be my lawyer. I assumed he'd set things right, but my call went through to voicemail.

The message I left him was a plea for help.

TWENTY-TWO

What is it about ocha that makes otherwise sane, frugal, smart people save up ten thousand bucks and, instead of buying a car or putting a down payment on a two-bedroom fixer upper, hand it over to an uncredentialed spiritual advisor who doesn't give receipts or warranties?

That is the question.

It's the question my parents were asking themselves and me when they came to California to attend my ceremony. They wanted to understand what I was doing. They wanted to believe their son was still in possession of his faculties, despite what they'd heard about the power of both AIDS and cults to steal them away. Life had not handed them exactly what they asked for. Or maybe they simply forgot to spell out their wish list in sufficient detail. They got a smart and handsome son, born healthy with all his parts. Breeder and Baptist, those were the boxes they forgot to check. The jury was still out on sane.

Picture them in their second-best suits, the ones they wore to professional conferences or Sunday church, one notch short of wedding and funeral attire, looking good the way black folks can at fifty, that is to say, not a day over forty-one or -two; plop them down on folding chairs in a California ranch house, fill in the chairs around them with people of all colors, heads covered and dressed in white, most with half a dozen or more strands of brightly colored beads around their necks. They sit very straight, my parents, the tight smiles on their faces expressing generic goodwill, the mirrored set of their jaws acknowledging how out of place they seem here, how wary and unmistakably bourgeois. If you

96

know them like I do, if you look close, you'll see their upper arms are touching and their thighs, they take comfort from touch and give each other courage skin to skin. They have always been this way.

An extremely large, very dark man in what appear to be loose fitting dark blue pajamas sits barefoot on a grass mat on the floor, his back against the wall. Madrina Michaela sits in a chair to the left of the mat, my assistant godmother Sophia beside her, pen poised to write down everything about to transpire here. My parents see their son, Archer, sitting a on short stool with no back and facing the very big, very black man in the blue pajamas, who will say the prayers and cast the shells and give the advices of the ita. "The man is the Oba," one my god sisters whispers to my parents, "the one who ran Saturday's ceremony. Oba means king."

I sat before Obanoshukua, dressed in my second best all-white iyawo outfit, with a white bath towel spread across my knees, I can only assume to shield the Oba from awkward views of my erogenous zone, and felt the flutters of pulse that announce Life's Big Moments. My hands were slick with sweat. Since I had never witnessed an ita before, I was entirely dependent on Michaela to tell me what to do. This put her in a position to instruct and correct, two things she liked very much to do. Even though Obanoshukua was center stage, it was Michaela's show.

Soon enough we established the rhythm of the ritual. A priest passed Obanoshukua a plate with an orisha's hand of cowrie shells upon it, that and a small cross made from the jawbones of a sacrificed goat and a small brown envelope holding the Oba's fee in cash for speaking to that orisha. After a long prayer, in which he called the ancestors and the orishas to the mat he threw four pieces of coconut to ask permission to proceed. Once that was secured, the Oba passed the plate of shells to Madrina. She scooped them up in her hands. As instructed, I knelt at her feet, my face trained on hers, while she told me about the orisha whose mouth she held, not just his or her agreed-upon powers, but how she expected that orisha to behave toward me, and me toward him or her. Each time, at the end of her homily, she put the shells in my hands and when she told me to, I dropped them on the mat.

Obanoshukua and Madrina studied the fall of the shells and pronounced the odu. In fact, I think they raced each other to count and name it first. Now I sat down on my stool, and the Oba took up the shells and cast odu number two of the composite. Did it come to me with blessings or bad luck? The Oba handed me two objects, a chunk of powdered eggshell and a black stone, to shake between my hands and separate secretly, one object concealed inside each closed fist. He dropped the shells again, which told him which hand to choose, and pointed at one fist or the other, at which point I opened my hand, revealing the hidden object and so, the nature of my situation. The process may sound exotic, but it's really just math, an algorithm executed by a kind of aboriginal computer, synched up to a library of folk wisdoms.

In Yoruba-land, in the old days, in Cuba even fifty years ago, the initiate was told the sayings associated with his composite odu and given the rest of his or her life to figure out exactly how those sayings, or refrains, played out their meaning. It was Michaela's assertion that the modern US way, her way, was better. That is, a personalized life reading, a co-production of odu, spiritism and amateur psychoanalysis that had as its object the creation of a devout and obedient godchild. What the shells said alerted the godparent to the character strengths and weaknesses of the iyawo as well as to his destiny. They also laid out a list of new business to be transacted with the Madrina. Each item on it had a price, ranging from sixteen dollars for cleaning the head to more than ten thousand for receiving cuchillo, knife, and the authority to use it to perform blood sacrifice.

The Oba was a Cuban man and spoke in Spanish, way too fast for me to follow. He and Madrina spitfired back and forth for a while, and then she'd say a few English sentences meant to shape the rest of my life.

I must not be a lawyer.

I should respect my godmother.

I should not wear clothes with holes in them.

I should plant a ceiba tree in my yard when I have a home of my own.

I was abused as a child.

Chango and Olokun will help with health problems.

I am intelligent.

I have an Indian spirit who walks with me.

No pork. No apples. No dark-colored drinks.

I should study divination.

Anything I give Ochun will bring her blessing.

The advices piled up as the orishas spoke, one by one. My back ached from sitting on the little stool. I didn't dare look at my parents. Finally, it was Yemaya's turn to speak, to pronounce the odu that would henceforth rule my head, and my life.

Yemaya spoke in 8-6, Ogbe Obara.

There are many refrains associated with the sign, but the only one that mattered to Madrina Michaela was this one: *The king is dead, but a new prince is crowned.*

To Madrina, that meant a rival had just been born. Madrina had once had a godchild with that odu who criticized and left her. For the rest of the week I was resident in her house, she dismantled my throne bit by bit, a little more each day, to keep me from doing the same. She barely spoke to me. I asked if I had offended her, and she replied, "I will do what I can for your health, Archer, but don't expect me to teach you anything you could use to depose me."

"Madrina, I'm a queen. I have no desire to be a king."

"Odu don't lie," Madrina said.

I was desolate, judged guilty of crimes I had no intention of committing. Yemaya took the ocean away, leaving me stranded on dry land. Obatala was my father in ocha. Omi Ode, Water Arrow, was my name.

Lance, having a gentler odu on his head, fared better. Madrina named him Chango Gumi, after a famous dead priest of her lineage. She still joked with him and went out of her way to teach him things. Over time, it drove a kind of wedge between us. That day, when everyone was gone and we were alone on our throne, we were too stunned and exhausted even to speak but slept deeply, head to head, without touching.

The next day, my parents left Oakland without saying goodbye. My father spent the rest of life protesting that his son had never been abused. In due season, I came to see the wisdom of another of Ogbe Obara's sayings: *The dove was once menaced by the snake, so he opened his wings and flew away.*

TWENTY-THREE

Our holding cell emptied and filled up again while I waited for Terry to call me back. The drug dealers got bailed. The shooters got charged and jailed. The pimps were back on the street faster than I can pull on pantyhose. By the middle of the second night, it was just me and the Samoan, a lush-bodied kid with a broad, sweet face and big hands. Probably too young and not quite my type—I've always respected the local statutory rape laws, even if they were thinking about girls not boys when they made them, but I was touched by his air of stoic melancholy and wondered how come nobody was setting him free. Of any ethnic group in Oakland, I'd always heard the islanders had the tightest families. At three AM, neither one of us had managed to fall asleep. The benches were too narrow and way too hard.

Finally, I decided to break the ice. "I'm Archer. What's your name?"

"Filiki," he said.

"Filiki. I like that."

"Most people call me Fil."

"Almost nobody calls me Arch. How come you're still here?"

"My family disowned me. Everybody except my grandma and she's real sick."

"What did you do?"

"I was stealing drugs for my grandma."

"Hardly seems fair," I said.

"I was stupid. I got caught." He folded his hands between his knees and stared at them.

"Why did your family disown you?"

"I came out to them." He looked up. "That means I like men not women."

"Oh, I know what it means."

"Do you want to have sex?"

"Sure," I said. "But not here." I could tell by his face he thought I was rejecting him and not our circumstance. "I like privacy and I use a condom."

His face brightened a little. "You're a top. I thought so."

In spite of myself and our circumstance, I was getting hard. I imagined how soft, how smooth his skin would be. "Tell me about stealing drugs," I said. I was trying to talk myself down.

"I tried to hold up the drug counter at Walgreens, on High Street. You know the one?"

I shrugged. All Walgreens look the same to me.

"My grandma can only take one kind of painkiller. She likes Percodan and they won't give it to her at Highland."

"What's wrong with her?"

"She's dying, man. Cancer. She just wants to go without too much pain. So I waited till the middle of a weeknight and I went in and pointed a gun at the pharmacist. I told him to give me all the Percodan he had. Grandma can't do morphine."

"So what happened?"

"They have this button behind the drug counter. They push it and it calls the cops. I didn't hear nothing."

"Jesus," I said. "That's armed robbery. You must really love your grandma."

"The gun wasn't loaded," Filiki said. "I'd never shoot anybody. Not even a fly."

"It's hard to shoot flies." My tongue is sharper than a knife sometimes. As soon as I saw the look on his face, I regretted the dig. He'd probably been hearing shit like that from teachers all his life. Instead of trying to talk my way out of it, I went over to his bench and sat down beside him. I put my arm around his shoulders and felt the warmth of his skin. He turned toward me and lifted his face to mine. His lips were dusky, plump and shapely.

I kissed him. He kissed back, deep enough to make me dizzy. It was impulse, not intention, one of those great unzippings of the superego that lets the id shine through. We softened and stiffened, as lovers will. I wanted to melt into him. And then I said, "We can't. Not here. They have a camera." I took one of his hands in mine and kissed it, then got up and returned to my side of the cell.

"You're a beautiful boy," I told him. "I wish we could."

"What do you know about Maria Victoria Fidelio?" Dixon asked me. We were back in the interrogation room, back at the table varnished with snot and palm sweat.

"Not a thing. Who is she?"

"Cuban," Dixon said. "They say she was your Madrina's girlfriend."

"Madrina had a Cuban girlfriend? That's news to me."

"Folks seem to think she's a gold digger."

When I didn't respond, he opened the manila folder he carried in with him and sifted through the sheaf of rumpled papers inside. Even upside down, I could see the sloppy writing and the atrocious spelling. "No literacy test for joining the force, huh?" I said.

Dixon looked puzzled for a minute, then he got it. Put his palm down flat on the evidence. "Gets worse every year. Some of the new guys think comic books are literature." He shuffled through his papers, then said. "You know Betty?"

I nodded. "Came to Oakland from Portland. Used to have money, till Michaela got it away from her."

"Something happened between her and the girlfriend. Night before the murder. You hear anything about it?"

"I've been indisposed."

"Happened at a…sounds like *mee-saw*? Something like that."

I couldn't resist correcting. "That's misa."

"Tell me."

"I don't think so," I said.

Dixon looked across the table at me, his face still as a statue, his eyes as hard.

"I don't know why I'm here," I said. "I don't know why my lawyer hasn't called me back. But I do know you can't just keep me here forever."

Dixon crossed his arms across what was, for a straight man his age, a modest belly. "Actually, the system is so fucked up, I probably can. The courts are understaffed. With forced furloughs, the city's only open for business four days a week. Public defender's office is swamped." He grinned at me, showing some old gold fillings toward the rear. "Rights are rights, but time is time."

Suddenly, I felt exhausted. That's what happens when you've been running on hope. My tank was empty. "Why me?"

"Motive. Intelligence. Opportunity."

"Oh, please."

"Our anonymous caller said to ask you what happened when Lance died."

I put my hands on my thighs, spread my fingers out like fans. "I hit a few walls. I screamed. I cried."

Dixon waited to speak until the silence around us was big and tense. "I heard you said some stuff."

"Maybe."

"I heard you threatened your godmother."

"I may have said she killed him."

"And?"

"It isn't strictly true. She led us to believe she could save him. We didn't have to take that chance."

Now Dixon lowered his voice. He sounded like my father, every stern and loving father since the world began, the kind of voice that makes you want to measure up. "Son, did you kill Michael Ann Krawczuk?"

"Wanted to. Threatened to. Didn't." The tears that filled my eyes humiliated me. "Lance was…. I loved him."

Dixon didn't say anything, just stood up, walked me back to the holding cell and locked me in.

A toothless white guy lay like a heap of trash on the far bench, the one I'd been thinking of as mine. His cheeks were seamy and his beard stubble was the color of rats. He was still alive enough to stink and snore at the same time.

Filiki was nowhere to be seen.

I tried my best to envision Yemaya, to imagine being washed clean by her giant froth-topped waves, but my spiritual mother had gone missing, too.

TWENTY-FOUR

We were at the old house, before Madrina Michaela moved uphill. I was in my iyawo whites, my head double-covered and my chin freshly shaved, my elekes hanging outside my shirt, Yemaya's seven not-really-silver bracelets tinkling on my wrist. Madrina Michaela made a lot of ochas that year, our year—nine, I think—and we nine babies lined up for her lessons, vied for her attention, did everything we could to make sure we got our share of the goodies, more if we could. Face time is favor. Knowledge is power. Siblings squabble, right?

Because I was an only child, I wasn't very good at squabbling. I sucked at Infighting, flunked Making the Other Kids Look Bad. Still, there were milestones, and my path between them, my aspiration as a child of the house, was to be impeccably respectful. I knew I'd never out-butch the Latino guys or have the visceral allure of the coffee-colored lesbians, so I went for reliable, available and alert, which was how I imagined the ideal disciple ought to be. In retrospect, I think it annoyed the shit out of Madrina.

As partners and twins, Lance and I always met our milestones at the same time, one after the other. That night, we were supposed to go over our life readings with Madrina, ask her to explain what we didn't understand. Lance went first, settled in at the kitchen table with Madrina while I waited in the living room and pretended to watch a *Law and Order* rerun on cable. Being too discreet to eavesdrop, I didn't know what they were saying, only how they were saying it—a constant flow of words that rose and fell, moved around obstacles and exploded into sprays of laughter. Spontaneous, in other words. Easy. Were they laughing about me?

After she met with Lance, Madrina wanted a break. She went to the bathroom, ate some leftovers, watched fifteen minutes of TV, checked her email, returned a couple of phone calls and finally said, "So iyawo, you still want to do this tonight?"

"Yes, Madrina."

Finally, the iyawo and his madrina sit together at the kitchen table. She opens his ita book, scans pages, mumbling now and then to herself. He watches intently, every neuron on full alert, an urban sparrow on watch for fallen French fries. Pages turn. Her silence grows. His anxiety balloons. With Lance, she talked and talked. Finally, she closes the book.

"Do you have any questions?"

In that instant, they solidify, my two big questions. I sense the clock is ticking. Which one is more important? I pick the one that weighs the heaviest on my heart. "In my ita, Ochun says I was abused as a child. My parents took it really hard."

"Were you?"

"Not ever that I remember."

"Abuse is not just sexual. It's not just physical."

"They never did either."

"Sometimes abuse is psychological," Madrina said. "Sometimes it's spiritual." She pushed her chair sideways a little, away from me. "My godfather told me I'd never have an ocha house because I'm too abrasive. I don't treat people well. He said it to hurt me. That's psychological abuse."

"I survived eighteen years in Texas."

Madrina flips through the pages of the ita, filled with Sophia's loopy script. Again, she closes it. Again, looks briefly at me until the dishes on the drain board attract her eye. She appears to address them, not me. "Your parents aren't bad people, but they're not spiritual people. They don't have aché. They don't understand the orishas or your path to ocha. You need to separate yourself from them, Iyawo. Yemaya has given you a new family. She's your mother now."

"I love my mother."

"That's good. You have the responsibility to respect your mother. You should always open doors for her and pull out her chair."

"I beg your pardon?"

"You know. Show her respect. Remember her birthday."

"I do."

"Eleggua says they put you through a lot. He would have said more if they weren't there. It was a difficult situation." She pauses, cocks her head as if she's listening to voices I can't hear. "If you have pictures of family on your boveda, you need to take them off. Take them to a church and leave them there."

"How come?"

"They need elevation. Boy, do they need it." Madrina laughs. "And you're not strong enough to give it to them. Get them off your table or they'll bring you down." Madrina looks at the clock. It's heading for eleven. She yawns. "What else?"

How do I say it? Does my odu mean I'm a bad person? Did you really wash your hands of me? How can I redeem myself? How can I prove myself to you?

Madrina's cell phone rings. She glances at the caller ID. "I need to take this." She gets up from the table, greets her caller in Spanish, leaves the room. I sit at the table for ten minutes, then fifteen. For a while, I hear her talking, staccato bursts of Spanish between silences, floating over the TV soundtrack. When I haven't heard anything for what seems like a long time, I get up myself and go into the living room where Lance is watching a different episode of a different cop show. I sit beside him. We wait.

After half an hour, as David Letterman is just tooling up, I call out, "Madrina?"

The third time I call her, she responds. "Goodnight, iyawos. You can let yourselves out."

When my father had a heart attack, later that year, Madrina said that as a iyawo, I was not allowed to enter hospitals. I went to Texas anyway, to be with my mom. I kept her company when she wasn't at the hospital and did a lot of housework. I took white baths. For a while, it looked as if my father might be coming home, so I stayed longer in Texas. One night he had a second, more massive heart attack and died. I told my mother what Madrina told me, that as a iyawo, I was not allowed to go to funerals.

My mother sat at her kitchen table. I sat on my mat on the floor nearby, drinking tea from my enameled blue tin cup. My mother's face was puffy and splotched from so much crying, her eyes were hollow. She turned them to me and studied my face. "Archer, I don't understand what's happening," she said. "I don't know who you are anymore."

I looked my grieving mother in the eye and said, "I am Iyawo." In our initiation year, it is our only name.

My mother lost her husband and her son at the same time.

Now Madrina was dead, never having answered my second question. The question itself had changed by then, no longer, *Am I a bad person?* but *If you didn't like me, why didn't you simply set me free?*

Lance had asked her when he could learn to make mazos, the magnificent beaded necklaces that new-made iyawos wear.

TWENTY-FIVE

I felt like a wuss, hating jail as much as I did. It wasn't Guantánamo. The food was starchy but passable. I didn't have to dig ditches or break up rock. The toll was mental, intense boredom leavened with anxiety. It was getting to hang out with Oakland's finest citizens, feeling their jagged brainwaves and smelling their unwashed bodies, their loud colognes. It was not knowing how to speak when spoken to, understanding that my standard English marked me as "other," despite the color of my skin. I've never been good at street vernacular, the elisions and rhythms, what gets swallowed and what gets spit out, never been able to talk ghetto without sounding like an asshole parody of the real thing. In the holding cell, I kept my mouth shut, as much from respect as out of fear.

The pimps talked trash about their bitches. The dealers mocked the white boys who cruise into East Oakland in their SUVs to pick up hash and speed. One of the convenience-store hold-up guys talked BBQ and two of my co-residents argued for a long time about who serves the best chicken n' waffles in town. Never mind the hypertension, the pre-diabetes, the chain smoking and the ZIP-code-shortened life expectancy, these men could talk like rivers flow, all sparkle and efficiency and surprising grace. They could laugh when nothing was funny.

My only slang is drag and I kept it to myself. I was so exhausted that I fell asleep, not before I heard one of the dealers say, What with the perfessor?—and felt the shadow of his pointing finger pass through my dream.

I had no idea if it was day or night, whether it was still the same day or had turned into the next one, when Dixon walked me back into the interrogation room. I tried to recall what he'd been wearing last time, but his de facto uniform was too drab to remember, the kind of cautious clothes colorblind people wear to protect themselves from clashing.

"So," he said and looked at me differently than he had before, with a little less accusation and a little more appraisal. Was he smiling? Dixon was so tightlipped I couldn't quite tell.

"So?"

"Several of your friends have reported you missing. The Santa Cruz police have been looking for you ever since they impounded your car."

I groaned. The last time my car got towed, it cost me a week's paycheck to ransom it.

"Don't you want to know who cares?"

"Samantha Steinman. Terry Gleason. Either my landlady or my boss."

"Steinman, yes. Your boss and your god brother Ernesto." After a beat, he said, "You look surprised."

I shrugged with theatrical nonchalance. Inside, not for the first time, I cursed Terry for a callous bitch.

"Gleason is representing Carlos Mendoza," Dixon said. "In fact, he persuaded me to release him with an electronic monitor, pending his arraignment on the negligent homicide charge."

"What about Madrina?"

"He's still my favorite suspect. You're number two."

"So give me an anklet and let me go, too. If I don't work, I can't afford my drugs."

"What are you saying?"

"My HIV drugs."

"Actually, I have a proposition for you."

"Sorry, detective. You're not my type."

Dixon looked puzzled, then got it and sort of grinned. "Not that kind of proposition. I'm not having a lot of luck getting answers out of the Santería community. Help me out and…."

Nosing around for Terry on Carlos's behalf was one thing, not that I'd done a very good job, but working for the cops? It felt like the wrong dress for this queen. The silence stretched as I tried to imagine myself wearing it.

Finally, Dixon broke it. "Look, Barron, I know you had issues with your godmother, but assuming you didn't do it yourself, I can't imagine you want her murderer to go unpunished. There's one sick fuck out there."

If I'd never been to a misa, never seen the ineffable in action or felt a spirit on me, what happened next would probably have left me whimpering in the corner. A silvery chill passed from the top of my head down the back of my neck, down my arms and legs, tingling every nerve and raising every downy hair along the way. It was like an electric shock and not—slower and more seductive, but just as other. For a moment, the air around me felt charged, as if somebody else was standing close and wanted me to know it. I took a long slow breath, both to steady myself and to help me hear the message if there was one.

Madrina, is that you?

The place fear lives in the belly closed like a fist. I saw the edge of darkness around the silver jolt. Then the moment passed, leaving me shaky and desolate, convinced I had just had a close encounter with one sick fuck.

Across the table, Dixon watched me closely. "What happened?"

I shook like a wet dog does to get dry.

And then I said, "Okay, what do you want to know?"

TWENTY-SIX

The only person who was free to pick me up from the police station was my god brother Ernesto. I was touched and puzzled that he'd reported me missing. He was just rising in the house, coming closer and closer to Madrina Michaela as I was on my way out the door. If he had a reaction to my going, I'd always figured it was Good riddance. Most dictators, like most gods, only have one right hand, and from the day he appeared on the scene it was clear that Ernesto meant to be Michaela's. I offered to pay for his gas if he'd take me back to Santa Cruz. He accepted, as long as I helped take care of some business first.

"We got to move the trucks," he told me, hands tight on the wheel of his own old Dodge pickup.

"The trucks?"

Ernesto looked sideways at me, one dark caterpillar eyebrow climbing. Did I really not know? "Madrina's other business," he said.

"I know next to nothing about trucks." It's true and I said it with a femmy edge.

With the side of an index finger, Ernesto dredged his mustache for sweat and wiped it on the thigh of jeans. On top he always wore a guayabera, loose enough to cover what was a bigger-than-was-good-for-him belly on a body that had to be ten years younger than mine. Today's shirt was light green, with a panel of frayed embroidery on either side of the front closing.

"Hundreds of guys are going home to Mexico now. Half of them bought a truck here, been sleeping in it for months, some of them. Fucking recession," Ernesto said. "These guys, they need money to get home, so Madrina buys them out for cash, way below Blue Book. Then she turns around and sells the truck at a profit."

"Don't you need a license to do that?"

"Madrina had a few rules. All cash. No paperwork. As is."

"Buyers didn't get the registration?"

"If there was one, it came with the truck. New owner could go to DMV and make the changes. Nothing was ever in Madrina's name."

"What about inventory?"

"Ha. Madrina was smart. All the vehicles lived on the street. She figured out which streets were safest, knew when the streetsweeper came around. Once a day, we went out and moved all the trucks."

"We?"

"I got laid off. Year, year and a half ago. I helped Madrina out with the business."

"So I guess you're the only person who knows where the merchandise is?"

"I guess that's right."

"That's a good inheritance."

"It's a lot of work, man. Weekends, you have to drive all the trucks to International in time to get a good spot. You know, down by Seminary. You got to keep your phone on all day. It takes two people."

"You have anyone in mind for number two?"

"Not yet. You interested?"

"I need something with benefits."

"Ha ha. That's right."

"So, are all your customers happy campers?"

Ernesto ha-haed again.

"The cops have her cell phone, right?"

"Madrina used a separate phone for trucks and ocha. She didn't want anybody showing up at her house, right?"

"Right," I said.

"The cops have got her ocha phone. I tossed the other one into Lake Merritt."

"Good thinking," I said.

Ernesto pulled an off-brand smartphone out of his shirt pocket. "I got a new one. Now I gotta make new signs to put on the trucks."

We took MacArthur into the Laurel, then turned east. With each passing street, the neighborhood got quieter and better groomed. Another turn
and we came upon what looked like a gardeners' convention, both sides
of a tidy street lined by a small army of dusty pickups, many with business names painted on the doors. I counted nine in all. Ernesto parked his
Dodge around the corner and we both climbed out. "Today's easy," he
said. "We put em on upper High Street till Friday noon." He pointed at an
elderly Toyota and handed me a chain with two keys. "You drive a stick?"

"Sure." My father tried to teach me but he was not a patient man. It was
under my mother's tutelage that I learned how to release a clutch and
change gears at the same time. I'm more comfortable in a sports car than a
pickup, but I managed to pilot my share of the vehicles to upper High. On
the fifth round, I drove merchandise and Ernesto followed me in his own
truck. It took us almost two hours to move the whole lot. Then I bought
him an In-N-Out cheeseburger and a tank of gas and we headed for Santa
Cruz, just ahead of the worst of the commuter traffic.

For a long time, I was content to look out the window, watching traffic
thicken and slow, watching the yellow haze belly up to the hills and the sun
get fiercer the farther south we went. When Ernesto put the radio on, jan-
gly Mexican lieder filled the cab. All around us, fellow travelers were texting and driving at the same time. After a couple of days of cold turkey, my
digital obsessions had eased up, my consciousness was no longer mapped
to the round of newsfeeds, chat, email and Facebook and I was beginning
to take the longer view. Everything could wait to be seen, said, shared. This
was freedom and it felt good.

I was appreciating the companionable silence when Ernesto broke it.
"What do you think is gonna happen to the house, with Madrina gone?"

It was not something I'd really thought about till then, whether "house"
as concept or community could survive without Michaela. As I pictured
the weave of our relationships, everything radiated out from the center of
the web, Madrina the all-powerful spider, binding each of us to herself
and only peripherally to one another. The thread might be drugs or health,
depression, lost love, betrayal, domestic violence, ambition, trouble with
money or the law. It was Madrina who promised to make the orishas solve
our problems and heal our hurts. The rest of us were doo-wop singers. She
strummed the lead guitar. "Is there a house without her? I don't know."

"The house isn't just a house, it's a business," Ernesto said. The tightness in his voice matched the white of his knuckles on the wheel. "Madrina was teaching me."

"Not just the prayers and rituals?"

"Everything," Ernesto said.

"People have to love you or fear you or want something from you," I said. I'd heard my mother say something like that about teaching and it seemed to fit the case. "Preferably all three."

"I want it so bad." I wasn't sure if Ernesto said this out loud, or if I was hearing his thoughts. Either way, his urgency was alarming. Had I ever wanted anything that much? Not besides Lance.

It occurred to me then it would be smart to make sure Ernesto didn't see me as competition. I'd heard his spirits were "no joke." So I said, "Good luck, man. These days, all I want to do is surf."

Just as we got to Santa Cruz, he took a call and sounded like a lover. "I'm on my way. Be there soon." It wasn't the words so much as the intimate whisper, the tenderness in his voice that gave him away. I never knew he had a girlfriend. He dropped me off. I left a message for Terry, telling him he better have a damn good excuse for letting me rot in jail, and another one for Doc Sam, telling her I was home safe. Since I hadn't figured out what I was going to tell my boss in UCSC security, I decided to wait another day to make that call.

The next order of business was to ransom my car. In Santa Cruz, that was physically easier and financially much harder than anyplace else I've ever lived. The city gives tax breaks to its rich inhabitants and squeezes traffic violators until they squeal. My savings were shot and I was whimpering by the time I was back behind the wheel. I needed the beach.

I was too tired to feel safe surfing but I wanted to walk on the sand, to listen to the ocean and not the nattering voices inside my head. Yemaya, reset my frequency. Rock me gentle in your big blue arms. When I got there, though, my mother was in a fury, casting up twenty-foot waves and throwing them down, a brash challenge to the sanctity of solid ground. A sign warned walkers that they might be sucked out to sea. No surfers I could see had ventured out, but a few guys in wet suits sat in their vans in the parking lot, watching and waiting. It takes guts to plunge into a high sea, even when it's calling your name.

TWENTY-SEVEN

I exfoliated. I depilated. I masturbated. I steamed until my fingers and
toe pads looked like raisins. I shampooed and shaved and stayed in
the shower until all the hot water was gone and my whole apartment
reeked of bergamot. Jail had failed to meet my personal hygiene stan-
dards. With my pores wide open and a thick-napped bath towel tied
around my waist, I felt like a new person. I was just attending to my toe-
nails when my smartphone started to sing.

The caller ID read *Doc Sam Cell*, but no one responded when I said
hello. I might have dismissed it for a pocket call, but I sensed a living
presence on the line. "Hey, what's up? Talk to me."

No response.

"Are you okay?"

I thought I heard something, a ragged low breath.

"Sam? Doc?"

"I'm here." Her voice was flat and seemed to originate in a distant
galaxy. The light years it traveled to reach me had stripped away all the
energy and joie de vivre. Maybe, I thought, the aliens abducted her and
left a robot in her place. The computer-generated voice was not convinc-
ing. That this is where I went testifies how weird it was that the strongest,
most generous being I knew had lost her affect and her volume switch.

"Tell me."

"Oh, Archer...."

"I'm here," I said. "What's wrong?"

"I'm down." To call her voice a whisper makes it sound more vivid than it was. I might have been conversing with a dust mote or a slug. The silence on the line was gray green, the color of despair. Once in a while, I'd hear a breath she'd managed to wrestle out of her gloom, like a thin strip of near-transparent cloth held aloft by a chill wind. Just hearing it made me shiver. I grabbed the kitchen towel and draped it across my bare shoulders. I had heard Sam angry, sad, disappointed, vindicated, exasperated and triumphant but never like this, so...*down*. It was her word and it was right. Flat as a Frisbee. Dark as the minute before the movie starts.

She was my rock. My hero. She took care of me.

Slowly, almost reluctantly I realized it was my turn to take care of her.

"Shall I come over?" I asked her.

"Yes, please."

Half an hour later I was there, turning on lights as night impinged, in the kitchen making us tea, in the living room, sitting across from her anxiously, not knowing what to say. Finally, I crossed the space between us, sat down hip to hip beside her and put my arm around her shoulders. Doc Sam collapsed against my chest. I don't know how long we sat that way, with her tucked up in my armpit, simply exchanging warmth, that fine electrical current called life, across our skins. Her fragility made me aware of my own strength. When my mind wandered, it was into a nearer past, to kissing Filiki in our cell. Sam's breathing changed, got longer and deeper and noisier, so that I knew she was asleep.

When my legs were all but numb from sitting, I disentangled myself, leaned her back on the sofa and stood up. When she opened her eyes, they were so wide and blank I felt as if she were staring at me out of a nightmare that was still playing inside her head.

"Hey there. My foot was asleep. You feeling better?"

"A little," Sam said. Her hair was messed up, her mascara smudged, her expression beyond artifice, one-hundred-percent authentic sadness.

"Is this about your mom?"

She thought about it, then shook her head.

"What?"

"Maybe my mom, a little. Everything." She pushed a hand through the thickets of her tangled hair. "It's so dark and dead and so far down."

"I know," I said.

"I'm afraid I'll never come back up."

"You will. You just have to ride it out."

She sighed.

"You probably ought to go see another kind of doctor."

"Okay."

"Everybody ought to get shrunk once."

A thin smile.

"How about I tuck you in?"

She changed into a nightgown, had a piss. I washed her face, rubbed in her drugstore moisturizer, brushed the snarls out of her hair. I made her brush her teeth. I held her hand in mine and inspected the haphazardly cut fingernails. "This week, we're going to get ourselves manicured. It'll be fun. Okay?"

"Okay."

I walked her into her pale blue bedroom, straightened the linens and folded back a neat triangle of sheet and blanket. Dutifully, Sam climbed in.

I turned off the overhead light, pulled the covers up to her chin and kissed her on the forehead, things I knew how to do because my father had done them. My mother had. In her sadness, Sam who is older than I am seemed very young. I turned off her bedside lamp.

"Good night, Doc. Sleep tight. I'll call you in the morning."

She caught my hand and held it tight. "Please stay."

I must have looked frightened or confused. "Don't worry, I won't molest you. Please. We'll sleep."

It wasn't until she promised to let me wear her pearl-pink silk nightgown that I agreed. It was tight but the fabric felt delicious against my skin, cool and slinky, even though the lace trim itched a little. The sight of me in it made her laugh. Doc Sam snuggled against my side as I stared at the ceiling and thought about Lance, about Filiki, about my mother and my father and everything in my whole life. And then, curled around each other, we surrendered to our separate terrors and slept until the sun rose on another day.

~~

"Arch, man, I'm so sorry," Terry said. "I was in Hawaii when you called."

"You could at least have texted."

"The hotel was on the north end of Oahu. No service till I got back to Honolulu."

"I spent three days in jail."

"Me, too," Terry said. "Only they call it Continuing Legal Education. You have to do it or you can't play. I was overdue. But it's resolved, right? They didn't charge you with anything? I mean, how could they. And the experience is invaluable. Just think how well you'll be able to relate to your clients once you pass the bar."

"I was planning to practice estate law."

After a beat, Terry said, "You're kidding, right?"

"Right."

"You sound angry."

On a phone call, silence substitutes for the shrug.

"Look, I promise I'll make it up to you as soon as I get back. They're calling my flight right now. Kisses, Arch. Can't wait to see you."

After we hung up, I gave myself the old welcome-to-reality lecture about not expecting more from people than they're capable of giving, the one that's supposed to dull the edge of disappointment and make it possible to continue being friends even after somebody treats you like shit.

It was a nice try but it didn't work. I'm not that Zen.

TWENTY-EIGHT

⊙━✦━⊙

Betty's got half a century in her trunk. She's a genuine entrepreneur, built herself the first and best African American beauty salon in Portland, Oregon. At her peak, owned two duplexes besides the salon. Betty's almost as light as I am. She bleaches and straightens her hair, which not only eats up most of what would otherwise be spare time, it makes her hair look even more like plastic than if she actually broke down and wore a wig. If I wanted to "do" Betty, I'd need four pillows, two to tie to my trunk, armpits to waist, and two more rolled up to make the bosom-shelf. She's not a centimeter over five foot four.

Betty was born and raised in Atlanta and made to Ochun when she was still a kid but she never practiced the religion after she left home at sixteen. Madrina found her on one of her dillogun reading junkets through the Northwest and turned on the charm. Pretty soon Betty had sold her Portland real estate and moved to Oakland with her pockets full of cash. She helped Madrina lease a big newly spruced up storefront right at the place the barrio rubs up against the hood. In the Botánica Aganju, Michaela did the readings and Betty moved the merchandise, at least until Betty's family, whose existence she'd neglected to mention, began to gather round her with their hands out. The family consisted of a recently paroled husband and two grown-up, hard-luck sons. As her bankroll dwindled, so did her status in Michaela's house, except as a vehicle for spirits of all kinds, whom she passed somewhat indiscriminately and in abundance.

"Archer, baby, it's been too long."

"Bendición, mami. I've missed you too."

"Santo, sweetheart. Isn't it terrible, about Madrina? I was devastated."

"Totally shocking. The worst of it is, I didn't come around to see her before she died."

"She wasn't intending to die, baby. None of us do."

"Still."

"I understand how you feel, but you know what Madrina always said, Oh Archer, he's just sowing some wild oats. He'll be back next time he ends up in the hospital with pneumonia." Betty did a surprisingly good Michaela imitation.

"I'm glad I'm so predictable."

Betty laughed. "You know Madrina, always willing to take the bleak view of human nature."

"A lot of the time, she was right."

"Love many, trust few, always paddle your own canoe. My mother taught me that."

"Do you think Madrina Michaela actually loved people?"

"It's just an old saying, Archer."

"You know one thing I've really really missed? The misas. I haven't been to a good misa in two years." Insert pause. "How about you?"

"Last Monday night was pretty wild, I understand," Betty said.

"Weren't you there?"

"Yes and no. In and out. I woke up the next morning with bruises all over my body."

"Girl, what happened?"

"They tell me that Esmeralda got in a cat fight with Madrina's new girlfriend."

I whistled. "Madrina had a girlfriend?"

"Brought her home from her last trip to Cuba."

Silence, Archer. Sometimes silence is the most effective interrogation tool.

"Half Madrina's age and definitely out for number one. I'm not even sure she's really a lesbian."

"I thought every woman was a lesbian at heart."

"Not this one, baby. Seriously, you know how those Cubans are. They have so little they'll do just about anything for money."

"Who was the misa for? What happened?"

"It was for her, Archer. For Maria Victoria. It started out normal enough. We all read prayers. Madrina sat back from the table, like she does. Ernesto and I were head of the table, running things. Pretty soon Eric passed his Indian spirit who said that Maria Victoria had hidden secrets that would shock us if we knew.

"Then Ernesto passed Niñita and she wanted everybody to cleanse Maria Victoria so we all got up and cleaned her with flowers and Florida Water and in the middle of it Maria Victoria passed this giant ancient spirit, something not quite human. Like a troll or something. Then Esmeralda came. That's the last thing I remember."

"The troll beat up Esmeralda?"

"I'm not sure what happened and no one will tell me. Madrina swore everyone to secrecy. I was supposed to meet with her on Wednesday night."

"Sounds like I missed a show."

"Me too," Betty said.

We talked a little bit about the arrangements for Michaela. Without a head, it appeared that the body of the house was running around in circles.

"You need an oba to do the itutu ceremony, right?"

"Right, little brother," Betty said. "But Michaela had managed to piss off just about every oba on the west coast. I think they're calling around New York and Miami now."

"Oooh, look at the time. I have to be at work in half an hour and I haven't had anything to eat. It's been wonderful to hear your voice."

"Same here. I know you and Madrina had words, Archer, but I think I speak for most everybody when I say we'd love to have you come back."

"Those are kind words, Betty. Thanks."

After we said goodbye, I microwaved a bowl of homemade lentil soup, then had to wait while it cooled down, blowing on every spoonful before I put it in my mouth. Idly, I considered the idea of coming back. I felt like a mini-Colossus, one leg on each side of the river, a place of precarious balance and no firm identity, where everything felt alien and familiar at the same time. Jerry Dixon was right. In my condition, I made the perfect police informant.

Finding out about Madrina's girl friend was the next thing on my list.

First, consider how hard it is to imagine your parents having sex. Hard meaning, makes you feel weird and dirty, like you need a bath. You know they did it at least once per offspring, they had to, but that doesn't mean it's fun to think about in too much detail. If you ever caught them in the act, you probably still have the psychic scars. Start there and escalate. Imagining Madrina Michaela in flagrante almost exceeded the limits of my erotic imagination, not just because she was the least demonstrative of people, prone to flinch at human touch. Other disincentives included how judgmental she was, how distrustful and how competitive. None of these attributes, in my experience, contributes to one's ability to enjoy a one-night stand, much less maintain a longterm sexual relationship.

That was one of my issues with investigating the girlfriend. The other one was Spanish. Cuban Spanish and Archer's Texas high school Spanish are pretty much two different languages.

Maybe Cubans can talk so fast because they drop or mash up so many syllables. My one field trip there with Madrina, back in '04, didn't last long enough to let me adapt. Even listening so hard it made my head hurt to the conversations of my elders, I was able to catch maybe seventy percent of what was being said, enough for a broad sense of the topic but none of the details, forget the niceties of time and tense. When I tried to talk Spanish with them, the Cubans were polite but puzzled most of the time. To my shame, I ended up behaving like an ignorant American, letting Michaela speak for me instead of suffering myself to sound stupid so that, with enough practice, I might eventually sound less stupid. Blame my too big, too fragile ego.

What I really couldn't imagine was why Maria Victoria Fidelio, who recently (lost or murdered) her (What was their relationship, exactly? Fill in the blank), would want to have a candid conversation, or any conversation at all, with Archer Barron, house defector and police informant. And then, I had an idea. To make it work, I needed an accomplice, a character, and a trip to the Goodwill.

⌐⌐

Shawnita swooped down and kissed Luisa's cheek. "Girl, it's been too long. Who's your friend?"

"This is Maria Victoria, from Cuba."

Shawnita sidled into the booth. "Hola. ¿Cómo está?"

As I'd guessed, Maria Victoria was Madrina's femmer half. Her velour track suit and Shawnita's might have come from the same thrift store. Both were tight, both tops unzipped low enough to show some boob. Maria Victoria was several shades darker, a pretty copper color.

"Pleased to meet you," Maria Victoria said.

Luisa said, "Maria Victoria speaks good English."

"You do," Shawnita said. "And I just love your accent. It's so…buttery."

The waiter came by. Shawnita ordered a Corona with lime.

Maria Victoria gave her the once-over. "Is that a…" she turned to Luisa, "peluca?"

"Wig," Luisa said.

"Is that wig?" Maria Victoria said.

Shawnita flipped her blond ends. "It is," she said. Actually, she'd borrowed Elizabeth's wig, teased it and added some jeweled bobbies. That's where the resemblance between them ended.

"It is nice," Maria Victoria said. "I want to buy a wig."

"When you're ready, call me. I'll show you where to get the best deal."

To Maria Victoria, Luisa said, "Shawnita got her elekes from Madrina Michaela but she doesn't come around often."

"Too busy," Shawnita said.

I searched for ghosts in Maria Victoria's smile and found a whiff of detachment but nothing that looked quite like rue.

Luisa said, "Did you hear what happened to Madrina?"

Shawnita shook her head no.

"Madrina's dead," Luisa said.

Maria Victoria said, "Somebody killed her. That's what the policía believe."

"Oh my god." Shawnita's reaction was big. She clutched her throat. After she was able to speak, she said, "I don't believe it. Who would do such a thing?"

"Madrina wanted me to sleep at her house on Tuesday night, but I went home instead," Maria Victoria said.

"Where do you live?" Shawnita asked.

"I live with my husband. I live with Antonio."

"But Antonio is…."

Before I could say *gay*, Maria Victoria smiled and said, "Gay. Sí. Madrina arranged everything. I pay him to marry me, he gets the money for his cuchillo, I get my green card. Everybody is happy." She took a pull on her beer. "But I am not happy that I went home."

"Girl, you can't feel guilty," Shawnita said. "Shit happens."

Maria Victoria shook her head. "I did not want to sleep overnight because Michaela is so gruñona when she wakes up."

"Grumpy," Luisa said.

"I am selfish. And the spirit el monstruo possessed me on Sunday night."

"What's that?"

"It is a how do you say, grim spirit. When el monstruo visits, somebody suffers."

"You don't really believe that," Shawnita said.

"Maria Victoria es una bruja," Luisa said. "Muy poderosa."

"Oh my," Shawnita said. And then, "I'll tell you what. Next round is on me. We can drink to Michaela."

My companions were game. We ordered the best dark rum, straight up, with a Diet Coke back. Three-layers-closeted Archer winced at the damage he was doing to his diet protocols. His heart was full of regret, of gratitude and spines. Luisa looked pained. Maria Victoria was hard to read.

Shawnita, the least conflicted among us, raised her glass first. "To Michaela de Estrella, who gave me elekes. One powerful dyke."

Luisa's eyes widened. Maria Victoria's snort turned into a laugh. We clinked and drank.

Luisa lifted her glass next. "To Madrina Michaela, who promised us so much."

We sipped her disappointments.

Maria Victoria's eyes traveled around in a way I took to mean she was remembering. "Michaela brought me from Cuba," she said. "Michaela was the first woman who ever touched me. Rest in peace."

We emptied our glasses and carved a space of silence around the ritual. Then Shawnita made a show of looking at her smartphone. "I've got to move on, ladies. Luisa, so good to see you. Thanks for the invite." She stood. Reached out and took Maria Victoria's hand. "Good to meet you. Welcome to California."

Maria Victoria cocked her head to one side and looked up at Shawnita. "You need to make ocha soon, I can tell. Maybe with your Madrina gone, you will call me. I am twenty-two years crowned to Ochosi." She laughed softly. "My padrino made me when I had seven years old," she said.

Shawnita, bless her, had the last word. "What I really need is a misa," she said. "How about we start there?"

⁓

The armpit of the night, sometime between three and four AM. Unless I've been dancing or working ocha till dawn, it's a time I'd rather not see. I have no defense against Terror then and Terror is beyond naming—it's not about death, though death partakes, it's not about failure, though the fear of failure always lurks nearby, it's not about how age erodes beauty or how being sick or always afraid of getting sick annihilates the future or even thinking you might never have sex again or not knowing what happens after you die. All of those dark starlets dance in Terror's chorus line but Terror itself is monumental and irreducible. You can't divide and conquer, you can't diminish your enemy by imagining he's naked. Terror was born naked. Terror never sleeps. Terror shocks you awake in the middle of the night just to have some company.

I woke up to sweat-soaked sheets and the silence that's so deep it has nothing to do with sound. The only thing you *might* hear then is the slight buzz of the bond between electrons and in its absence you have to wonder if it's you or the universe that's died. That and you're pretty sure it's all your fault.

It took me an immeasurably long time that night to deduce from my dry mouth and the collar of achiness around the back of my neck that Alcohol had invited Terror over to Archer's house to play. There was that cold glow like sheet lightning along my synapses and the dull midback discomfort that convinces you your kidneys have stopped working. A slight tremor in my hands. Loose bowels. All these symptoms together slowly testified against the idea that I had killed my Madrina and gone to hell.

I first met Terror in Texas, when I was no taller than a footstool. Being a Baptist baby, my defense then was to fold my hands tightly under my pillow and say little prayers inside my mind until Terror got bored with me and Sleep came back. More than once, one of my teachers asked my mother what time I went to bed. As a man, I learned that all the daylight drugs metabolized into that one dark creature. After I made uneasy peace with my AIDS rage, I invented my own abstemious AIDS ways with the unexpected benefit that Terror started to let me sleep soundly through my short nights more often than not. Shawnita's rum and Coke had brought on Archer's wrestling match with dread. Slowly, the night air dried my clammy sheets. My breathing deepened and my heart rate slowed down. I absolved myself of most of the sins that come with being human. Hallelujah! It was the booze.

TWENTY-NINE

We had a boon time, not just Lance and me but a wider circle within a circle, some of us Santeros, some not, a pack of San Francisco gay boys intoxicated by freedom, emboldened by community, at home under the city's high flying rainbow flag. Harvey Milk had paved the way for us, had died for us, some might say, so we could live in the city without shame. We were out, out, out, out and proud, out and about, out and outrageous beyond the wildest dreams of our deep-closeted back-home years. Lance and I were not promiscuous but we were not strictly monogamous, either. Our pack was all positive but for most of us that was no longer a death sentence but only a moral obligation to come clean before we came. We took our pills, we struggled to afford them. We accepted the responsibility to disclose our status. It put certain partners out of reach, but that was mostly okay. There were plenty of horses on our side of the fence. And we rode bareback with each other.

Lance and I, Benny and Lev were a high-functioning foursome in more ways than one. We made a kind of bloc inside Michaela's house, appointing ourselves handlers of the animals used in rituals. We goofed and giggled but did a good job, so while Madrina was often telling us to shut up and pay attention, she was usually happy enough with what we did. On our own, in the city, we were a stable social entity, a strong magnet that collected shavings from a lot of different quarters. Because we all did different work, our net spread wide, gathering up geek and glam, artist and advocate inside it. Lance's ex, Terry Gleason, became part of our circle. As our ochas settled on our heads and in our lives, we felt more centered and more sane than we ever had before. I know I did.

We shopped and went to the gym and had facials, went dirty dancing and to drag shows and art shows and foreign films, saw the opera when we could afford it and played Gay Charades at home. We had extravagant potlucks and the occasional Big Night Out. When Madrina called on one or more of us to help her, we usually all showed up. Her prejudice against me was clear to everyone, but my friends took the sting out by passing on the lessons she withheld and including me as soon as she looked the other way. We had an adventurous erotic life and an exotic spiritual practice. We were Adams in Eden, not missing Eve.

Then one day in the spring of 2003, on the flimsiest of pretexts, our country invaded the foreign sovereign nation of Iraq.

I was making vegetarian spaghetti, long on spices to make up for missing meat. Lance was on his way home from rehearsal with a loaf of French bread. Benny and Lev were bringing wine for them and Martinelli's for Lance and me. It was not unusual for us to eat together a couple times a week, their place or ours, our own version of a moveable feast. What was weird was how bad I felt that day. I stared into the bubbling pot with no enthusiasm for stirring, not caring if the hot steam burned me, not hungry, in some strange way, not even there. The ache inside me had driven the thoughts right out of my head. I'd been depressed before, back in Texas, but this was not the same sad animal. Tears splashed down on the spaghetti sauce. Damn, I felt bad.

Lance got home. His eyes were flat, his mouth hung part way open without making a readable expression.

How was your day? I asked him.

I feel like shit.

Benny, when he got there, looked like he'd seen a ghost.

On arriving, Lev threw down his messenger bag, then unfolded the grass mat in front of my ochas and flung himself down, flat on his belly. For a long time, he just lay there. None of us said anything. I had the oddest feeling that we were all lying side by side on the floor.

Lance broke the silence. I feel like my heart is breaking, he said.

Lev, rising, named the demon. It was compassion.

Politically, we felt shame but it was a till then unexperienced byproduct of our spiritual journey that the world's heart beat inside us. We felt the suffering of war. It wasn't even about taking sides; we hurt for everyone. Something we'd done for ourselves had grabbed us by the scruff of our selfish little necks and shaken until we were involved with all mankind. I'm not claiming we had become holy men, only that our emotional depth and breadth had grown alarmingly. It was not comfortable.

Holy shit, Lance said, speaking for us all.

⁓

Some of Lev's co-workers at Channel 4 had helped to organize the Day X protest, a demonstration that was planned in every detail except the actual date. Now that the invasion had happened, the time had come to put the plan in action. Before we finished eating our spaghetti that Friday, Lev's friend had called to invite us to help. Marchers from all directions would converge on City Hall Plaza for speeches and prayers. It was our job to build an altar where people of every faith could light candles, pray and sing, to contribute a spiritual dimension to a political event. Or, as Benny put it, to temper rage with hope.

We sprang into action and worked all night, fixing on a concept, then harnessing our individual skills to make it happen. We wanted to write a prayer in three (or more) dimensions, to make it clear that people are more than meat sacks, to focus the faith and goodwill of the thousands who would come together in one place, to give them something to do once they arrived. Because we'd all been in the habit of building elaborate thrones for our ocha birthdays, we had a lot of stuff to use and a habit of working together to create sacred spaces. Our inner queens joined with our inner priests, making the four of us a decorating team of eight. Dawn was breaking when we set the last of the flowers just so at the base of the banked altar, cued tape on a beautiful Obatala song, and asked a homeless guy to take a picture of the four of us together in front of our work.

The space was so compelling that all the religious types at the rally naturally moved to it to deliver their mini-sermons. Between speeches, real people came up, added flowers, lit candles, knelt, crossed themselves, wrote their own prayers on the little pieces of paper we furnished and put them in the basket we provided to accept them. The news crews took pictures of our creation. One of them even interviewed Lev and me.

If you've ever doubted that no good deed goes unpunished, consider this. Around the planet, newspapers reported protest turnout numbers divided by ten. In San Francisco, thousands of people who weren't there got arrested and had to post bail. The war went on for eight years more. On the other side of the Bay Bridge, our Madrina saw us on television and got mad. "Priests have no place in politics," she told us. "Where the hell were you when I needed you? You knew I had an ebo meta yesterday."

Madrina drove her point home by punishing us with a fine. Each of us owed her a goat to appease our sins except for me. She was sure I'd led the others astray, so I owed her two goats. If you've never shopped for livestock, take my word for it—goats are expensive. Madrina added a hefty fee for sacrificing them.

Eventually, Benny and Lev got new jobs in Los Angeles. Eventually, Lance died. I moved to Santa Cruz.

The sad thing is, our best selves were what Madrina Michaela liked the least.

PART THREE

Annie don't wear no panties.

Erykah Badu

THIRTY

B ring Darla.
These words hand scrawled on the bottom of an invitation to Terry's thirty-ninth birthday party, the hand his, like him more grownup than the last time I saw it. It was an invitation to bury the hatchet, for one thing. I took it as an apology for not being there when I needed him to lawyer for me. But it was so much more.

Did he know what he was asking?

Probably yes.

Nobody still in my life had such a long view of Archer except my mother and she lived in Texas. Some things one keeps from mom. Terry knew, knew me as Darla came into being, knew me in sickness and in health, knew me in love, knew me in makeup, knew me in iyawo whites, knew me in grief. Besides the ocean, the most important thing they took away in my ita was drag.

I've pored over that lined notebook time and again. I know the name of the odu, I've memorized its refrains, I've looked it up in every book I could find that promised to explain the meanings in good fortune and bad and the offerings to mitigate it, and there is not one thing that pertains to dressing up, to disguise, to gender-bending. I've questioned my elders: Where do the advices come from?

"The Oba knows," Madrina Michaela said. "Orishas speak to him. Sometimes his eggun, or yours, will tell him things."

"Why doesn't it say that in the books?"

"The books are trash," Madrina said. "This is an oral tradition."

"But…"

"Sometimes it's hard," Madrina said. "You can't pick and choose. A good Santero obeys."

"What happens if you violate your prohibitions?"

Madrina shrugged, her perfect gesture, one square shoulder raised expressing her utter contempt, a physical judgment passed on cosmic questions too trivial to merit serious consideration. Attitude as answer. But Madrina, if Archer becomes Darla, will Archer die? If Archer eats corn chips, is stomach cancer far behind? As the faith knot loosened, two more questions rose up. Why do they take things away from us? Madrina, was it really you, whispering in Obanoshukua's ear?

I didn't care about the corn meal or the white wine or the pork chops, I didn't care when they said I wouldn't have very many godchildren, or that I shouldn't work late at night or go out in the fog. *Law. Surfing. Drag.* If three things made Archer Archer, if three words defined his true and higher self, that was them. Somebody knew me well enough to understand just what to cut away to leave me broken.

"If I do everything my ita says, perfectly, where does the benefit reside? My luck? My character? My soul?"

Madrina answered with her perfect shrug. Or sometimes with its verbal equivalent: You just don't understand.

Archer's newest question: Madrina, if you understood so perfectly, if you behaved so well, if you had so much aché, how come you're dead?

Bring Darla.

She with the hair, the lips, the eyes. Those cheekbones. The slender ankles, the narrow waist, the perfect nails. Oh girl, those titties. All that glitters. Have you heard her sing? That bitch is witty. She got sass.

Darla had not walked this earth for eight long years. What remained of her lived in my closet in two still taped-shut boxes. I trembled to open them. Archer was not the same canvas now as then. The years coarsened his skin, the meds thickened him. He had less hair. I fought, I did. I ate right, I exercised, I meditated, I abstained. I did it for Archer and in Lance's absence, his yawning, gaping absence, I did it for Archer's mom and maybe, I saw it then, maybe for Darla in her box in the back of my closet and the bottom of my soul. When I sliced the tape and opened the flaps of that first box, color and sparkle flew out, silk whispered to me, Estée Lauder's Beautiful escaped its prison and spread its wings, dispersing sweet tendrils of Darla's signature scent, and what popped into my head was my favorite line from Shakespeare, also a kind of signature: *Age cannot wither her nor custom stale her infinite variety.* Shakespeare was talking about Cleopatra. Who in Shakespeare's time would have been played by a man. I opened my mouth and started to sing.

In the week before Terry's birthday, I threw out the old makeup and bought new, not everything I wanted but enough to do the job. I ironed eight years of wrinkles out of my gowns and replaced my laddered hose. I restyled Darla's wig and discovered that if I used surgical tape under it, I could give myself an instant facelift, raising my brows and tightening my jawline, flipping off time for as long as the illusion stayed taped in place. I walked around the apartment in my highest heels, loving how they cantilevered my ass and made my hips swing when I walked, and tried to convince myself I could wear an evening gown with a day old beard and hairy armpits, only to find once again that although I appreciate gender shock as much as the next girl, I could not go there myself. I shaved. I got my nails and eyebrows done. I was kind to my skin. I flirted with Pete and Don and the guy I buy my morning coffee from. I escaped the prison of Archer and felt my humanity expand.

Terry's birthday party was over the top. His guests were all white or shades of Asian, the kind of guest list that makes me feel viscerally unsafe and opens my ears to racial insult. One of Terry's uptown friends had contributed the venue, a private party room at a downtown restaurant, a couple more stocked the bar, another guy brought flowers, mostly yellow, which is Terry's favorite color next to brown, a DJ spun, Pat and Sal, two dykes with a catering business, made the hors d'oeuvres out of tasty things not on my diet. Everyone was buff and stylish, the outward and visible manifestations of money and taste. I came as Darla. Neither she nor I knew anybody there.

After hugging the wall for a while, I'd just fallen into conversation with an off-the-charts intense young journalist in Ralph Lauren horn-rims when Terry wandered up.

"You two met each other," Terry said. "Good."

"I don't know his name," Darla said, "and he hasn't asked me mine."

"Oscar, this is Darla," Terry said. "She's just about to sing for me."

Until they're scared, who knows they have a fist inside their gut? Mine clenched. My hands trembled at a steady low vibration. "Terry, it's been a long time…."

"A long wait. I know."

"I can only do two songs anymore."

"I love them both."

"Damn it, Terry, I'm scared."

He flashed me a silky grin. "Get over it, bitch. This is my birthday. Do you have your backup tracks or not?"

I pulled the thumb drive out of my cleavage and handed it to Terry. He walked it over to the DJ and leaned into the mike. "Tonight I give you an amazing chanteuse, my dear friend…DARLA!"

For just one interesting instant, one I remembered keenly from Before, I was two people fusing, Archer and Darla. The alchemy is in the voice they share. Picking songs, Archer has to be careful to find ones they can both believe in, not just the lyrics or the mood but the tempo and the beat and the range. How to sell it is Darla's problem.

She took the mike, blew on it, smiled at the audience, then especially for Terry, eyes fixed on him, and sang.

> *Dig if you will the picture*
> *Of you and I engaged in a kiss*
> *The sweat of your body covers me*
> *Can you my darling*
> *Can you picture this?*
> *Dream if you can a courtyard*
> *An ocean of violets in bloom*
> *Animals strike curious poses*
> *They feel the heat*
> *The heat between me and you*

Our version of "When Doves Cry" is more like Patti Smith's, smokier and jazzier than the original and I used her arrangement, which has a bass line, but it's still Prince. I had them by the end of the first verse. I let my voice out and felt my body fill up with light. Archer's ghost, yin to his invisible yang, I moved, danced in the musical interludes. Became Darla. Not so different, really, from being ridden by Yemaya.

Voices rose with the applause, reached out and wrapped around me. Terry came over, stretched up and kissed Darla on the lips. My cheeks were on fire. Sweat drops big as pearls rolled down the back of my neck. The young journalist's eyes burned into me. I couldn't quite tell if he was smiling or not.

"Ready for number two?" Terry said.

Darla was ready. In fact, she couldn't wait. I filled my lungs with all the air I needed to deliver the next song, Billie Holiday via Cassandra Wilson, whose voice is eerily like Archer's own.

> *You don't know what love is*
> *'Til you've learned the meaning of the blues*
> *Until you've loved a love you've had to lose*
> *You don't know what love is*
> *You don't know how lips hurt*
> *Until you've kissed and had to pay the cost*
> *Until you've flipped your heart and you have lost*
> *You don't know what love is*
> *Do you know how lost I've been*
> *At the thought of reminiscing*
> *And how lips that taste of tears*
> *Lose their taste for kissing*
> *You don't know how hearts burn*
> *For love that cannot live yet never dies*
> *Until you've faced each dawn with sleepless eyes*
> *You don't know what love is*

Damn. Darla belted the song out despite the stupid tears that welled up in her eyes. I hoped the glue that held my eyelashes in place was waterproof, that the rush of emotion would play as theatre. Behind his horn-rims, the journalist's eyes were big, and beside him Terry's face looked like a mask, frozen expressionless.

Cruelty or catharsis?

The two songs we remembered how to sell are not easy on the heart.

THIRTY-ONE

꩜

That's part of the story of that night but not all.

Let me move the camera a little and shoot a B-roll.

The place is a room and the room is for private gatherings, the sort of room where rich people hold wedding receptions and fundraisers for chic and esoteric causes. That is to say, wood paneled, discreetly lighted, furnished with an elegant severity, bold reflective surfaces and touches of brushed aluminum, all attention subtly driven to the wall-that-is-window and the San Francisco street outside. The people who fill the room are overwhelmingly of the queer persuasion, one queer persuasion or another, which means that in general they are better dressed and behave with more cachet than the same size random sample of straight folks would. A few brightly turned-out queens light up an otherwise somber fashion palette. Darla and Oscar stand at a tall round table near the window, which allows them to look outward those times looking at each other or looking inward gets too uncomfortable. Because neither of them drinks alcohol, there is nothing to blunt the edges of their encounter. Archer—that is, me—hovers near the ceiling, watching. I am there and not.

Oscar of the horn-rims is slim and muscular, Semitic, a Jewish boy with curly black hair and surprisingly blue eyes. His skin is pale with a dork-ish pallor that does not excite Archer's racial antagonisms, nor, evidently, Darla's. You have to understand Darla's situation here. She is innocent as a newborn, or a zombie newly awakened, maybe, after eight years in the crypt, a fledgling creature who is just beginning to master herself as entertainer, never mind a sexual being in an evening gown, so that even though she is older by at least a decade than the young man she's talking to, she is in some ways far less experienced. At the same time, she is waking up inside that self. *I have a dick. I have tits. I feel desire.*

Darla didn't have much time to figure it out before ocha took her nail polish away. Hardly any at all. And this boy Oscar is something else.

"Honey, I feel like you're collecting me," Darla says.

"That's what writers do."

"You're saying the personal is political. I'm saying girls just want to have fun."

"I find intelligence sexy. Sparring is fun."

"Oh, are we sparring?"

"Girl, we are mixing it up." Oscar touches Darla's arm, a touch as electric as live wire brushing skin. The physical rhythm starts to develop, a promising groove.

Oscar's brow knots. "Still, don't you think," Oscar hesitates, starts again. "I mean, drag is necessarily subversive. Undoing gender norms is a political act. That's the whole point."

"The whole point? Honey, that's bullshit," Darla says.

"How so?" He says it mildly, but Darla can see how focused he is. If only she were a little surer of herself.

"It's not the norms that come undone, it's the self. Archer doesn't control me any more than I control him. Drag is the one great opportunity to be instead of to know."

Oscar giggles, which makes him girlish. Darla likes surprising him. "Nice," Oscar says. Then, "Young gay men are fierce. We have to be. We came out young, into a hostile world. We've been through so much already."

"Come back and talk to me about 'so much' when you've lost a man you loved." Unpremeditated, that.

"You've got stripes," Oscar says.

"Damn straight. I earned them."

"I didn't mean to sound smug."

"You couldn't help it, baby boy."

Oscar lowers his head, penitential. Probably mock penitential. "My blog is about gender politics. And social history. And you're right, I'm always collecting material."

"Yes, Virginia, there *is* a generation gap." Darla waits a beat, then says, "The question is, can we rise above it?" Puts her hand on her hip and lets the question hang. Around them, half the party moves to the music.

"Are you asking me to dance?" Oscar says.

"You asking me?" Darla says.

Oscar takes Darla's hand and leads her into the mash of dancers. Each stands utterly still for a moment, letting the beat find them.

Near the ceiling, Archer—that is, me—watches, waiting to see what will happen next.

THIRTY-TWO

Jerry Dixon called at 7:30 the next morning. I wouldn't have answered the phone, might not have heard it at all if I hadn't fallen asleep with it in my hand. I was wiped out but not hungover.

"So what have you found out?" Dixon said.

"Yrrrrgh," I said.

"I was thinking we could get some breakfast."

"Arrrrmmmg," I said. "Let me call you back in a while."

"I'm in Santa Cruz," Dixon said. "You're my one big chance to get out of the office."

"You've got to be kidding," I said.

Now that I'd found my words, we agreed that he'd cool his jets while I cleaned mine. At 8:30 I slid into a booth facing him at a downtown diner. We made an odd couple in Santa Cruz, not least for being two black men. He was nursing a cappuccino and looking bourgeois.

I ordered orange juice and a tofu scramble with whole wheat toast. Dixon went for huevos rancheros with a side of bacon. Waiting for my juice to arrive, I realized I was ravenous. Darla had been too nervous to eat anything before she sang and too busy after. I tossed back the first OJ, hailed the waitress and ordered another one.

"How about bringing me one of those, too?" Dixon said. He pulled a Moleskine notebook out of his jacket pocket. "So, here's the rundown on Michaela's house: Six former crack addicts, seven AA regulars, one doctor, a museum curator, three day laborers, a database designer, two salesmen, three part-time baristas, a nurse's aide male, a nurse's aide female, a clinical psychologist…" He glanced up at me. "A night watchman…."

"Security professional," I said. "Go on."

"Exotic dancer. Sex shop owner. Three school teachers. One prostitute, reformed, two occasionally active. Landscaper. Babysitter. Roofer. Plumber. Wal-Mart greeter. A legal secretary. Baggage handler. Cleaning lady. Recreation director. Four social workers. Two gang members. Two professional musicians. Nine have criminal records. With the recession, fifteen are underemployed or out of work."

"That sounds about right," I said.

"So what have they got in common?"

I thought about it, not for the first time. Gave him my standard answers. "Crappy childhoods. Spiritual longing. An excess of reverence. Looking for an edge." Said out loud, my standard answers sounded glib. "Maybe the biggest thing is, people want to feel special. They want to feel unique. When we're initiated, they dress us up like royalty. We're 'crowned.' The Christians aren't giving you that. Neither are the Muslims or the Jews." I drained the OJ. "The music's irresistible. There's lots of obedience but very little piety. We get protection. We get to mess with the odds."

"Where do I sign up?" Dixon said.

"And if you stick with it, show up, study hard and kiss ass, you can have your own house and your own income stream some day."

"How much can you make?"

"It's all under the table, off the books. But it's not unreasonable to assume that Madrina took in at least a hundred thousand a year, tax free."

"Not shabby."

"It's pretty hard work," I said. "A good manager with good business skills could make it a whole lot less so. And then, for some people, it's their religion, not their business. That's a whole different trip, I think."

"What about race?" Dixon asked.

"There are houses in the Bay Area that are close to all black. Some of those folks had no use for Michaela and how she mixed it up."

"Michaela was a Pole from Pittsburgh."

"Yeah, but who knew? She claimed she grew up in Panama. She claimed she had some kind of melanin disorder that made her skin look white."

"A real wannabe," Dixon said. "So, if I showed up on her doorstep, how would Michaela have treated me?"

"Older straight black cop? She would have treated you really really well. Madrina loved watching cop shows and having black god kids. And in the religion, there are some things only straight men can do."

"I like what I'm hearing."

"Go to hell."

"Touchy."

"It's a sore point."

Breakfast arrived. My stomach gurgled with joy. "There's something else, too," I said. "About the whole African roots thing." First forkful. Warm and worth waiting for. I chewed before I spoke. "Michaela practiced the Lucumi tradition. That is, Africa enslaved, Africa pushed through the food mill of Cuba, Africa adapting. Black, but not exclusively African. More like a new religion for a new world."

Dixon dabbed a smudge of egg yolk and salsa from the corner of his mouth. "Syncretism," he said. I must have looked surprised because he said, "What? I can read."

"After two years' vacation, I'm just unwinding what's the tradition and what's the Roman Catholic overlay and what's spiritism and what's strictly Madrina Michaela."

Dixon cocked his head. "Religion is dangerous because people are dangerous," he said. "When I was a kid, this deacon in our church was always trying to touch me where he wasn't supposed to."

"That's icky," I said.

Dixon stood up from the table and picked up the check. "Pretty much made an atheist out of me," he said.

The fog had burned off while we ate. The tide was high and frisky. A bunch of tourists clustered at the railing of the pier, watching a family of seals ride the waves. Their voices, carried back to us by the wind, were happy and shrill.

"Want to walk out that way?" Dixon said. "Want to tell me what you found out?"

"Only if you reciprocate."

"You start," he said.

Without mentioning Shawnita, I told him what I'd learned about the Cuban girlfriend. "She's an opportunist," I said. "But that's not illegal. The most interesting thing there is that she passes a nasty spirit. Which she did during a misa on Sunday night. Her spirit got in a fight with Betty's spirit. They both have marks to prove it."

"The husband gives her an alibi."

"Unless el monstruo can travel without her."

Dixon stopped walking and looked at me, hard. "Do you believe that shit?"

"It's part of the mythology. It's part of what I've spent two years trying to wash out of my brain."

"Okay," he said. "What else?"

I told him about Michaela's moveable car lot. "Damn, that's good," he said. "But I'd hate to think a pissed-off customer did her in."

We joined the seal watchers at the splintered railing. Dixon pulled out his phone and took a picture. "My wife loves animals," he said.

"Why do people kill each other?" I asked him.

"Money and love, mostly. Except in war."

"Isn't it like doctors say, if you hear hoof beats...."

"Don't think zebras. Yeah. But this case is so exotic. I'd hate a pedestrian ending," Dixon said. "What else you got?"

"That's it," I said. "Your turn."

"What do you want to know?"

"Everything."

Dixon leaned up against the railing, back to the sea. "So, according to the sister, Grandma Krawczuk was one mean old bitch. She wanted Michaela to be feminine and submissive, with ribbons in her hair. Michaela wanted to play football."

"Seriously?"

"Yep. They let her play Pop Warner till sixth grade. Michael Ann wanted Grandma to take up her cause with the school board, so she could try out for the junior high team. Sister remembers a knock-down drag-out between Michael Ann and Grandma that left them both bruised and bloodied. Michael Ann ran away the summer after her sophomore year of high school. She doesn't really show up on the radar again until she's picked up for shoplifting in Miami six years later."

"That's where she found the religion."

"So I hear. The sister's coming out to deal with the remains. She favors cremation."

"Lots of luck with that. What else?"

"The autopsy's not complete yet, so we don't know cause of death, not for sure. But there's a chance that the killing and the butchering were separate events."

"That doesn't make sense."

"It does to somebody," Dixon said.

We left the seals behind, wandered past the souvenir shops and the eateries, silently watching the far horizon and the sky full of fat clouds and the tourists in their vacation t-shirts. Couples mostly, mostly heterosexual and, on a Monday morning, mostly old enough to be retired. Diving around us, gulls cried like cranky babies. We walked in silence. At pier's end, we both stared outward, at the horizon.

"You know I've been reading," Dixon said. "Do you do this divination stuff?"

"Some. Not very well. I'm not sure I believe in divination anymore."

"What would you say if I told you I want to get a reading?"

My laugh was bitter as a seagull's. "I suppose I'd take you to a Babalawo, then," I said.

In my pocket, my smartphone gave its metallic text-message burp. I palmed it and read: *How Can You Mend a Broken Heart. Al Green.* It was from Oscar.

"Boyfriend?" Dixon said.

"None of your business."

Most of the way back up the pier we didn't talk. When my phone rang, not far from the surfing seals, I saw it was Ernesto calling. "God brother," I said, and punched ANSWER.

THIRTY-THREE

❦

Any illusion that I'm a fast driver evaporated on that ride. Dixon blew
me out of the water. When a CHP guy on a motorcycle pulled us over
near the summit, Dixon flashed his Oakland badge, explained we
were on our way to a crime scene, and accepted the offer to escort us to
the Alameda County line. The two of them might have been pair skating
through traffic, they moved so much in unison. After our escort left us,
Dixon slid into the car-pool lane, pointed the car north and stepped on
the gas. As agreed, we picked Ernesto up outside the Buttercup Café.

The truck was parked in Maxwell Park, up above Mills College, a red
Chevy pickup that needed to visit a car wash. I don't know much about
trucks, but this one looked old. With the street cleaners due in twenty
minutes, it was the only vehicle on the east side of the street. Ernesto
handed Dixon the keys. "Do you mind if I stay in your car?" I trailed
behind as Dixon reached the truck, unlocked the door, did a slow motion
double take and blew his huevos rancheros in the street. After that, he
called CID. "We'll just wait right here until they come," he said. "Nothing we can do."

The crime scene team arrived about ninety seconds in advance of the
street-cleaning truck and diverted it in case there was anything to deduce
from the dust and debris on the street. I sat in the car with Ernesto while
Dixon filled them in. After a while, he motioned to me to join him. I gave
the pickup and the police team a wide berth.

"I need you to identify the victim," Dixon said.

A glance was enough to recognize her and a lifetime too short to forget what I saw. It was Betty. Someone had opened her chest and removed her heart. It sat on her stomach, cased in too much yellow fat.

"It's her. Betty Winslow." I turned away from the truck, stepped far enough away to thin the stench of blood and entrails. Pale sun touched my face.

"Next of kin?"

"I may have a number for one of her sons." The number I had was old and had been disconnected.

The investigators wore surgical gloves. They were less pretty than a TV forensics team, a chinless Chinese guy and a pudgy white kid. After a few minutes, the Chinese guy emerged from the cab holding a blood smeared three by five card between thumb and forefingers. He waved it at me. "What does this mean to you?"

Machine printed in capital letters it said: ONE'S LUCK IS A FICKLE THING.

Maybe because it was on a card, I recognized the refrain from my own days of study and self-quizzing. "Oche meji, I think. It's a religious text, like a proverb."

"Kind of like, 'The explosion of the volcano is your daily life'?" he asked me.

"Yeah, that's one too. I couldn't tell you the number right now."

Behind me, Dixon said, "That's 4-6."

I realized three things in so close to the same instant they seemed like one thought: He was right; he'd seen this before; madrina. "That's why you've been reading," I said.

"It is."

"Does anybody know?"

"Not outside the department."

I'd known for ten, fifteen minutes my legs felt shaky. Now I realized my bladder was about to pop. "What do cops do when they have to take a piss?" I asked.

"Step up real close to the car and unzip."

Ernesto looked the other way while I hosed down the passenger door of Dixon's car. A lean mom running with her two year old in a stroller just missed the excitement. She swerved to the other side of the street and pushed on uphill. Then Dixon and another cop got in the front seat.

I climbed in the rear next to my god brother, who was sweating hard. Since the day was cool, it had to be from nerves. For the first time, I noticed he was wearing cheap imitation Crocs, pale blue. After a couple hours' steady gnawing, his fingernails were pretty much gone. I remembered him saying he'd quit smoking not too long ago.

"Start from the top and tell us what happened and what you did," Dixon said. His tone was not unkind. Ernesto explained the truck scheme pretty much the same way he'd told me about it. "This morning I got up and started my rounds, moving the trucks that were on streets with sweepers coming. I had a cup of coffee in my hand. I just spilled some on my pants, so I wasn't looking when I opened the door." The second, older patch of vomit was his. His empty coffee cup had rolled to the curb. "Then I called my god brother Archer."

"Why did you call him?"

Ernesto shrugged. "He went to law school. And I told him about the trucks." After a moment, "And I was scared."

I asked him what had been eating at me. "Does anybody else know about the trucks, Ernesto?"

"Only Carlos. Since Sunday he's been helping me." Ernesto looked desolate. He seemed to understand he was not helping Carlos.

An ambulance came and collected Betty. Dixon drove Ernesto back to the Buttercup to pick up his truck. There remained the problem of what to do with me. "I've got to get home to babysit by five thirty. My wife goes bowling," Dixon said. "The city will buy you a bus ticket."

Ernesto said, "Man, I have to keep moving trucks."

I called Terry and got through.

Terry's office was in the Financial District, in a narrow building occupied by startups and non-profits, one of those buildings with late nineties décor in the lobby and strictly seventies on the worn back stairs. The receptionist left soon after I arrived. I admired Terry's suit, dark blue with a barely visible stripe, sleek but with enough fabric to ripple slightly when he walked. His red tie was loose around a loosened collar.

"Court today," he said.

"If I'd known I was going to see you I would have changed."

"So what's going on? Why are you carless in the North Bay?"

There must a hundred refrains that tell you don't gossip, don't tell your business, a secret told is not a secret anymore. Every odu has its own variations on *keep your mouth shut.* Since odu were on my mind, I held those thoughts for a minute or two before I told him everything. As usual, he listened well.

"So, are we having dinner in San Francisco or in Santa Cruz?"

"Do I get to choose?"

"Sure."

"Here. In the city. I miss it."

He took me to a Turkish meze place with enough depth in the menu to please us both. We talked about Carlos. "I need you to testify at his hearing," Terry said. "I want it in the record that apparently sane people believe that ocha saves lives."

"Can I get you a pinch hitter?"

"I want to hear you sell it," Terry said.

"I don't know that I can."

"Sure you can," Terry said. "You have to."

For a minute, I thought there was a mean glint in his eyes. We talked about Oscar. "Isn't he adorable?" Terry said.

"Is he your special friend?"

"God, no. I can't handle that many words per second."

"He's awfully young."

"And yummy."

I sighed. "I'll be careful. And honorable."

"Better you than me," Terry said. "I've already killed too many friends."

Finally, we talked about where we were going to spend the night. I realized that after everything that had happened, I didn't want to be at my apartment. We went to his instead.

THIRTY-FOUR

I cannot even imagine the first wave. The sudden betrayal of the body, the world's creepiest diseases piling on, no "syndrome" then, no rhyme or reason, just improbable unceasing insults to the organism. One day you're nature's pinnacle, you're an engineering miracle and next, almost that fast, you're on the recall list. How did they stand it, our forebrothers, half a generation and a whole world before us? Kushner made it okay to say it was hard, freaking impossibly sometimes undoably hard, to die. To watch a perfect human being disintegrate before your eyes. To help a lover go.

Everything was ad hoc back then.

Now at least there are names for things, expectations, known series of if, then, next, now, what now. Now that the enemy has a name and a dossier, we can pick our weapons and train for the fight. With each year that passes, more of us win. Having a common enemy makes community. We know the drugs, the clinics, the hospitals, the hospices, the mortuaries, the decisions about what to do with what's left after all the rest is said and done. We make dark jokes about the inevitable. Sometimes we start again.

We slept on the tiled floor in the front room of the house in Matanzas. The tiles were faded, broken here and there, but the Moorish pattern, reds, greens and dull golds, cast a wash of color upward across the whole beautiful ruin. From the street, the house receded in a straight line, one room at a time—salon, sitting room, bedroom, bedroom, what must have been a dining room, last in the string a kitchen, with a once-working bathroom to one side, a provide-your-own-water toilet and a shower stall that frankly scared me. In the side yard there were rickety benches, scarred tables, a laundry sink, a cistern, a crisscross of lines strung to dry wet clothes and rags and, sometimes, skins. A backyard full of palms and animals waiting to be sacrificed, the poultry in crates, goats and sheep tethered by rope to the trees and prone to swoon in the heat, as if they were resigned. Coconuts, bananas in the backyard, and an outdoor shrine for the ancestors where all the rituals began with songs and prayers. The house had no windows but tall wooden shutters that opened between the bedrooms and the courtyard. When the neighborhood had electricity, so did the house. It was midsummer, breathtakingly hot, and municipal water trickled through the system for about an hour a day if that long. The rest of the time, it came from the cistern in pots and gourds—water collected without prejudice from pipes and sky.

In the room where Lance and I slept on the floor, frogs lived in the walls and sang all through the night. Mosquitoes danced over our bodies and sipped our blood while we slept. When summer storms ripped the sky, the sound of thunder filled the house and the rain came so hard the roof was no barrier. The ceiling rained like the sky. Lance was sick by then, always feverish, coughing through the night. Our elders slept on lumpy beds in the bedrooms, two rooms away. It was my moral challenge to find a way to detach myself so completely from the racket Lance made that I could sleep beside him.

Not his fault. I am separate. I am centered.

"You boys got everything you need? Did you put your bug spray on?"

It was Sophia, my assistant godmother, my ayubona. While the godparent performs high ceremony, the ayubona does or directs the grunt work and the heavy lifting. Sophia had looked after me at our ocha and since adopted my twin as her favored foster child. Later in the week, she would be receiving Ideu and hosting a drumming for Madrina Michaela's Aganju. At home she was a software saleswoman, an account rep, blackness and double X-chromosomes making her a token times two. Sophia had graduated from Berkeley, a Cognitive Sciences major, drove the only sports car in Madrina's house, had the nicest apartment in the best neighborhood and ate sushi more often than anymore else. If she'd been a little thinner or a little bit less smart, she might have moved to LA and tried to make the film thing happen. The nice word for her younger brother Perry was "slow." Less politically correct folks called him retarded. Perry lived with her parents in Rockridge and slept with her in Matanzas. He was receiving Asohano with us the next day.

"Try to get some sleep," Sophia said. "Tomorrow's going to be a big day and a long one." She knelt to kiss us both goodnight, me on the cheek, then dabbed the sweat off Lance's forehead with the hem of her faded gingham apron to make a dry place to put her lips. "Sweet dreams," she said. Outside, the thunder rumbled so deep I could feel it in the ground, just like car bass in the ghetto back home.

San Lázaro is the patron saint of Cuba, a miracle healer who gathers Christ's resurrected Lazarus and the leper kings of Africa up under one burlap cloak, Babaluaye from Dahomey, Asohano of the Arara, maybe more, mixing ocha, Congo, adding a dash of the power of the dead. You receive him for your health. It costs a lot. I won't be a spoiler and describe the ceremony, in case you need to stand there yourself one day, only say it is the most profound ritual I have ever experienced. During it, you are sure you have been transported to the dawn of time, to the first healing magic, birthed by the Neanderthals or handed down from the stars. During it, I felt a swirl of curious spirits around me and small cellular shifts inside me, as if the ritual had the power to rewrite my DNA. Scientific scoffing to the contrary, I believe it strengthened my immune system, improved my luck, gave me the will to keep on fighting for my life.

What about Lance?

He felt the ceremony deeply, soaked up the aché and generosity of the Matanzas priests who came to help us, got plentiful advices and many blessings from Asohano in his reading two days later, went through the same process I did without experiencing the same surge of health and optimism. Maybe it helped him handle the end. Maybe it helped make me strong enough to stand by him through what was coming. Perry got as caught up in the ceremony as a kid at Disneyland. Asohano himself cleaned his head. Maybe it made him smarter, I don't know. He made us laugh.

How to explain the rest?

There are probably more ocha priests and more Paleros and Babalawos in and around Matanzas than anyplace else on earth. Every kid on the street knows more than you do about your religion, having been born into it and the elders are its keepers, its ancient avatars. They know the songs, the dances, the prayers, the spells, the procedures, the curses, the incantations, the herbs and flowers and the powders, the recipes, the refrains and the names of the ancestors stretching all the way back to Africa. In Matanzas, even the crickets know secrets. While it's part of Castro's revolutionary socialist nation, it is other things, too, a living museum of West African religions and a colony of the United States of Santería.

Our trip to Matanzas was arranged by the Cuban priest Esualaomo, a shirt-tail relation of Obanoshukua. He found the house we stayed in and did our ceremonies, he rallied the community to assist, hired the drummers and the singers and the dancers, bought the goats and chickens, hand-made the artifacts, dug up the bones, provided the fabrics to build the thrones, made sure everyone who helped got a hot meal on site and went home with a portion of protein, meat from the birds and four-leggeds that had been sacrificed. All the cash we paid passed through his hands, or so we believed until one night when Michaela was out collecting lore from the elders and the rest of us were left to our own carless, penniless devices at the old house, eating the granola bars and Top Ramen we'd brought with us in our duffel bags, playing dominoes, all except for Perry who was drawing pictures with his colored markers, and Esualaomo came by to visit, bringing us paper cones of peanuts as a treat and two of his kids to play with Perry, whom they adored.

We sat outside in the courtyard until it was too dark to see and then went in, sprawled in Sophia's bedroom to shoot the shit and pass the time. Lance stretched out with Perry on the bed. Esualaomo, shirtless on a hot night, compact, medium brown and quite hairless, foiled teeth reflecting his relative prosperity, sat in the carved rocking chair. In Spanish, he asked, "How much have you all paid your Madrina for this trip?"

Sophia translated for the rest of us. I anted up a number, doubled it for Lance, tripled for Perry. Sophia added her ceremonies. She was about to tell him the result, but he shook his head urgently, no.

"I don't want to know your number," he said. "I want to show you mine."

He pulled a folded sheet of paper out of his cutoffs pocket and spread it flat on the floor, a detailed accounting of everything he'd spent on our behalf, rent to rogations, including his own derecho. That means fee.

The difference between our number and his was more than ten times his number.

"Oh my god," Sophia said.

On the way home, we were stranded in the Havana airport for eighteen hours. After ten days of getting used to temperatures over a hundred degrees, the icy air conditioning assaulted Lance's lungs. He trembled and burned. Bored, Perry ran up and down the open terminal, bouncing off fellow travelers. To keep from going nuts, Sophia and I switched up responsibility for our charges every hour or so. Madrina sat on a barstool, nursed mojitos and "read" her fellow patrons to pass the time. Back in the States, Sophia confronted Michaela with the numbers we'd learned from Esualaomo. Their relationship never recovered. Sofia disappeared from the ilé and from the area, apparently in disgrace.

Lance never recovered either. Six hard months later, he was gone.

THIRTY-FIVE

"**I** probably owe you," Terry said. "For cleaning up my mess." He was spreading raspberry jam on an English muffin, the most ordinary of actions. We were having breakfast in the diner near his apartment. I knew what he meant but didn't like how he said it. I didn't know what to say back so I kept my mouth shut.

"You did a good job," Terry said. "Better than I would have."

"People rise to occasions," I said. "You just don't know."

"I know I'm selfish and squeamish," Terry said, looking up at me, head tilted to one side, smiling, so the words felt as much like flirtation as confession.

"So am I." Serious but not flirty.

This was us without Lance. He still had a place at the table but it seemed like he was shrinking. My phone sang. I assumed it was Pete at the Clinic calling to chew me out but when I looked I saw it was Ernesto. I let it go to voicemail.

"This is a little weird," I said.

"It is, isn't it?" Terry-of-five-years-ago showed up in his smile.

"**B**endición," Ernesto said when I finally called him back. "Archer, I need your help."

"What, did you find another body?"

"God," he said. "Thank god, no."

"Look, Ernesto, I don't want to be mean, but I have a life. I'm on a time out from the ilé. From the religion, too. I may never come back."

157

"The morgue released Michaela's body to the funeral home. Her sister flew in. She wants to meet us there."

"Us?"

"I was thinking you and me."

"I have to go back to Santa Cruz, man. I have to work tonight. Call somebody else."

"I would have called Betty, ibaye. She was good at this kind of stuff."

"May she rest in peace," I said. "You can handle it, Ernie. You were Madrina's right-hand man."

"That's the problem, man. I'm a great right-hand man. I'm the best. But to be a leader? I suck. My ita says so."

"Did it ever occur to you that your ita said exactly what Michaela wanted it to say?"

He was quiet for a minute. Then, "Naw. It's odu, man. Odu don't lie."

"Odu are subject to interpretation."

"I've always seen you as a leader kind of guy," Ernesto said. "And I'm scared to meet the sister by myself. What if she's like Madrina?"

I like to believe I'm immune to flattery. It was curiosity and his promise of a ride home in time for work that finally made me agree to come along.

⌇

Bowman's Funeral Home is deep in the 'hood and close to the cemetery. The cemetery has resting places for all the city's people, even though you could probably guess a dead person's race by his date of death, Chinese people being the newest occupants, then African Americans and so on back to the early German burghers. It was the only cemetery in the world that would make a place for the nameless children who died in Jonestown. Their mass grave is close to the crest of a hill and marked by a simple stone, with a handful of fading plastic roses lying on the grass in front of it. I'd been to Bowman's Mortuary once before, when my god sister Orchid's youngest son was shot dead in the street. The place was creepy, the way it tried to look like a rich people's house with fat red sofas and fresh flowers on the end tables and gilt picture frames on the wall and even a probably fake fireplace, when you knew it was really all about the business of death, a few degrees cooler than was quite comfortable and weirdly quiet. Ernesto and I sat a couple of feet apart on one of the squishy sofas and were weirdly quiet ourselves.

Things got even weirder when a simulacrum of our madrina came gliding through the automatic doors. It was her and not, Madrina in a blue dress with hair below her ears, two, three times as much hair as Madrina ever had, black streaked with silver. Her trip to the other side had changed Madrina's body language, too, pushed her chin back and lengthened her neck, instigated the aforementioned glide where there used to be nothing but swagger. This Madrina was slim compared to ours, maybe thirty pounds lighter on a close to six foot frame, and little gold crosses dangled from her earlobes. The weirdest thing of all was the lines on her face, those lines that your personality carves into your skin after you've put in a few decades on the planet, so you wear a kind of signature expression even when your face is at ease. This was not Madrina's expression. These were not her lines.

The creature glided up to us and put out a hand that was Madrina's with a different manicure. "I'm Esther Ann. Sister Immaculata," she said. "I'm thinking you didn't know Michael Ann was a twin."

Ernesto took this as permission to stare. It was hard not to. I introduced us. "I'm sorry for your loss."

"I hadn't seen my sister for a long time," Esther Ann said. "After birth we got less and less close."

"Wow," I said.

Esther Ann had a laugh that sounded slightly loony in the hushed funeral home. "Not to overstate the obvious," she said, "but you look like you just saw a ghost." She extended her arm. "Pinch me, if you want. I'm real."

"Twins are magical in our tradition," I said.

"Twins are magical, period," Esther Ann said. "Michael Ann and I finished our growing up apart. We didn't see each other for more than twenty years. But I'm the mother superior of a Roman Catholic convent."

"Nature or nurture?" I asked.

"I'm a lesbian, too," she said.

The same and not. Esther Ann wore a fur glove on Michaela's iron fist but was no less adept at getting her own way. "Unless my sister left an insurance policy or a will with enough assets to cover burial, she's going to be cremated. Her—what do you call yourselves?"

"Godchildren."

"You can do whatever you want with the ashes."

"If we raised the money, would you let us pay for a cemetery plot?"

"How much have you raised so far?"

"A hundred and fifty bucks," Ernesto said.

Sister Immaculata put her hand on his arm. Gently. "It's hard times. People are hurting. Once the spirit's gone, the body is just a thing." After a beat, she said, "I've scheduled the funeral mass for Monday, at the new cathedral by the lake."

"That's a huge venue," I said.

"That's why I need your help making sure everyone who cares knows about the service," Sister Immaculata said.

Ernesto the good lieutenant stepped up and joyfully agreed. At that point a thin man in a dark brown suit appeared in the lobby, looking for all the world like a Jehovah's Witness dressed up to canvass the neighborhood. "Are we all here now? I'm Lawrence, your service-planning consultant."

We followed Lawrence into his office, where he did his best to up-sell us. Some of the coffins in his display book cost more than a new car. I could feel Ernesto wanting to waver, but Esther Ann held firm and ordered the cheapest casket it was legal to burn a body in. She declined the offer of a pre-immolation viewing and afternoon tea there at the home.

"Think of us as *your* home," Lawrence said.

Sister Immaculata declined both his hospitality and ours, saying she would be staying with her order while she was in town. She wouldn't mind help at Madrina's house, though, going through Madrina's things. Once again, Ernesto was happy to oblige. They agreed to meet up there first thing the following morning. Then it was time to disengage, an odd process between strangers who've just shared the intimacy of making funeral arrangements.

"Well," Ernesto said.

"Very well," Sister Immaculata said.

"What was she like?" I couldn't help asking.

"You know, I was asking myself that the whole way here on the plane," she said. "Brilliant. Mean. Insanely hard working. Maybe crazy." Sister Immaculata pushed the hair back from her left ear, which revealed that the top half of the ear was gone. "My sister did that," Sister Immaculata said. "Even as a child, Michael Ann was fascinated by knives."

—

"I didn't think it was going to be like this," Ernesto said. We were driving south out of Oakland, just ahead of the commuter traffic.

"Which part?"

"I just wanted to learn the business," Ernesto said.

"Do you really see it as a business?"

"Well, sure. Madrina always said people who study hard should be well paid for their knowledge. That there will always be enough people with problems to fill up a hundred houses." His laugh was bitter and prideful. "Fuck knows how hard I worked to be the one she was teaching."

"I bet."

"After Sophia ran off, there was an opening. Everybody wanted to be the one."

"Not me."

He laughed, not kindly. "Everybody and their dog, man. It got ugly for a while."

"How did you get to be the one? Your innate good character?"

"Very funny. I did two things. I made an alliance with Betty, ibaye."

"And?"

"I turned myself into Madrina's Hebrew slave."

After that, we were quiet for awhile. Traffic thickened around us as we approached San Jose, strings of semis separated by singleton commuters in their fuel efficient cars.

"Who's killing Santeros?" I said.

"I know, right? Shit. Who would do such a thing?" He steered with his left hand and crossed himself with the right. "I had them put a safety lock on my door, right after Madrina. I still don't feel safe."

One of the scars of Santería I'd been trying hardest to heal was the paranoia, the chilling conviction that the universe is both purposeful and by default, innately hostile. Theologically speaking, that sense of impending doom, the fuck-up always waiting to befall you, is human life in neutral, improvable through ebo, disaster the inevitable product of disrespect. In the old stories, the orishas are full of faults and foibles, they play tricks on each other sometimes, but as far as I can tell, there's not too much affection for flawed humanity, no finding the humor inside the darkness. Every other odu tells you you have no friends. To be fair, I'm sure being a slave on a sugar cane plantation did not inspire irony. But this is California, 2010, and I can't live without it.

I thought of one of my mother's sayings and passed it on: "Locks keep honest men out." Then, "Seriously, Ernesto, I think you're next. It's an occupational hazard of being the right-hand man."

I meant to be funny in a smartass kind of way, but I might as well have hit him in the stomach with a baseball bat. Ernesto slumped behind the wheel and his knuckles went white around it. I repented my flippancy. "Hey, don't freak out, man. It could just as well be me."

THIRTY-SIX

⚬━┼━⚬

Dark and quiet. Peaceful campus. I may have actually formed the thought: *I am the security guy at the safest place on earth.* I may have saluted the notion *My alma mater is a civilized institution* as it wafted by. I was glad to be there in that plain, scuffed useful space. Sometimes bad taste, or no taste at all is comforting. I was glad to have a strong Wi-Fi signal so I could watch *RuPaul's Drag Race*, Episode Three, "Country Queens," in between scans of the video monitors.

On a standard night, maybe one scan per twenty turns up something you want to look at closer. You read the screens as pattern, not detail. When something's wrong with the pattern, you zoom in. Some little glitch at the edge of perception says, TILT, so you do. What read first like *Fistful of Half Drunk Boys Coming Home from a Night Downtown* resolved into *Four Boys Carrying Girl*. I watched until they moved beyond range of the camera. When I picked them up next, they were on the grounds of Crown College, headed toward the apartments. Something hungry in the way they moved said I was not witnessing an errand of mercy.

I worked for the UC Santa Cruz police department. They paid me one grade lower than the sworn peace officers and made me wear a slightly tackier uniform. If I saw something suspicious in my sweeps I could escalate to the campus cops—since the recession, that was "the cop," one per shift—or I could check it out first myself. In this case, I left a voicemail for Angela, the cop on duty that night, telling her where I was headed and why, watched the security camera up by the Crown/Merrill apartments for as long as I could see the boys, to get a sense of where they were headed. I saw them shift their burden roughly, getting ready to carry it up the stairs. At that point I headed for the car. A can of mace and a cell phone were the weapons I had on hand. In five minutes, maybe less, I was in the Crown parking lot, orienting my body in the space so it matched the security camera shot. *Over there. Now up.* Logic said they'd taken her to one of four apartments, but which one? I asked Yemaya for a sign. My first guess was wrong. A pink coed with a bed sheet wrapped around her squinted out at me, on a scale of one to ten, medium-pissed.

"Campus security," I said. "Sorry to wake you up. Have you seen or heard anything unusual in the last fifteen minutes or so?"

"Besides a rent-a-cop at my door at four AM?"

"Besides that."

"Besides the assholes who live next door coming home drunk again?"

"Which next door?"

She pointed to the right. I thanked her. Then I pounded on the door next door. Inside, men swore. It sounded like they were bouncing off walls. I thought I heard a female voice rising above the male rumble, thin and fretful, a strand of silk piercing leather.

"Security. Open the door now." They talked it over. "Now," I said. I did not say Now, or Else. I didn't really know what else I was going to do until I wrapped my fist in my Security windbreaker and slammed it through the front window. From there, it was not hard to reach around and unlock the front door. I was thinking in imperatives, not consequences. Those four tough boys more or less wilted at the sight of me, fell back from the kitchen table and the naked girl on it. One, maybe more of the boys was still zipping. Furious movement, then everyone stood absolutely still. The girl moaned and turned her head without opening her eyes. Her legs were still spread apart. There was a gob of cum high on the inside of one thigh.

I grabbed the nearest junior rapist by his shoulder and slammed him against the nearest wall, which happened to be the kitchen wall, with enough force it knocked a frying pan off its hook. The noise startled us all.

"Take your hands off him." The voice came from my right. I turned toward it. From my left, "You can't just come in here and break up a private party."

These guys were so quick at concocting a story I could only think they'd done it before. I had an inkling where this was headed—thuggish black security guard goes rogue, violates civil rights of college students. I un-handed the creep—he had curly light brown hair and one of those nasty pug noses that white folks do sometimes, pulled my cell out of my pocket and started taking pictures of the scene—a naked Chinese girl, a quart of gin, four white boys and a butt plug as big as the Ritz. The boys started yelling all around me. They wanted my cell phone. If they hadn't rushed me, tried to pile on, tried to rip it out of my hands, I might have stayed calm. But just like sensing a shift in the pattern is a visceral thing, so is reacting to an attack.

My mother's immediate response to my coming out in Texas was to enroll me in karate class and make me go. I hated it but I learned. After I learned, I liked it better, stayed with it until my belt turned brown. I don't use it often, but any set of tricks you spend years mastering, your body remembers, even if your mind doesn't. I time traveled back into the zone (Mr. Lim Kee's Karate Studio, 1981) and neutralized my opponents, not before I unintentionally broke one freckled Caucasian nose and took a few hits myself. I felt the violence hormone surge inside me, traveling brightly along my limbs like any good drug does. My skill encased my rage. I wasn't out of control, but the edge was in plain sight. "What the hell do you think you're doing, you little pieces of shit?"

The conciliator of the group stepped toward me, palms up. "Hey, no hard feelings. You can do her next. Nobody needs to know about any of this."

Wrong answer. I picked him up and then I tossed him down. "What did this woman ever do to you?"

Unaccountably, a couple of them laughed. The conciliator said, "Fuck-ing bitch destroyed the curve."

"You mean to say you're gang-raping this girl because she gets better grades than you do?"

That uncorked the volcano. They started to spew, stuff they no doubt learned at home from their mommies and daddies. Damn Asians and In-dians coming over here and taking advantage of our educational system. Taking jobs away from Americans. Damn drudges make it so we can't have a life. Fucking know-it-all bitch. You don't think we'd fuck somebody that ugly because we wanted her.

As they ranted, the Chinese girl raised her head a little and inched to-ward the edge of the table so she could puke on the floor and not herself.

That uncorked me. To the broken nose, add a couple of cracked ribs, a couple of lost fillings, and two black eyes. Did they fight back? In a manner of speaking, they did. Was it a fair fight? Who knows. Angela said that when she got there they were all huddled in the bathroom, nursing their hurts. I'd carried the Chinese girl, her name was Ling-Si, to the sofa, covered her up with a blanket I found in one of the bedrooms and was washing her face with a cool cloth. One by one, Angela brought the boys out of the bathroom and took their statements.

Ling-Si started to come around. Her eyes when she first opened them were wide and blank. Slowly, my image took shape in her brain. "Hey, welcome back," I said. "How do you feel?" I prayed she wouldn't scream. Instead, she rose up weakly and emptied what was left in her stomach on my lap.

"Do you remember what happened to you?"

If she did, she didn't want to talk about it, just lay back on the sofa and closed her eyes. Angela appeared beside me. She was early middle aged, motherly, although she and her husband didn't have kids. They'd "retired" to Santa Cruz from the LAPD a few years before. He was a Santa Cruz city cop. She worked on campus. "Can she walk?" Angela asked me.

"I don't know."

She leaned down and gently opened the blanket. I had not ministered to Ling-Si's injuries down there, only covered them up. Angela whistled at the sight. "I think I better call the ambulance."

She made the call, then turned to me. "How are you doing, Archer?"

"I gave better than I got."

"Better than you should have, probably. One of those kids is claiming to be related to half the Orange County Republican party."

"What's he doing at Santa Cruz?"

"You *are* naïve," Angela said. "Don't you see the swastikas on the bathroom stall walls?"

"I try never to use public restrooms," I said. "Those little monsters raped this girl, for god's sake. Because she wrecked their fucking curve."

"At very least, they're going to claim you used unnecessary force."

"I caught them red-handed, committing a violent crime."

Angela sighed. "One in every four undergraduate women is subjected to sexual assault during her college years."

"Here?"

"Everywhere, Archer. Better you should have caught them stealing her purse. Property, that's worth fighting about."

Two paramedics came. They put Ling-Si on a stretcher and carried her away.

"Where do you want to give me your statement, Archer? Here, or back at the security office?"

"If you need to wait for the city boys, we can do it here."

"We don't have to wait. The city's not involved."

"You're not arresting them?"

"Until we have a medical report and until we know if Ling-Si wants to file a complaint, this is a campus matter."

"I want to file a complaint."

"You're a witness, man. You have no standing," Angela said. "Actually, let's get out of here. This place has got a nasty vibe."

I handed her my cell phone. "First take my picture." Fat lip, bruised jaw and upper arms. "I want proof those shits were in a bad mood." I turned my head side to side and she snapped the pictures.

"Good call, Archer. I'm not sure I would have thought of it."

"Document everything. I learned that in law school," I said. "Not bad advice for a black man."

My shift ended about the same time I finished giving my statement to Angela. I thought I was eager to get home, but when I finally got to the safe bubble of my car, I just sat there for a while. It was like I had an off-switch and someone threw it, or maybe a circuit breaker and it blew. I had no power left and not much feeling. It was times like that I missed Lance most, when I talked to him out loud as if I thought he could still hear me and talk back.

Daylight comes slow beside the ocean. The sun has to climb over the tops of the mountains first, time measured in vertical degrees. Morning had just touched Santa Cruz when I put the key in the ignition, started the car and drove home.

Ling-Si was the number one student in the bioengineering program for her year.

THIRTY-SEVEN

<hr/>

Oscar sent me an email with the link to his blog: http://www.thetablet.com/gendernationX. He'd told me it was syndicated, so many backlinks, so many hits, plus it got printed in an alternative paper somewhere, maybe in Palo Alto, I forget. "It's really weird to watch your thoughts turn yellow" he'd said. "Digital thinking is forever young."

I'd just brewed my second morning mate when I logged on. I don't know what I expected but it was not to see Darla, microphone a few inches from glistening lips, her face twisted up with the emotion she was wringing out of the song or it was wringing out of her. She was shiny with ladylike sweat. She looked scary and hot. Darla resembled Archer less than Sister Immaculata looked like Madrina. Oscar must have taken the picture with his phone.

Mad about Darla: A Lesson in Details

"Black queen" traditionally gets two hits in my memory bank: The proud and desperate ladies of *Paris is Burning* and in the glamor campy camp, RuPaul. Much as it's my job and my bent (yes, I'm bent) to explore cultural phenomena as they pertain to gender, I've always been a little reluctant to step across the racial divide. I don't like to be called a poacher.

Darla is both black and a queen, not a professional performer but a polished persona with a voice that at its purest wraps itself around your heart. I met her at a friend's birthday party last week. She sang. After she sang, I asked her a lot of questions. Darla responded generously, not always to the questions I asked. About halfway through our conversation, I understood that I'd been trying to herd her toward my own foregone conclusions.

That's what journalists and scientists do, seek to prove our hypotheses. We believe such and such is true and then pile up evidence to prove ourselves right. If someone were to engrave the words *He spotted trends* on my tombstone, I would not feel insulted. If I got credit for defining and naming what I spotted, so much the better. I came at Darla with a sheaf of psychic specifications for Men Who Wear Women's Clothes and another set for Drag Queens, all of my ideas congruent with the latest in queer theory.

Darla shot the theory and its proponent down. "Cross dressing," she told me, "isn't just about gender. It's insurgency against the paranoid colonizing power of the ego. It makes 'the other' real. Every time I dress up, every time I put on makeup I'm feeling with somebody else. Life is too short to get trapped inside just one body or just one way of being." Darla laughed. "Drag is when you get into something that you don't control. It's not about thinking, baby boy."

It took me five days to find the lesson in our exchange. For me, it's something like this: Journalists and academics generalize, that's their job. Artists particularize. We come at truth from opposite directions.

Darla, honey, I really love your dress.

Oscar Applebaum

Hot damn. The picture was one thing. The word picture was something else. Pleased and violated, I felt both ways—not, when you think about it, so different from what makes sex interesting. After I blushed and fluttered for awhile, it came down to this—Darla liked the attention.

A few people had left comments in response to Oscar's blog. One of them said he should get over himself. Another one said there are as many reasons for gender-bending as there are people on earth. Somebody else just said, Fun! The site wouldn't let me comment unless I registered. I signed Darla up for her own account. Then she signed on and left a note: *Baby Boy, Give me a call. Darla*

I wanted to tell him about whaling on the white boys. Not five minutes later, Archer's phone rang.

～

"Totally loca," Ernesto said. "You're not going to believe what she did."

"You mean Sister Immaculata."

"Yeah, her. She said since Madrina had paid cash for the trucks, they all belong to her now. She's giving them to that Catholic church in Fruitvale, St. Elizabeth's. Any member of the congregation can check one out for fifteen bucks a day plus gas. It's like, a memorial to Madrina, she said."

"You're the only person who knows where the trucks are."

"Not anymore," Ernesto said. "Sister Immaculata is very persuasive."

"How about the house?"

"Forget the house. Madrina was just about to get foreclosed on."

"The things we didn't know."

"Madrina bought at the top of the boom, with this crazy-ass non-conforming no-credit-check jumbo loan that just adjusted up. She was paying close to six grand a month."

"Or not."

"Not. Nobody's got that kind of money anymore. Sister Immaculata wants to have a yard sale this weekend. She'll give the proceeds to the house to pay for Madrina's itutu."

"That's creepy."

"It kind of is, huh? You want to help?"

"No thanks."

"I'm going to put it on Facebook," Ernesto said. "You think I ought to put the Mass there, too?"

"Why not."

"Just friends or friends of friends?"

"Damn, Ernesto, I don't know."

"At least nobody else got killed lately."

"That's a good thing," I said.

～

After that, I drove out to the north end of town, where the wetsuit of my dreams is on layaway. The shop doesn't really do layaway, but Don who owns it is old enough to understand why I want to do it that way. It's how I bought my first bike. It's the complete reverse of credit-card debt. I gave him another ten bucks and shot the shit for a while. When I'm around Don, I talk like that, like the drag version of a Vietnam veteran. Don's got watery blue eyes and skin that looks like it was cured by a crazy taxidermist, in this case, the weather, wind and sun. Don started surfing the year I was born. He's smoked a lot of weed. Just seventy-six dollars more and I take the wetsuit home with me.

Home. My split lip hurt. I was going to try icing it when I got upstairs even though it was probably a little late for ice. My box was full of bills and junk mail. I rifled through the envelopes while I climbed. One was plain white, with no return address. My name and address were laser printed in capital letters. There was nothing inside but a three-by-five card.

THE CAT WEARS GLOVES, it said.

THIRTY-EIGHT

Dixon's house was in the hard-won hills, on the high end of 98th Avenue just below the golf course. The houses are split-levels that hug the upward climbing streets, built in the seventies by a new black middle class. Standing in his driveway, I could see the bay below, San Francisco across the way and the glow cast up from the horizon by the very last of the late day sun. When it touched the bellies of the brooding clouds, it turned them gold around their bruises. I stood there long enough to watch the color drain out of the sky. Dixon was, by his account, one of only a couple of OPD detectives to live in Oakland. Walking up to his front door, I felt weirdly hollow inside.

The door opened almost before I touched the bell. There was Dixon, minus his suit coat, his tie and his shoes. His black socks were intact but thinning at the heels. He gestured at the small regiment of footwear inside the door, then at expanses of pale gold carpet beyond. I kicked off my sneakers and lined them up with a pair of sturdy black oxfords. Dixon's shirttail had escaped his trousers in back and his belly looked bigger than it did when he was wearing his jacket. He oozed man-of-the-house authority and homeowner's pride cut with an edge of wariness that made me wary, too.

"Thanks for coming up here," Dixon said. "I try not to leave home on my nights off." He led me past a formal living room, past a staircase and on into a sprawling kitchen where I met Leslie, Mrs. Dixon, a handsome woman a couple shades lighter and maybe a decade younger than Dixon himself. Her style appeared to be haute Macy's and she wore it well. She

was standing at an almond-colored stove that matched all the other ap-
pliances except the stovetop, which was mostly chrome, stirring something in a big pot. When Dixon introduced us, she put down the spoon
and took my hand in both of hers.

"Hello, Archer. You will join us for dinner, won't you?" She stepped out
of the kitchen and drew me toward a little family room where a woman
I first guessed to be her mother slumped in a Barcalounger in front of
the flat screen TV. A green metal tank stood like a faithful dog at her feet
and fed oxygen to her nose through a tube. Scarred, mottled skin, skinny
arms and legs, big belly. What hair she had was coarse and gray. "This is
my sister, Juanita. Juanie, say hello to Archer."

Juanie's eyes strayed briefly away from *Jeopardy*. "I don't like mushrooms," she said.

"No mushrooms tonight," Leslie said. Juanie reinvested her attention
in Alex Trebek. "She likes the theme music," Leslie told me. "Juanie
was a trivia queen back in the day. She could answer every question."
I followed Leslie back toward the kitchen, where she confirmed what
I suspected. "Between the dementia and the weed, she's pretty far out
there." Late-stage AIDS. My silence was a question and Leslie answered
it. "Juanie was a junkie. She's been positive more than ten years. She
came to live with us when she couldn't take care of herself anymore."

"How long?" I asked.

"Almost two years."

"I lost my partner, almost five years ago now."

"I'm sorry."

"Me too."

Juanie didn't join us at the dinner table. Leslie said she was pretty much
subsisting on Ensure. I turned down the beef stew and piled my plate
with bread and salad. From my place at the table, I could see a bank of
framed family photos, their parents and their kids, I guessed, all pro-
fessionally shot, all better than average looking. Inside a silver frame, a
beautiful young Leslie fed a piece of wedding cake to a young man with
not a touch of silver in his hair.

Dixon said, "So here's the strange thing. Leslie actually had dealings
with Michaela. She knew her."

"How long ago?"

"It was before Juanie got diagnosed. Twelve years, maybe more."

"I was probably around then."

Leslie studied me, subtracting the years and the beating that comes with them. "You do look sort of familiar," she said. "There was a lot of interest in Santería in the Bay Area back then. You remember. It was half black history, half black magic, and a lot of stories passed around about people kicking crack because of it, beating Hep C and cancer and AIDS."

"Yeah, I remember."

"Authentic African spirituality." Leslie smiled. "I knew the Christians didn't have a thing to offer us. I checked out that woman in San Francisco, the one who wrote the book. I liked her, but I didn't want to go to church in San Francisco, so I started looking for houses over here." Smiled at Dixon. "Jerry was skeptical."

Dixon smiled back. "But supportive."

"Tolerant. So my friend had started to get involved with this woman called Michaela de Estrella. She brought me along to a couple of bembes. Once I went for some kind of ceremony and plucked some chickens. It was sort of fun, but Jerry thought I was nuts."

"You stayed out late," Dixon said. "And you stank when you got home."

"That's true," Leslie said. "Still, I loved the music and the dancing part. Then my friend took me and Juanie to Michaela to get readings."

When most people tell you how they came to the religion the first time it's the same story—an orisha talks to you at a bembe and then you get a reading. Themes emerge.

"It was the first time I'd been one on one with Michaela," Leslie said. "My friend was there to take notes, but she stayed in the background, you know? Michaela was seriously creepy."

"You figured that out right away?"

"Leslie is very intuitive," Dixon said. "She'd make a great detective."

"She wouldn't look me in the eye. And I felt like she was trying to sell us something. Especially Juanie. Something called lickies, like that."

"Elekes."

"Nine hundred dollars," Leslie said.

"Most people say they feel like Eleggua could see inside their heads."

"You know, I just figured Sophia had been telling her our secrets."

"Sophia? Oh my god. Sophia was my ayubona."

"I know," Leslie said.

"Oh my god. Do you know where she is?"

Leslie nodded. "I do. And she'd like to see you."

"I heard she went to Miami."

"She didn't like it there. She's been back for what, honey?"

"A long time. She lives over in South San Francisco."

"Lessy? Mommy! I peed myself." That was Juanie, in the other room. Leslie pushed away from the table. "Hold on. I'm coming."

That left me and Dixon at the table. By filling my mouth with bread, I meant to buy some thinking time.

"Sophie says you're sane and honest, as Santeros go. That I should take you off my short list."

"Sounds good to me."

"Where were you today?"

"I was at home most of the day."

"Can you prove that?"

I thought backwards and saw that I could not. "I called you as soon as I checked the mail."

"You could have sent that card to yourself."

"I guess so."

Dixon refolded his paper napkin and put it on the table.

"We found another body today, with another saying pinned to it."

"Where?"

"Down at the MLK wetlands. In the shrubs. Somebody's dog found it."

"Who?"

"Woman named Carly."

Carly. Sixtyish, a refugee from New York who had adopted Michaela, or the reverse. Fabulous spiritual hustler. At misas, she passed more spirits than Tyler Perry makes movies. The woman could find angles in a round house. Carly. "What was the refrain?" I asked him.

"*The one who knows the truth does not die like the one who does not know,*" he said. "What does that say about Carly?"

"Sounds like an accusation."

"How did she and Michaela get along?"

"You scratch my back, I'll scratch yours."

I folded my hands in my lap, squeezed one hard in the other, breathed.

As if he'd just peered inside my private mind, Dixon said, "This time we know where Carlos was."

"Good. That's good," I said.

Leslie called from the back of the house. "Jerry, I need your help putting Juanie to bed."

"Coming." Dixon disappeared into the family room. A couple of minutes later, he passed back through, carrying his sister-in-law in his arms. "Say goodnight, Juanie," Dixon said. "Here we go." He headed for the stairs, moving as if she was light as a butterfly. In the rear of the house, I heard a washing machine start to churn. Leslie came back. "I'm going to have a glass of wine. Want one?"

"No, thanks."

"It won't be long now," she said. "I couldn't do this without Jerry."

"Why not hospice?"

"She's family." Leslie tossed back half the contents of her wineglass. "Sometimes I wish she'd hurry up already. Then I feel guilty."

"I know," I said.

Dixon came back and followed his wife to the Chianti. "Want some, Barron?"

"Naw."

"Are you going to the mass for your godmother?"

"I haven't made up my mind."

"I expect the killer will be there," Dixon said. He sipped his wine and stared at me. "Barron, I want you there. I want you to help me watch the crowd."

I was starting to feel like a chewy toy in the jaws of a police dog, used and abused. "What if it's me you're looking for?" I said.

"I'll keep an eye on you. You watch everybody else."

Leslie leaned across the table. "If you don't mind, Sophia would like to go with you. She's nervous about going alone."

"Okay," I said.

Dixon emptied his wineglass and filled it up again. "We don't normally drink till Juanie goes to bed. Did you bring the letter?"

I passed him the envelope that came in the mail. He studied the envelope, then reached inside, pulled out the note card and set it down on the table. Leslie craned to read it while he did.

"'The cat wears gloves.' What the hell is that supposed to mean?"

"I've never been quite sure. But the odu, 5-5, means the priest will never birth the orisha that's speaking."

"So it's a dead letter."

"Maybe."

"This stuff makes my head hurt," Dixon said. He drank more wine. "This is the first time we've had advance warning."

"Maybe it's a joke," I said.

"I don't think so. I think he's toying with you."

"He or she," Leslie said.

Dixon sighed deeply. "Do you always need to be so fucking politically correct?" he said.

"So first I sent it to myself and now somebody's playing with me?"

Dixon played with another big swig of Chianti. "I don't know what the hell's going on. If you help me out, I'll take it as a sign of your good character. I might be able to squeeze a per diem out of the consultant budget."

A voice in my head advised me it was time to say good night. I was worn out. The week had had its way with me. Dixon's head games had put me off balance. On the other hand, damn it, I was afraid of the dark. When Leslie invited me to catch Nancy Pelosi on *Charlie Rose*, I pretended to be a lot more interested in Obama's healthcare legislation than I really was. I joined the migration to the living room and sat with the family in front of the flat-screen TV.

"Charlie's more alert since the bypass surgery," Leslie said.

I confessed to not owning a television. I admired Speaker Pelosi's new do, an ash-brown newscaster bob, and speculated about Botox, too. She looked almost hot, considering. And I felt safe.

Dixon's phone rang then. He said, "Shit," and went in the other room to answer. When he came back he was pulling on his jacket.

"Come on, Barron. Let's go."

"Where?"

"Your Madrina's house." He was already tying his shoes.

Madrina's house in the hills was only a mile or two away. The lights were blazing when we got there. In the driveway, Sister Immaculata was locked inside her rented Prius, ashen-faced and big-eyed, and didn't come out until she was sure she recognized us. We followed her down the sloping driveway around the side of the house and into Michaela's triple-wide garage—besides the over-size lot, one of the features that sold her on the place. A good ocha house is private and sound proof, has lots of storage, good ventilation, more than one sink, a floor that's easy to clean—Michaela's garage had its own drain. She'd installed vast amounts of shelving to accommodate all the ritual necessities, everything from animal cages to washtubs, low stools and terra-cotta bowls for making omiero from herbs and water, plastic buckets, Costco-size packages of black plastic lawn and leaf bags, bundles of clean rags and shelves full of honey, rum, molasses, toasted corn, dried fish and rat, cascarilla, candles and surgical cotton, stacks and stacks of plates of all colors, hundreds of them, and plastic storage boxes where she archived artifacts of her godchildren's ochas that wouldn't be touched again until they died. I was used to seeing the room full of Santeros working ceremonies, full of sacred songs, call and response, or late night gossip, I was even used to hosing and scrubbing that smooth concrete floor until there was no trace or scent of blood left when all the other work was done, of being the last one there and turning out the lights. It was one job Michaela had trusted me to do.

Now every light was on. Five cat traps, the kind the ASPCA loans you to capture ferals so they can be neutered and released, stood in a neat row, doors open. In front of them, five neatly gutted cat bodies, five plates laden with neatly excised cat bones and bits and organs, a grisly parody. I was dimly aware that cat entrails smelled different from goat or fowl.

"We spent the whole day getting ready for the yard sale. After Ernesto left, I went out to get a hamburger. I ate in the kitchen," Sister Immaculata said. "Then I came in here."

"Barron?"

I shook my head. "Santeros don't sacrifice cats. At least, not that I ever heard of." Then I saw it, Madrina's knife with its sharp blade and beaded handle, clean and shining and squarely placed at the exact middle of the row of plates, as if to claim credit for work so neatly done.

"I expect the cat wore gloves, don't you?" Dixon said.

My heart slammed once, hard, and my vision wavered for a moment, as if I'd seen a ghost.

"When we were children," Sister Immaculata said, "Michael Ann hated cats."

In a voice meant to abet and not disrupt reflection, Dixon asked her why.

Looking at the cat carcasses, she shook her head minutely, side to side, a sad and thoughtful gesture. "I've always believed that people hate what they're most afraid of," Sister Immaculata said.

PART FOUR

When you meet a stranger in a lonely place, greet him warmly and with respect.

Traditional Proverb

THIRTY-NINE

⊂━✕━⊃

Don gestured toward the visitor's chair. Once I sat, I felt less like a third grader. My lip was still messed up and I'd made no effort to cover the aging bruise. I wanted my boss to see that the altercation had not been all one way.

"So," Don said.

I sat tight.

"This is a dilemma," Don said. "Those boys from Crown have filed a complaint against you. Ling-Si has yet to make a formal complaint against them."

"Did you get my email?"

"I did. And if Ling-Si wanted to file a rape report with the city, those photos would make her case."

Don was a balding white guy about my age. He graduated from the New Jersey State Police Academy, back in the day. Less than a year as a rookie in Newark convinced him he was too attached to his personal safety to make a good city cop, so he interned with the campus police department at Princeton, then moved west, college to college, until he landed the top campus cop job at Santa Cruz. A decent, cautious guy, with about as much imagination as a spoon. I got points with Don for being a law school grad. "There has to be a hearing, Archer."

"Bring it on."

"The rule book says you have to be suspended until the hearing."

"That sucks."

"What really sucks is that I can't pay you during your suspension."

"Is that in the rules, too?"

"It's in the budget. If you're not working, I have to hire a temporary replacement. I can't afford to pay two people for one job."

"As long as I can keep my health insurance." I could tell this was a new thought. I watched him play with it. "It's cool," I told him. "You wouldn't offer health insurance to a temp."

"I'll look into it."

"Don't cut me off, man. I have a pre-existing condition."

"I hate this fucking recession," Don said.

"How's Ling-Si?"

"She's out of the hospital. Her parents came from San Diego. They're staying at the Comfort Inn on Plymouth."

"Is Ling-Si back in the dorms?"

"She's staying with her folks."

"Has she gotten any counseling?"

"Not that I know of."

"So those fucking little beasts are going to mess up her life *and* mine? That doesn't seem right."

"Sex crimes on campus are tough."

"What I saw wasn't about sex. It was about hate." Don sighed like a man unfairly burdened by circumstance. It pissed me off enough to say, "Why is it you're not sticking up for me? I may have saved a student's life."

Across his littered desk, past the snapshots of his pudgy blonde children, Don sent me a hangdog look. "The president of the university got a call from the governor. Arnold got a call from one of his big contributors. That's how the good old boys do it."

"So now you're one of them."

"Don't give me that shit, Archer. I'm doing what I can."

"Yeah? Like what?"

"Your health insurance. I'll fight for that."

"Good." Grudgingly, "Thanks."

"I'll get the hearing scheduled as soon as I can."

In the juju lobe of my brain, I could hear the ghost of my Madrina saying Santeros don't do politics, they do ebo. In the political lobe of my brain, I decided it was high time I took up the fight for justice. "You'll be hearing from my attorney," I told Don.

Doc Sam had my back. Her spirits had risen and she was ready for a fight.

We stood shoulder to shoulder at the door of Room 207. I was clutching a mid-price floral arrangement from Safeway in token of my get-well wishes for Ling-Si. When a well-groomed Chinese woman answered the door, I thrust it forward. "Mrs. Chen? These are for your daughter. I hope she's feeling better."

Mrs. Chen looked rightly suspicious.

Doc Sam stepped forward and introduced herself. "Mrs. Chen, this is Archer Barron. He intervened in your daughter's rape."

Hearing the R-word rattled Mrs. Chen. She thrust the flowers back toward me. I felt about as welcome as a vinyl siding salesman.

"Archer may have saved Ling-Si's life," Doc Sam said. "Certainly her reproductive capability." She paused a moment to let that sink in, then said, "May we come in and talk with you?"

"Wait, please." Mrs. Chen all but closed the door on us. Voices rose and fell inside, speaking Chinese. Doc Sam and I looked at each other, raised our eyebrows and stood our ground. And stood it. It must have been at least five minutes before Mr. Chen opened the door and invited us inside. The room was tidy, covers pulled back over two king-size beds. My flowers sat in the middle of a round table ringed by upholstered motel chairs. Mrs. Chen invited us to sit.

Doc Sam stepped up. "Archer works for the campus police. He spotted your daughter's attackers on one of the video-surveillance monitors. He went out of his way to investigate. I think it's fair to say that what he found both angered and appalled him."

The Chens kept their eyes on Doc Sam, their faces glazed by good manners.

"I don't know how much your daughter remembers," Doc Sam said.

"Very little, thankfully," Mr. Chen said.

"There are some things you should know. Archer, can you tell the Chens *why* their daughter was treated in such a terrible way?"

I folded my hands on the table in front of me. My fingers looked too long, too thin. "Those boys were angry at your daughter for setting the bar so high academically. They wanted to punish her for that."

The Chens murmured like doves. "We know that sexual assault is an act of war," Mrs. Chen said. "Until now, we didn't know which war."

"Racism was part of it, for sure," I said. "But their greatest concern was the curve."

"The boys' behavior was not just nasty, it was criminal, " Doc Sam said. "The efforts their parents have made to cover it up are completely unacceptable."

"What efforts are those?"

We shared what we knew. "The idea of buying indemnity for rapists makes us both a little nuts," Doc Sam said. "If Ling-Si is willing to file a criminal complaint against her attackers, there's a chance they'll be punished."

"Our daughter has survived one brutal attack. You really think she ought to invite another?"

It was a reasonable question. In a reasonable society, law and custom would mediate between our basest impulses and our behavior. Why should a victim be asked to turn into a crusader? I tried to imagine getting raped then making a fuss about it. Emotionally, it didn't compute.

Doc Sam said, "Nothing protects the next victim better than the courage of the last one." She lifted her chin. "Nobody else really cares, until it happens to them or somebody close to them."

"This isn't a Hollywood film about a spunky girl standing up," Mrs. Chen said. "This is my child."

"Your brilliant child," I said.

I didn't mean to make Mrs. Chen cry. Her face clouded, then the cloud broke, one continuous, lightning-fast shadow passing over her face, raining tears. She seemed deeply embarrassed to be crying. How you feel when somebody hurts somebody you love. When somebody you love hurts.

"Of course, it's her call," I said.

The storm passed fast. The woman had stripes in self-control. "I beg your pardon," she said.

The whole visit seemed more and more like a bad idea. I wanted to figure out how to let Doc Sam know how much I wanted to leave.

"Archer had the presence of mind to take photos at the scene," Doc Sam said. "And he was there. It's not like it's her word against theirs. They'll get nailed."

And then, Ling-Si came out of the bathroom, swaddled chin to toe in what must have been her father's bathrobe. She walked carefully, as if each step had a price tag and her face was woefully pale, her eyes swollen above and purpled underneath. At the sight of her, I stood up, less a vestige of my southern boyhood, I think, than the impulse to salute her status as a survivor.

She stared at me. "I recognize you," she said.

We stared at each other. "I hope you're feeling better," I said.

"I'm starting to heal." She looked down at her seated parents and Doc Sam. "What to do *is* my decision," she said. "I haven't made it yet. I'm still trying to figure out if I can finish the term."

"We want her to come home." Mr. Chen reached for his daughter's hand but she kept it just out of reach. He tried again. She took a full step to the right. These were small gestures, gracefully performed.

"She has that choice," her mother said.

"I think I need to take a nap." Ling-Si backed up until she found the bed then sat down on it.

"We should go," I said.

Doc Sam got up. "You're a brave young woman. If there's anything you need, please call me at the clinic." She gave Ling-Si her card. "Do you mind if I ask you one question?"

Ling-Si shook her head. "No."

"What's the last thing you remember? How did you end up with those cretins, anyway?"

"I was having a beer with my girlfriend. Celebrating our mid-term grades. The guys came over and said they wanted to buy me a drink."

"That's all?"

"I remember the waitress bringing a new beer," Ling-Si said. "I remember thinking they'd finally got over their competitive bullshit." Reflexively, she added, "Sorry, Mom." To Doc Sam, "That's it. That's all I remember. I have a few random pictures of this man's face. He was there when I was waking up."

"Archer stopped the assault," Doc Sam said.

"I've been listening to everything from the bathroom," Ling-Si said. In the face she raised to me I saw less the particulars of age and race than the universal anguish of the victimized. "Thank you for taking care of me," Ling-Si said. "If I'm brave enough, I'll fight. The law gives me a little time to decide."

I thanked her and we left.

"So you'll represent me."

"Shit," Terry said, "I'm spoiling for the chance. I'd love to slap those GOP dickheads around."

"That's a relief."

"Don't worry about it."

"There's something else."

"Shoot."

"I bled."

I could hear him take a deep breath two counties away. Then, "Did any of it get on them?"

"I don't know. Maybe." At first I read the sound he made as a laugh, then decided I must have misheard. "What I want to know is, do I have to tell them my status?"

"Did you have to tell HR before they hired you?"

"Nobody asked."

"Because they can't," Terry said. "It's not legal to ask."

"Don't ask, don't tell."

"Gives it a whole new meaning, doesn't it?" he said.

"I don't know. There's an ethical issue here. It troubles me."

"On a scale of one to ten, how do you rate the rapists? Ethically speaking."

"I don't want to be like them."

"Look, Archer, if you tell them, you're asking for a very expensive lawsuit against you and the university."

"I know."

"If you don't tell them, maybe one of the fuckers gets sick. Maybe they all do. Maybe not. Is that so terrible?"

"I don't know."

"Blood is a weapon, Archer." Terry said. "My advice is, let it do its work."

FORTY

○━━✕━━○

So there I was, at the intersection of Bad Idea and Why Not, lounging against a stage-set lamp post, my imagination of myself more debonair than the blue-jeaned, sweater-wearing, sneakered reality, that guy with the slightly thinning hair, with the little lines that outlasted his expressions, those changes in the skin of his hands, from calfskin to rawhide, well, maybe not that bad, with a seed in the heart of him just starting to open, puzzling and problematic for how it brought memory and lust and ethics together in one skin, and how much it hurt to feel that opening.

What Terry and I had been doing was functional and fun, an erotic halfway house between self-relieving and full engagement with another human being. I suspect we both closed our eyes and dreamed of Lance. With my Madrina gone, with my faith in hiding, with everything in my life up for grabs, springtime was coming to my body.

How exciting the pain seemed. How scary it was.

How to welcome it.

How to do no harm to anyone, myself included.

I picked the restaurant and got there first, got a two-top by the window with a northward-facing view. One of us would see open ocean. One of us would see both land and water. I ordered a Perrier and chose the boundless view for myself. When Oscar arrived, I was willing to negotiate. With Darla in his mind, he would meet Archer. By looking outward, I gave him a moment's privacy to process the metamorphosis. The ocean calmed me, until a touch on my shoulder announced his arrival. He looked out at the headlands, the explosions of surf against stone, ceding the horizon to me without discussion. For a ghost of an instant, I played the scene with Lance, who always wanted both.

Oscar looked really young.

"Wow," he said.

"Wow."

"I didn't know what to expect." He didn't try to hide his curiosity or soften the scrutiny. "Wow."

"Be kind," I said.

"Always."

It was enough before the lunch hour that the bartender was covering the tables as well as the bar. He was a young surfer type, a couple of piercings, a couple tats, gently high.

"Mind if I have a beer?" Oscar said.

"Go ahead."

"Social lubricant."

"I thought your blog was that."

"You can never have enough lube," Oscar said.

"Seriously, do you use the journalist thing to pick up men?" This was nowhere I had planned to go.

He grinned. "Sometimes. But you should know that I'm absolutely serious about my research. That it sometimes has benefits is a side issue."

"I understand. You're a good writer."

I liked how he took pleasure from the compliment before he parried. "Do you know the difference?"

"I do. Law school flattened my style some, but I'm a pretty good writer myself."

"Law school. Terry said that's where you met."

"It is."

"But you're not a lawyer."

"Nope. I was a night watchman, but I got suspended yesterday. I guess that makes me unemployed."

"Why did you get suspended?"

"I did the right thing."

"Do you want to talk about it?"

"No. Tell me about you. Where's all the research headed?"

His grin was easy and self-deprecating. It appeared to be backed by a giggle, always ready to erupt. "A book, of course."

"Do you want to talk about it?"

"Maybe later."

"Is it about drag queens?"

"Only in part. But you've got to admit, drag queens are fascinating. I find them magical."

"Have you done drag yourself?"

The giggle, high and a little manic. "I've tried on this and that. It makes me feel wicked."

"Wicked is good."

"Indeed."

Outside the window, the colors of the day had intensified, the light yellowed as the sun burned through the ocean's breath. The level of Oscar's beer sank. "Want to go for a walk?" I asked.

"I do." He finished the beer. We squabbled briefly over the check, then headed out, left the boardwalk for the sand. He seemed shyer outside. "I want to take off my shoes," he said. "Do you mind?"

We sat down side by side and shed our shoes, rolled up our pants legs, wiggled our toes and burrowed deep enough to find the warmth inside the sand. Then we headed to the water's edge. With the ocean in our ears, there was no need to talk. We crossed the outposts of foam, stepped into the shallows, powerfully cold. Oscar's feet were broad and pale, with dark hair on the tops of his toes. I pointed at them. "You're a hobbit."

He laughed, then tucked his hand in mine. "Me Frodo, you Sam." And tugged me farther out into the surf. We stood side by side and let the waves find us, rock us, climb our thighs and soak our trousers, before it receded, sucking the sand from underneath our feet. I felt all these things but none quite so intensely as the place our hands joined us up, skin to skin. It felt so innocent.

When he was tired of playing in the little waves, Oscar pulled me out of the water, across the firm sand to the soft, dry stuff above it. He appeared to be on an expedition, searching for the best place to plop down, with the biggest sky above and the fewest eyes upon us. When he found it, he sat and tugged me down beside him. "That was fun," he said. "I love the ocean."

"Do your surf?"

"Never have," he said. "Will you teach me?"

"Maybe," I said.

We stretched out on our backs, side by side. I crossed my hands under the back of my head and stared up at the clouds, aware of how close our bodies were and careful not to let them touch. As soon as I'd established my friendly autonomy, he closed the gap, erasing the no-man's inch between us until our bodies touched, shoulders to anklebones. That's an approximation, given the difference in our heights. It felt like my nerves were glowing the whole length of that long frontier. After a while, I realized I could hear him breathing. I concentrated on my own breath, letting it nail me to the planet's sandy skin. We stayed like that for what seemed like a long time. Then Oscar rolled over, climbed on top of me and kissed me deeply on the mouth. I participated fully, I admit and imagined more, but when we came up for air, I said, "We need to talk, baby boy."

"Ha. That sounded like Darla."

"You know I'm positive."

"Everybody I've been attracted to for the last three years has been positive."

"You're hanging with the wrong crowd."

"A lot of guys my age are saying fuck it, might as well just get it over with."

"It may sound all existential and romantic, but that's a crock. You gotta love your latex."

"Don't you think it's my choice?"

"I think you need to be smart."

Oscar rolled off me, sat looking out at the ocean over tented knees. He spoke to me sideways. "Everything I've done since I knew I was gay has been about legitimizing my desire. I hate fences."

I sat up, too, mirroring how he sat and stared. "Me, too." The ocean filled our petty human silence with her voice. I imagined Yemaya was saying, Lust in. Fear out. Over and over again, just that.

While she repeated the mantra, driving it deep into my shuttered heart, my brain took little pictures of the man beside me, what I could see, knees and ankles and toes, the shape of his fingernails, the delicate curled back of his ear, a small patch of stubble where his razor scraped less close. All these things were powerfully other, making a wave of wonder and desire rise up inside me.

He was not Lance.

I was trembling when I reached over and ran my hand over his thigh. The ocean breeze had cooled the surface of his skin and I could feel the goose bumps among the hairs. He half turned to face me. I knew I could please him. I knew we would fit.

"If I'm honest and you're smart, we can do anything we want," I said.

FORTY-ONE

⟨━✦━⟩

A day later, after our bellies were full of lunch, Oscar headed back to San Francisco. He left me bouncing off the walls of my suddenly too-quiet loft. We'd packed more pleasure into thirty-six hours than I'd experienced in the last five years, not just sex but food and music and mutual self-revelation. I even let him explore my closet and try some stuff on. I felt like a sausage stuffed with sensuous delights. I also felt exhausted. One of the few indulgences we had not engaged in was sleep. A long nap swallowed what remained of the day. I woke up with my head groggy and my penis hard. When the phone rang, I hoped it was Oscar calling even though it was probably too soon.

"Archer, you home, man?"

The words were so slurred I couldn't tell who was saying them. I padded downstairs in my flip flops and found Ernesto on the front porch, clutching a half gallon of José Cuervo Gold and looking mysteriously blurred, the way drunks do.

"Bendición." Ernesto lurched at my shoulder.

"It's okay, man. Santo." I steered him through the door. "How the hell did you get here?"

"Drove."

"Like that?"

He lifted up the jug of tequila. "Me 'n' José."

I followed him up the stairs, shoving from behind now and then, ready to catch him if he started to fall. To be honest, I hardly knew the guy. In my apartment, he collapsed onto the futon. "Can I smoke?"

"No."

He tossed his Camel Filters on the coffee table and set the tequila down beside them. "Wan' some?"

Weirdly, I did. I got us juice glasses and poured them full. We half emptied them in one big gulp.

"Ever been to an itutu?"

"Uh huh. Lance's."

"Jesus."

"Madrina's?"

"We foun' money in her pots. Mucho dinero, man."

"Who did it?"

"Obanoshukua." He drained his glass. "Came up from San Diego."

"I thought he and Michaela weren't speaking."

"Yeah but then Sister Immaculata got on the phone. Totally shamed the guy. Shit, I'd hate to be in her class." He refilled his glass. I took another mouthful and felt the inner fire crawl down my arms and legs. Is booze alive? It felt like it. "She said as long as there was money to pay for it, Michaela ought to have the ceremonies she needed."

"Big of her."

"Very strong woman." Ernesto drank. "Jesus. That ceremony, man. It blew my mind."

"It's supposed to."

"I would have invited you but some of the others didn' wan' to."

"It's okay."

"It tore me up, man."

I nodded.

"All of her ochas wanted to go, except Ochun. She's staying with me."

"Maferefun Ochun." I downed the rest of my tequila.

"None of 'em stayed with the Cuban whore."

"Uhm." I remembered Lance's itutu, some of it, anyway. Archer was only there for an instant or two before Yemaya borrowed him, just long enough to see some of the others get possessed before he did. The next day my throat was sore and I had bruises I didn't remember getting. I felt desolate and cleansed.

"It was heavy, man."

"In Cuba, the body would have been there. They make omiero and wash the body, right in the room."

"I couldn' handle that, man."

"No."

"I'm all messed up."

I nodded.

"I got this card in the mail. It had my name on it."

"Another odu?"

"*The dead are not so dead.*"

"I got one, too."

More tequila, then, "I'm scared."

"Me too. Why did you come here?"

"I needed to talk to somebody in the religion. My partner, he doesn' unnerstan."

"You're gay? I didn't know you're gay."

"I hide it good, huh?"

"I always thought you were a macho asshole."

"Jus' a good actor, man. Mi madre doesn' even know."

"That's sad, man."

"Can I use your bathroom?"

I had to help him get there. Through the closed door I heard him piss, then puke. After a while, he staggered back to the futon.

"You want something to eat?"

"Jesus, no."

"So are they burying Madrina after all?"

"It was too late, man. They already burned her." He belched, juicily. "You goin' to the mass tomorrow?"

"Uh huh. I'm going with Sophia."

"Sophia? Used to be in the house?"

I nodded.

"Tha' bitch. She was suppose to make me but she stole all my money instead an disappeared."

"Maybe."

"What maybe. Madrina said. Madrina made me for free."

Never argue with a drunk. That was one of my father's precepts and I followed it then. "Whatever you say, man."

"You wanna see something freaky?" Ernesto reached inside his shirt and pulled out a five-by-seven photo, warmed by his belly and nicked here and there by his belt buckle. He handed it to me.

It was black and white with a matte finish, an exceedingly strange image, as if the photographer had re-staged a random detail from Bosch's *Garden of Earthly Delights*. At first look, it was a huge bird or an angel, a human-size figure nearly obscured inside a full-length cloak of blindingly white feathers. A black leotard subtracted mass and detail from the body inside the cape, so it registered on the senses as a life-size shadow, inseparable from the black background. Inside the brilliant feathery hood, the head and much of the face were covered in black. Through the holes in a black mask, Michaela de Estrella's big eyes stared out inconsolably.

It made me feel creepy, as if I'd been caught looking at a particularly kinky kind of porn. "Jesus. Where did this come from?"

"Sister Immaculata and I found it in Madrina's drawer."

"What did Sister Immaculata make of it?"

"She said something like, We are the Dow."

"The Tao, maybe?"

"Yeah, maybe. Then she laughed and threw it away. I took it out of the wastebasket when she wasn't looking. What do you think it means, Archer?"

Michaela wanted to die and she didn't expect to die anytime soon.

I would have told him what I thought but he wilted. Passed out. Tilted his head back, closed his eyes and started snoring, loud and strange as a wild animal. I eased him down on the futon and covered him up. The change of position silenced the snores, but as soon as he settled in, he started up again in a lower register, an even more random rhythm. The photograph I put face down in the far corner of the room.

It was another night in camping mode. I dabbed lavender on my pillow, though, put on my satin sleep mask and stuffed my earplugs in, all of which obscured the intrusion without quieting my mind. For that, I recited prayers and nursery rhymes until I finally fell asleep.

I didn't wake up until the rock came through the window. Ernesto didn't wake up at all.

TRAGEDY, DECEPTION AND DESPAIR ARE NEAR. That's what the message said.

FORTY-TWO

The window glass rained shards on my sleeping bag. The big stone landed near my head. Whatever I'd been dreaming got sucked up in a waking nightmare. I crawled out of my sleeping bag and made my way to the nearest light switch, managing to catch a splinter of glass in my naked heel. Once there was light, the stone could speak. Tragedy, deception and despair. It sounded liked the law firm from hell.

I grabbed my flip-flops and staggered to the window, stepping over the big pieces of broken glass. Cold damp air flooded in through the hole and made the hairs on my arms and legs stand up. There was too much light behind me, too little in the street, but I thought I saw a whoosh of motion out of the corner of my left eye. Gone? Hiding? The shadow moved too fast through too much darkness for me to see its shape. It could have been a dog or a cat or squirrel. Do squirrels hunt at night? My thoughts were sharp and scattered as the broken glass. Was someone hunting me?

Tragedy, deception and despair.

Ernesto emitted a nasty semi-human sound, eerie in the night chill. His face was slack, the jaw darkening with beard, bushy black eyebrows drawn together, maybe in response to the crash. I thought about waking him up, then pulled on my sweatshirt and grabbed the heavy cane I'd beaded red and white for Obatala in the long nights of my iyawo year and raced downstairs, not much concerned about my landlords' sleep. Out on the dark street, tossing the cane from hand to hand, I stopped to listen. What I heard was the rush of my blood in my own ears.

Tragedy, deception and despair.

Come and get me, assholes. Step out of the shadows. I wanted an enemy I could see.

Slowly, the night cold cooled my head. If I called the Santa Cruz police, all I'd have to report was an act of vandalism. I could call Dixon in Oakland, but there wasn't a hell of a lot he could do from there. My cane was only a useful weapon if someone came in range of it. In fact, I was gloriously exposed. I heard a car door slam a street or two away. An engine growled to life, tires engaged with pavement. It was the rock thrower, I was sure. I wanted nothing more than for him to turn into my street. It didn't happen. The car sounds diminished. Since I hadn't bothered to consult a clock, I had no idea what time it was but I started to feel pretty stupid standing where I was.

Upstairs, Ernesto had turned from his back to his side while I was gone. I shook out my sleeping bag and swept up as much of the glass as I could see. My nerves questioned the night and told me the immediate threat was gone, but I was still pissed off and the impulse to take up arms was strong. Since I don't own a gun, I headed for the kitchen, studied my knives in their block and picked the biggest, sharpest chopper of the lot. Carrots begged for mercy before this knife. I could dice an onion in seconds flat. Carnivores are not the only ones with skills.

I lay down corpselike in my sleeping bag, holding the knife in one hand, the cane in the other. Eventually, I metabolized the adrenaline surge. I may have dozed. As soon as it was light, I went downstairs, let myself into my car and called Dixon on his mobile. I told him about the message on the rock. "This is starting to freak me out."

"I'll be at the memorial service," Dixon said. "Not that we'll find anything useful on it, but bring the card."

"Nothing on the others?"

"Not a thing. About all we know is that our guy is good with a knife and knows his odus."

"They're all in the book. Madrina was pissed off when that book came out."

"I bought a copy on Amazon," Dixon said. "At the service, keep your eyes and ears open, okay?"

"What am I looking for?"

"I wish I knew. Look closely, though. See who's there. Watch how they act."

"It's a big space. Where should I sit?"

"Best view's from the back, but you have to get there early or you won't see people's faces when they come in."

"Where will you be?"

⌒

When I got out of the car, I saw Ernesto staring out the smashed glass of my attic window, careful to blow the smoke from his cigarette outside. The jagged hole looked like an open wound in the tidy Victorian façade. By the time I got upstairs, he'd put out the cigarette but the acrid smell lingered.

"Shit, man, what happened here?" he said.

"We had a night visitor."

"I didn't hear nothing."

I handed him the three-by-five card. He read it out loud. "Boy, that's a nice one. You ever notice how many odus sound like death threats?"

"It's a pretty bleak world view."

"I got a couple in my ita practically make me cry," Ernesto said. "And that's with blessings."

"I hear you."

"Would you look at that?" He'd spotted my weapons on the floor beside my bed. Kitchen knife and cane. By light of day, they looked pretty tame. Ernesto picked up the knife and tested its sharpness against his thumb. "Holy shit," he said. "You could do some damage with that."

"I was hoping for the chance."

"Looks like we're both on the list, huh."

"Yeah, I don't think that rock was a greeting card."

"Or a holy card." Ernesto laughed at his own joke and then regretted it. "Oh, man. I feel like shit."

"I'll make coffee."

Ernesto combed his hair back with his fingers, a gesture I suspected had less to do with grooming than not smoking. "I gotta get home," he said. "I gotta get cleaned up and practice what I'm gonna say." He hitched his pants up and tugged his tee shirt down. "I hope Arne's not too mad I didn't come home last night. Knowing him, he's thinking the worst."

"Have him call me. I'll tell him we both passed out."

"Poor guy's starting to freak out," Ernesto said. "First I spent all my time at Madrina's house. Now somebody wants to kill me."

"What does he do when you're tied up with ocha stuff?"

"Oh, he keeps himself busy." Ernesto sat down on the futon to tie his shoes.

We had coffee and he left.

＿＝

Santeros wear white to funerals. It signifies purity, brings protection, repels sickness and death. Was I a practicing Santero or not? I posed the question to my closet and found the idea of putting on a dark suit unimaginable. I took a white bath and packed my navel with cascarilla, all the while riding the teeter-totter between conviction and disbelief. Putting powdered eggshell in your belly button to keep the evil spirits out may sound a little bit superstitious, until you consider that just about every spiritual and martial practice on the planet shares the idea that the life force manifests in just that spot. Who knows? It had been a long time since I put on my dress whites, a Kenneth Cole linen blazer, white slacks, white shirt, white silk tie. I topped it off with a Panama hat and slipped into a pair of Italian designer oxfords, brown snakeskin, that I'd found for half price at Nordstrom Rack.

The outfit looked good. Inside I felt raw. The mirror told me I looked it, too.

＿＝

"Archer!"

When Sophia hollered my name, all my apprehension blew away. "Ochun Bi!"

Picture us approaching. Now we are face to face. We study the effects of time and pretend we're not.

"Call me Sophia, please. I'm not really practicing anymore." Her skin is clear, her eyes are bright. She's doing a smooth bob Michelle Obama thing with her hair. The pounds too much ocha adds are pared away. She wears a yellow suit.

"Damn, you look good."

She grabs my upper arms and holds me still to inspect me. "So do you, Archer. A little tired, maybe." A shadow crosses her face, and I remember she's like that, as transparent as sunlight.

"What's wrong?"

"I owe you so many apologies. Leaving without saying goodbye, not being in touch when Lance passed. I am sorry. I did think of you, often."

"I was mad at Madrina, not you."

"I still can't believe she's dead. I guess I thought she'd live forever." She laced her arm through mine. "I'm hungry. How about you?"

We'd met at La Méditerranée on College Ave, a place we'd often gone together before and after I got made. They never got weird when I pushed my food onto my blue tin iyawo plate and ate with my own spoon and they always took my stuff to the kitchen, after, and returned it clean. I was hungry for hummus and baba ganoush. Inside, we ordered and gossiped and got used to being in each other's company again. She told me about the meditation classes she'd been going to.

Later, after I'd inquired after Perry, after our food came, I asked her why she left like a thief in the night.

Sophia poked at her salad greens and looked at me in a bird's darting glances. "We had a terrible, terrible fight. I really thought if Michaela didn't kill me, I'd kill her. It was that intense."

"You loved her."

"For a while, I suppose. I loved the idea of her."

"What happened?"

"It started in Cuba. Remember? When I asked her about the difference between what she charged and what she paid the Cubans, she went nuts. Aganju or no, her fury wasn't hot. It was ice cold."

"I can imagine."

"When she couldn't break me down with words, she started hitting me. Her eyes changed, Archer. I didn't know who was there. I only hit back once, but it cut her lip. She went to the bathroom. I took a hundred bucks out of Ernesto's sopera for gas money and headed out."

"You took a hundred bucks?"

"I know I should have sent to him as soon as I had it. I'll give it to him today."

"Madrina gave everybody the impression you emptied the pot. Ten grand."

"What?"

"That was the story. You took the money and ran."

"I took a hundred bucks. I kept driving until it ran out. That was in northern Arizona. I got a job at Starbucks and saved up until I could afford to move on. I went to Atlanta. I thought I could be a Santera there, but I hate the South. I hate being black in the South. I'm a California girl.

I'm a Berkeley graduate." Again, sunlight. She grinned. "I have a master's degree, for Christ's sake. So I snuck back to the Bay Area and made myself invisible in plain sight."

"How long have you been back?"

"Almost three years." She said it with an imp's pride.

"Not practicing?"

"Only in my own heart. Leslie told me that you'd gone AWOL, too."

"I moved. It seemed like the easiest way."

Our food had gotten tired of waiting for our attention and wilted, cooled, coagulated, all the things that neglected food does. We picked at it for a while. Then, "Tell me something, Sophia. Did Madrina hate me or just my odu?"

She thought about it and then spoke carefully. "Let's put it this way. Even if you had the most innocuous 'good child loved by god and his mother' odu in complete ire, I doubt you would have made the inner circle. You had too many strikes against you."

"Like?"

"Too smart and too gay. Too middle class."

"Why would she even bother to make me then? Wouldn't it have been better to send me on my way?"

"Michaela wanted to be known as the iyalocha who could heal her children. She wanted terribly to be remembered when people say their mojubas a hundred years from now."

I said what I'd been thinking for some time. "Everybody dies, Sophia. You can fuck around with death all you want to, but time is something else. It's the mightiest substance. Time is always going to win."

Sophia took her iPhone out of her bag and consulted the screen. "Speaking of which, it's time to go." She reached across the table to put her hand on mine. "Stick close to me, Archer, will you? This is going to be just too weird. But I can't not go."

I promised to take care of her.

And so my ayubona and I, reunited, paid our tab and arm in arm set sail for the Cathedral of Christ the Light and Michaela de Estrella's funeral mass. Even though we deliberately went early, the nave was already filling up fast when we arrived. At the front of church, projected high above us, the holographic Christ looked pleased.

FORTY-THREE

‹──✦──›

Let us assume the best of everyone who came to church that day. Let's assume that those who spurned and smack-talked her in life, those elders of the community, leaders of other houses, came not because they were curious, or smug or wanted perhaps to recruit an orphaned godchild or two for their own ilés but because they repented their unkindnesses to Michaela de Estrella and wished through their prayers to speed her journey to the feet of Olodumare, God. Let's assume they were not curious about how she died, or about the whispers of a twin or the rumors of other deaths in her familia. Let us assume they did not wish to gloat or curse, that their interest in her passing was not prurient, that they were above that simple, base human desire to be seen by others at their pious best.

Let's give everyone, *almost* everyone, the benefit of the doubt.

That would include me and Sophia, arriving not first but in the first wave, awed like all the rest by Oakland's miracle of a new Roman Catholic cathedral, Christ the Light, a space that Sophia likened, with some accuracy and no intended disrespect, to a giant glass and wood vagina, enfolding within its soaring fecund shape an elegantly exposed pipe organ, modern confessionals carpentered of fir slats, a string of tiny chapels to either side themed by their resident icons and real candles blooming on tall metal stems, and the nave itself, ribbed like a ship and full of filtered light. Like ancient churches, it was built above the bones of the dead, or to be accurate, spaces waiting to receive bodies and ashes both in a mausoleum as beautiful in its way as the space for living worshippers was and in the long run probably expected to produce more revenue. Santería is not the only religion with a strong profit motive. Christs of varying degrees of fitness suffered on crosses of different artistic materials and styles, but the main attraction was the digital man up front, wearing a monk's robe and lifting one hand to bless all of us below.

"Wow," Sophia murmured.

"Wow," I agreed. You could tell the Santeros from everyone else by their light clothes—I'd say the split among the mourners was about 75-25 in favor of initiates—and in the more than ten years I'd been coming around I'd never seen so many of them in one place before. Michaela's godchildren present and estranged were clustered in the first rows of pews and as we moved upstream toward them I was aware of the recognitions that exploded like a string of caps, *oh my god, look who came.* This was followed by *I haven't seen him for so long, I wonder if I should speak to her,* whispered behind hands or simply pondered so loudly inside individual brains that the thought leaked out. Familiar faces, many beloved, watched us come and something inside me throbbed painfully at the sight of them. Beside me, Sophia looked as if she were seeing ghosts.

Rosario, bless her, stepped forward, greeted me and took both my hands in hers. Carlos separated himself from a small knot of apparently straight men and joined her. "You remember Sophia?" I said, and they fell upon her, too. Their faces showed their sorrows and also their resilience.

"My hearing is coming soon. My lawyer says you'll be a witness for us," Carlos said.

It took me a moment to conjure up Terry from the words *my lawyer.* I nodded.

"He's coming today," Carlos said. He scanned the crowd. "I don't see him yet. He wants to see if anybody else will testify for me."

Maria Victoria from Cuba joined us, looking rather beautiful and out of place in a short white cocktail dress, a white lace shawl and tall white heels. Rosario introduced us. "I heard a lot about you, Archer," Maria Victoria said after she bumped shoulders with me, then, "You look sort of familiar."

"Really? I don't think we've met. How do you like Oakland?"

"Okay until people started dying."

"Nice outfit, by the way."

"These shoes are killing me. I hope we sit down soon."

I felt a hand on my arm, half turned and saw Lev, old college chum, my first real lover, he who first tugged me toward Michaela and this day. Loss and the fight for his own life had changed him from that slender boy and he looked deeply middle aged in his brown suit. Benny had died of a heart attack sometime after they moved away. I threw my arms around him. "Oh man. Oh man. How long's it been?"

"It was a funeral," he said.

"Too long," I said. "How are you?"

"Persisting."

"Not practicing?"

"Not for a long time. You?"

"In recovery," I said. "It's hard."

"This is hard. But I had to come."

I glanced behind us, to find the crowd had almost doubled while I wasn't looking. Was Dixon out there?

"I was so sorry to hear about Benny," Sophia told Lev. "He was such a bright spirit."

"I miss him."

Three defectors together acted as a magnet, drawing the few of our elders who remained and the younger priests who knew us. We greeted and blessed each other in a swirl of hierarchical aplomb and real affection. It was a day for laying grudges aside, or so I felt. Ernesto appeared from the inner sanctum and gave my shoulder a manly slap before we greeted each other Lucumi-style. His hair was slicked back, the beard stubble gone. He looked like a portly Caribbean banker in his white sharkskin suit, a style that echoed Michaela's of ten years before. He looked important and the familia affirmed his position. *Where's Madrina's sister? When does the service start? Are you nervous about talking?* His responses were genial. This was a smoother, more confident Ernesto than I'd seen before.

Spotting Sophia unmanned him, though. His smile fell off, his eyebrows joined together in perplexity. No words emerged from slackened lips. Sophia stepped forward and took his hand. "Ernesto, it's so good to see you. I pray for you often."

Ernesto stared, nodded minutely.

"When I left town, I borrowed a hundred dollars from your pot. It helped me start a new life. Thank you." Sophia pulled a packet of neatly folded twenties from her pocket and tucked them in Ernesto's, right where a hankie might have gone.

Ernesto touched his pocket. "A hundred dollars?"

"I should have paid you back sooner. But I felt so bad about leaving, not being your Madrina."

"Madrina was my madrina," Ernesto said. "It worked out okay."

"Good. I'm glad. I'm glad I finally got to pay you back."

"But a hundred dollars. Madrina said…."

I put my hand on his shoulder and spoke close to his ear. "We'll never know, man. At least you got your crown."

The organ sounded, speaking Mozart, and quieted the human voices in the nave. People sidled toward their places in the pews. I remembered that the better view was toward the back, but the surge of my god family carried me to a place at the very end of the fifth row on the right, Sophia on one side, the cathedral's center aisle to my left. Ernesto stood near the altar. The programs were in the pews. When I picked mine up, Madrina Michaela stared back at me, wearing a proud and piercing scowl. The picture was five or six years old. Behind a handsome wooden cross and an altar boy dispensing fragrant smoke, the bishop himself progressed up the aisle. I knew his title not first hand but from the program. Wearing a simple white robe, Sister Immaculata marched behind him, carrying a bronze urn. With every row she passed, each mourner who saw her exhaled a little sonic bubble of alarm, until that whole tall dome filled up with shock and awe.

Was it a joke? A miracle? Had Michaela de Estrella been resurrected from the dead? Even if you knew she had a twin, the visual effect was powerfully unsettling.

When the officiants arrived at the front of the church, the music stopped. The cross was holstered, the urn placed on a low table before the altar. Esther Ann, Sister Immaculata, stood at the lectern and smiled serenely at the assembly, then opened the Bible and began to read, a passage from Luke, the program reminds me. I didn't really listen and I doubt anybody else did either. It was a lesson in the realities of syncretism, African gods masquerading in the robes of Catholic saints, and we the people were numb to the cover, imagining the voices of the drums and the shrieking of the orishas come to earth to mourn.

At the end of the reading, Sister Immaculata crossed herself, then introduced herself and welcomed us to her sister Michael Ann's funeral mass. She hoped we would partake at the Lord's table. Later in the service, anyone who wished to offer a remembrance would have the opportunity. Committal of the ashes of the deceased would take place in the crypt, immediately following the mass.

She sat down and the bishop stood up. Instructed by the program, the congregation stood up too. The bishop prayed diligently, the words in English but the cadences Latinate, different from the lightning fast mojubas Madrina Michaela and Obanoshukua recited in Lucumi. At a certain point, custom or the program directed us to kneel, and we did, a movement that, intentionally or not, had the effect of separating our ritual oneness into hundreds of separate beings, most of us focused on one stiff back and two aching knees. It was this dispersed consciousness that allowed the egungun to magically appear.

Unnaturally tall, a multicolored armada of a creature, the underlying human form purposefully obscured by hundreds of colored streamers, the true face veiled, false shoulders crowned by a papier-mâché mask— I'm describing details but the impression the egungun made was not detailed but an all-at-once visual assault on the senses, one that pulled up the anchor of reality and set us all adrift on different seas, filled with wonder, slapped around by dread. The egungun moved with the lurching stiffness of a zombie. In Africa, the masquerade represents the dead come back to advise and punish the living. It was nothing I'd ever seen before except in pictures, but my central nervous system read the iconography more or less correctly and I'm guessing everybody else's did, too. The egungun lurched up to the bishop, who slowly sensed its presence, looked up from his prayer book and nearly lost his shit. His face drained of what little color it had to start with and he dropped his prayer book on the floor. That's the first image my mind holds on to.

The second is the arm that snakes out of the costume, the gloved hand, the giant dagger in it.

Maybe because of what had happened the night before, the glint of that blade freed me from the spell of the egungun faster than it might have otherwise. The creature corrected course and pitched forward, in the direction of Esther Ann. My mind surrendered to instinct and I rocketed out of the pew, closed the twenty feet between us fast enough to knock the arm off course enough that instead of doing any real damage to Sister Immaculata, the knife merely gashed her white robe open. I think she screamed. The egungun tacked to face me. I thought I could knock the knife out of its hand, raised my hand to try. The blade sliced across my open palm and I saw a bright gush of my tainted blood. No time for HAZMAT warnings. The creature took off, laterally, and I followed as it plunged through a fire door. I ripped off my tie and wrapped it around my hand, then listened. Footsteps descending. The rage that filled me was big and felt familiar.

The chase was on.

By the time I reached the mausoleum, the egungun costume was empty, carelessly heaped on a stone slab in front of a mounted cross. I could hear the mummer, though, his breath and the squeak of his tennis shoes just audible over the tumble of water in the fountain at the entrance to the crypt. There was no way to move quite silent on that marble floor. I didn't even try. After a long tense moment, I saw a streak of black, moving from crypt to crematorium. I thought I'd lost him until I caught his reflection in the glass front of a wall of niches, turned in time to see him plunge through another gray metal door. In little bits and pieces, I got a sense of his human form—medium height, compact, dressed head to toe in black. Gloved. Hatted. Gone.

The door led outside. For a moment, sunlight blinded me. By the time I could see, what I saw was that black form, racing across the street toward Lake Merritt. I set off after him, dodged cars that honked peevishly at me, made it safely to the other side but lost my quarry. Joggers saw me and looked alarmed, which led me to take stock of my condition. My hand was bleeding through the tie. My white suit was blotched with red. I felt fine. The only problem was, I'd lost him. I stood in the path, sweaty and clueless, until an old Chinese man in a flat straw hat and white pajamas flashed me a toothless smile and pointed his staff toward the boat ramp. I took off in that direction and was rewarded by a glimpse of speeding black. I ran on the sidewalk until the path veered down toward the water. Again, a dash of black.

I think now he wasn't really running away. He was leading me on. I was led. Sunlight bounced off the water. I saw him duck into the fenced yard where canoes were stacked like bodies in the crypt. I had death on my mind and a giant anger in my heart. I pulled the chain-link fence shut behind me when I entered the boat yard, moved cautiously toward the stacks of boats. He surprised me by stepping into clear view, maybe twelve feet away, planting himself squarely, feet spread. Under his black beret, a rubber mask caricature of George Bush's idiot grin. For a second, it stopped me cold. Then I charged.

I think it was the force of my attack that drove his knife into my gut. I heard a shot explode nearby and assumed that I was dead.

FORTY-FOUR

M ama?
    Mama?
       It's Archer.

I'm awake and Ochun Bi is here.

Ochun Bi means Ochun is Here. She is here and I need to say my prayers. I take her hands in my hands and my hands are very dark. They look old. Old and dark. I hold her hands tightly and begin to pray.

Mojuba Olofin, mojuba Olorun, mojuba Olodumare, mojuba Olojoni.

I pay homage to god in all his forms. I hail him by all his names. This is urgent work.

Oni odun macuedun. Olorun alabosudaye. Olorun alabosuinfe. Olorun alaye. Olorun elemi. Olodumare oba aterere kaje.

The words of the mojuba tumble from my lips. I know the meaning of every one. Ochun Bi prays with me so that our voices braid together, the way the voices of wind and water do, the way the voices of earth and heaven do. When it comes time to pay homage to the ancestors, I know all their names and as I say their names I see their faces. Their presence comforts me.

Ibaye bayen tonu.

For the first time, Aina Saide, Michaela de Estrella, joins the long list of the dead. *Ibaye bayen tonu.*

At last it's time to ask the living for the blessing of their energy, joined to mine.

Kinkanmache. Kinkanmache yubonna mi Ochun Bi.

Aché.

Ochun is Here is here with me. Swiftly and surely, we march on to the end of the mojuba. Our hands are clasped. We pray to receive every blessing, to ward off every evil. When we finish, homage has been rightly, fully paid.

The day can begin.

Sophia had tears in her eyes.

"Why are you crying?"

"Who was that?"

"What?"

"The old man."

"I don't know."

"He speaks Lucumi."

"Do you know where I am?"

"Oh, Archer, baby. You're back."

I was back, in Alta Bates Hospital in Berkeley, California. I was in intensive care. I had been gone for almost twenty-four hours, during which Sophia had kept vigil. I felt like shit. Even though the stab wound might have killed me, "it could have been worse." According to the resident who came to see me when word got out I was awake, the knife had not punctured my stomach. That was the good news. It had nicked a kidney. "Fortunately, you have two of those," he said. After a few hours, I was doing well enough that they downgraded my condition to serious and gave me a room of my own. I hadn't had so much company since I last celebrated my ocha birthday—what? Two, three years before. Given my HIV status, any infection could be deadly, so my visitors had to swab down their hands and put on disposable masks before they came in. The blue domes made them all look weirdly alike.

Sister Immaculata came and thanked me for saving her life. She brought yellow roses.

Doc Sam came to tell me that she expected me to stay with her until it was clear I was healed up enough to be on my own again. She brought a mixed bouquet, lilies, carnations and alstroemeria.

Don, my sometime boss, came to tell me I still had health insurance, not to worry. Ling-Si had decided to file a criminal complaint against her attackers. Don brought a bunch of camellias from his garden.

Rosario came and hugged me, hard. I didn't have the heart to tell her how much it hurt. She brought me daffodils. Trader Joe's had them on special, like every year. Piri loved them, she said.

Oscar brought the tackiest, most suggestive floral arrangement I've ever seen—anthurium, birds of paradise and palm fronds in one garish phallic display. I loved it to pieces. *Drag queen action hero, irresistible. Get well fast.* That's what the card said. Even without his own mouth and nose, he was adorable. I was grateful no one had let me near a mirror.

Terry brought white hydrangeas, as pale as he was. He came to tell me Carlos's hearing had been postponed till I was well enough to testify.

I could only have two visitors at a time and no one was allowed to stay for long. By the time visiting hours were over, I was out of steam and hurting in spite of the dope in my IV drip. I fell into a nap that was more like a swoon and woke up an hour later thick headed and heart sore. My cell phone had evidently been impounded, so I picked up the receiver of the old-fashioned desk phone on my bedside table. Dialing a full eight digits was beyond me—my right hand was invisible inside a fat and gleaming bandage, but I managed O. When the hospital operator responded, I asked her to dial for me. The phone rang four or five times.

"Hello?"

"Mama?"

"Archer? Are you all right?"

"I'm calling to say I'm sorry. I'm so sorry."

"Oh, baby, so am I. Do you need me to come?"

"No, mama. I'm coming to see you, as soon as I'm better."

"It's not pneumonia again, is it?"

"No, mama. I had an accident but I'm going to be okay."

"Is there anything you need, son?"

"Just your forgiveness, mama. Just your love."

"You got it, boy," my mama said.

I hung up smiling. It was the first time we'd talked in several years.

⌒

They had me on a liquid diet, so dinner hardly deserved the name. Dixon arrived, duly blue-masked, while I was sucking it through a straw.

"Visiting hours are over."

"I'm a cop."

"Where were you yesterday?"

213

"Right behind you. Who d'you think shot the asshole who was trying to kill you?"

"The guy in the Dubya mask? You shot him?"

"Yup. Want to know who he was?"

"Was. He's dead?"

"He is."

"Do you, like, get in trouble for that? Shooting people dead?"

"Mitigating circumstances," Dixon said. "He was your friend Ernesto's significant other."

I tried to get my head around that but it didn't make much sense.

"Guess what Arne did for a living," Dixon said.

"I can't."

"Head butcher for a boutique meat company."

"Where's Ernesto?"

"Don't know. When you took off after Mr. Thing, Ernesto managed to get lost in the confusion."

"I'm a little slow today," I said. "How about you just tell me."

"Okay. At their apartment, we found an open copy of *The Dillogun*, a computer with an incriminating memory, two boxes of surgical gloves and another one of those plastic booties doctors wear to protect their shoes. We also found a shitload of fancy knives."

"But no Ernesto."

"We've got a crime-scene tape on the apartment and a couple of guys watching it," Dixon said. "Which is why I'm thinking he'll turn up here."

"Now I understand why he didn't come during visiting hours."

"Very funny," Dixon said. "You were on the list, Archer. And the shrink thinks he'll blame you for Arne's death."

"What shrink?"

He shrugged. "We have a guy on retainer. It's pretty much SOP these days."

"So you grab him when he turns up at the hospital."

"Too loosey-goosey. We pick him up when he turns up in your room."

"Fuck, man. I'm hammered."

"I know. I know," Dixon said. "But I'll be right there in the bathroom."

"I want a weapon."

"You can have a tape recorder. As soon as he tells you everything, I take him down."

The eyes may be the windows of the soul, but I was missing the mouth view. When your opponent has no expression, negotiation is tough. "I don't like this," I said. "Did you ask my doctor?"

"It's a homicide investigation. Civilians can't get enough of that shit." After a slight pause, he added, "Actually, he said it's up to you."

"Why do I feel like fish bait?"

"Because you are," Dixon said.

FORTY-FIVE

Dixon was still sitting by the bed when my surgeon made his evening rounds. The doctor had met my insides but not my waking self.

"Niles Fusada," the doctor said. "I'd shake your hand, but under the circumstances it seems like a bad idea. How are you feeling?"

"Like you're pumping me full of opiates and I'm going to hurt like hell when you stop."

"I'd say that's accurate." He studied my chart in silence for what seemed like a long time, then looked at me above his blue mask. "I talked with your HIV doc before I operated," he said. "Medically, you're pretty remarkable. Your virus load is extremely low. Your overall health is strong."

"I work at it."

"So your doctor said. The surgery went well. It'll take a while to see how your damaged kidney responds. But the biggest issue for a patient like you is secondary infections. You're getting a big dose of antibiotics to prevent sepsis, but we also have to keep you clear of viral infections."

Up until then, it looked like he was talking to the chart. Now he put it aside and made eye contact with me. "There's something else I'd like you to try. My little sister is working on her PhD in nursing. She's designed a study to determine if and how much the use of Reiki speeds healing in post-operative patients. You might say I'm shilling for subjects."

"Didn't the pope forbid Catholics from using Reiki?"

"I'm sorry. I didn't realize you were a Catholic."

"I'm not. I just read that somewhere."

"Evidently the pope thinks only Jesus should be allowed to do hands-on healing," Fusada said. "But the fact is, with a little training, anybody can do it and anybody can benefit from it. Nurses have known that for a couple of decades, at least. My sister wants to prove it to the medical establishment."

"Okay. Sign me up."

Dr. Fusada's blue mask wiggled a little when he laughed. "That was too easy."

"I hope it works," I said. "Did you really tell this man he could use me as bait to catch a criminal?"

Dr. Fusada's eyes traveled from Dixon to me. "The way he explained it to me, you're probably in danger no matter what." His hands moved through the air, as if he were trying to grab hold of some better plan. "I hate violence," he said. "It makes no sense to me."

"It's not like I love it," Dixon said.

I know I was asleep because when the voice spoke, it broke into my dream. My subconscious tried hard to weave it in, like when you wander around a dream looking for a bathroom because you really have to piss, but it resisted incorporation.

"I didn't kill Madrina."

I opened my eyes and confirmed that it was Ernesto's voice, coming out of Ernesto's body. He looked battered and exhausted and like he'd probably been crying.

"Oh yeah?"

"Madrina liked the meat from Arne's company. He saved her a hanging tender. We just stopped by to give it to her."

Breathe, Archer. Stay cool. I saw that he'd pulled the door to my room shut. The bathroom door was open by a casual slice. Better not to speak.

"All the doors were locked, so I used my key. It was so quiet. She was dead when we found her. She hadn't been for long. She was still bleeding. God, there was a lot of blood."

"Sounds terrible," I murmured.

"I wanted to call the police right away, but Arne, he said, 'Hold on, let's think this thing through.' Arne was smart that way." He gave a little sob, like his choice of verb tense had just reminded him of his loss. "So we thought about it. We didn't want to get blamed for something we didn't do but we did want to make the best of a bad situation. It was like, there was business involved."

"Ah. Business."

"Madrina made a good living. And I was learning how. I was the one she was teaching. But Arne said there were too many elders in front of me. Too many people who didn't know half of what I do who'd try to take over everything."

I nodded sympathetically.

"Plus the trucks," he said. "All those trucks."

"Thousands of dollars right there."

His mouth twisted. "That damn nun up and gave them away. Like they were hers to begin with."

"Did you show her all of them?"

Ernesto laughed like a dog barks, a short, blunt sound. "All but three. I kept three for myself. By this time, Arne's put on a pair of those surgical gloves Madrina always kept in the linen closet and he's picked up her matanzas knife, the one that's beaded, and he says, 'Watch this, baby.' And he cut off her head. Just like that. I think I went into shock. 'Where shall we put it?' he said, and I pointed at Aganju's pot. She was still warm enough that more blood came out. I thought I was going to throw up."

"Did you?"

"Naw. Arne says, 'I always wanted to do that to a human being. Do you s'pose she's got a hanging tender?' And he started poking around with the knife. I said, 'Stop that right now, that's my madrina,' and he said, 'Baby, she always treated you like shit.' And I was like, 'I don't care, show Madrina some respect.'" Tears welled up in his eyes.

"That's good," I said. "You guys did a good job cleaning up after yourselves."

"Yeah, we did. Arne knows stuff like that." A short, grim laugh. "We even cleaned up for whoever killed her in the first place."

"How did they?" I said. "Kill her?"

Ernesto shrugged. "She bled out from that big artery up the side of the neck. The carotid. Her throat wasn't cut or anything. I don't know how they got it open."

"So you left?"

"Left and came back later and like, found her dead. That time I called the cops." Ernesto settled into the visitor's chair, leaned forward, looked hard at his own hands. There were little stands of black hair between the knuckles, strewn across the backsides. "It wasn't like I was pretending, either. It really hit me hard."

"So when did you decide to start eliminating elders?"

"You know, at first I thought Arne was overreacting, but then we had that meeting with the cops, everybody together at the house, and I saw he was right. People didn't respect me the way they should. It was all Betty this and Carly that and why not ask Archer. And Maria Victoria, she has twenty years made. That bitch is ambitious."

"You made a list."

"We did. And you were on it. You still are."

"I don't want anything Madrina had."

"People like you. They trust you, god knows why. Madrina didn't."

"No. How'd you decide to start using the odus?"

"That was pretty good, huh? You should have seen yourself, when that rock came through the window."

"I thought you passed out."

Ernesto smirked. "Odus made Arne crazy. Every time he got a reading from Madrina, it was all, you have no friends, death is looking at you, you're an asshole. Madrina said life is like that, and the religion understands. Arne thought it would be funny to make people take their own medicine."

"Tragedy, deception and despair are near."

"That's a good one."

"So, did you kill Betty and Carly, or did Arne do it?"

"What does it matter?"

"Just curious."

"I set them up. Arne cut them. We were a team." He made fists and attacked his tears.

"What about the cats?"

"The cats were fun," Ernesto said. "Madrina and Arne used to catch homeless cats in those traps and have races to see who could cut them up fastest. Madrina hated cats. They had a bet. If Madrina ever beat Arne, he had to be her goat opener. For free. For a year. She never did though. Arne was a professional."

"You scared the shit out of me."

Ernesto's laugh was tragic, the deep moan of wounded pigeon. "That was good, huh? It was Arne's idea. Kind of like his personal memorial for Madrina." He went silent for minute, his face went oddly blank, then twisted up. "Now I'll never know if he killed Madrina or not. He teased me about it, 'Wouldn't you like to know?' But he never said for sure." Real hatred in the look he turned on me. "That's your fault, you smug bastard. For you, I got something special."

"You know, you don't really have to kill me, Ernesto. Ibu Toke. I'll never compete with you. I don't even live here anymore."

"I just told you everything, asshole. And if it wasn't for you, Arne wouldn't be dead." Ernesto reached inside his jacket and brought out a huge syringe. "You get a shot."

"Of what?"

"Pentobarbital. I bought it over the counter, last time I was in Mexico. It's what veterinarians use to put dogs down."

I figured I could knock it out of his hand before he got the needle in me, but he had a different plan. Before I even grasped what he was doing, Ernesto plunged his giant needle into my IV bag.

"I wasn't sure about the dose but this should be enough to do the trick. It might take a couple of minutes for you to die."

I screamed.

Dixon came out of the bathroom holding his gun in both hands. It was pointed at Ernesto's head. "Move and I'll shoot you," he said.

The IV fed into my left arm. My bandaged right hand was almost useless and I couldn't reach the needle with my left hand. It took precious seconds to figure out I could rip the line out with my teeth, seconds more to actually do it.

"Go ahead. Shoot me," Ernesto said. "I don't give a shit."

"I do," Dixon said. The line dripped bitter fluid onto my tongue. I spat and tried to puke. Dixon cuffed Ernesto's hands together behind his back, not as smoothly as on TV but better than I've seen cops do it on the street. Fuck, how could I tell if I was dying?

"Okay, listen up," Dixon said. "Until the Supreme Court says otherwise, I still have to tell you your rights." Fast and mechanical, he rattled off the ritual disclaimer. A nurse and a uniformed cop came bursting through the door. "If you've got an antidote to pentobarbital, you better get it," Dixon said. "Right now."

"I hope you die, asshole," Ernesto said. I turned my face toward the wall and waited to see what would happen.

FORTY-SIX

t her dressing table, my mother puts on her face and takes it off again. Those are her words. I think what happens is this: She takes off her prettiness and there, underneath, finds her true fierce beauty. The ritual is fascinating to watch. When I was little, I hardly ever missed it unless I was already asleep. As grade school wore on and my life filled up with other stuff, I witnessed the transformation less and less often. Now I'm thirteen years old and this is where I choose to have the conversation.

Having made her brown face white with Ponds Cold Cream, my mother wipes off the whiteness with Kleenex. Her makeup comes with it. She is brown and strong again. Has she gotten older since the last time I watched?

"What's going on with you, baby boy?"

"I have something to tell you, mama."

"Shoot."

"Mama, I'm gay."

I'm ready to explain. I'm ready to defend. I have a brainful of datapoints. I've waited until puberty hit, until the hormones came flooding in and confirmed my suspicions. I'm ready to defy, to argue, to apologize and console.

Mama says, "I know."

"You do?" I say. "How do you?"

"Mothers do," she said.

"Why didn't you say anything?"

"Because it's your business, baby boy, not mine." Mama gathers up the soiled tissues and puts them in the wastebasket. She gives me her full attention. She smiles. I don't know what I expected but I do know this is not it.

"Don't you care?"

Mama thinks about it. "Yes and no," she says. "I don't care who you love or how you love them, as long as your love is true. I don't want you to get hurt. I do want you to be able to defend yourself. Most of all, baby boy, I want you to grow up to be a good man."

Why does this feel anticlimactic? "Is that all, Mama?"

Again, she thinks before she answers. "That's pretty much it. I know you're smart. I know I won't always be there to make sure you brush your teeth and eat your vegetables, so I figure I have to let that stuff go." Her smiles persists and it changes. "If I was totally honest, I'd say I'm disappointed I probably won't have any grandbabies."

"Gay people adopt babies sometimes."

"They do. But I'll tell you what, I'm not gonna hold my breath, okay?"

"Okay." I had so many words inside me and now they're gone. For a while we just sit there.

Then my mother reaches out her cool hand and puts it on my cheek. "I love you, baby boy."

"I love you, Mama."

Lance and I are on our throne. Madrina Michaela takes off her shoes and steps into our space. She sits between us on the floor, propped up against the red satin wall. "So, iyawos, what's today's question?"

Madrina has told us we can ask her one question every day. One and no more. So far we've asked her things like whether ire or osogbo happens when you're born or develops as you live your life. (She'll get back to us on that one.) Why can't iyawos touch people who aren't priests? (We are so clean, so pure, we mustn't let strangers steal that from us.) What happens at our three month ebo? (Our ochas are fed and lifted up.) We've been alternating. Today it's Lance's turn.

"What makes a good godchild?" he asks.

Usually, Madrina starts to answer before your voice rises at the end to make a question. She's studied hard and filled her brain with facts. She'd be a great quiz show contestant, especially because she's so quick on the draw. This question, though, she has to think about before she answers.

"A good godchild is obedient," she says slowly. "A good godchild is loyal, no matter what. He never questions his godparent's authority. He spends a lot of time at his godparent's house. He understands that he has a new family now and he turns to his godparent for advice, not to his old family. They're the ones who screwed him up." Madrina laughs. "That's a really good question, Lance." After another short pause, she says, "I used to think the best godchild was the best student, but now I know that's not true. I'd rather have respectful than smart."

Madrina sits with us a moment longer, then pushes up to her feet and leaves the throne. "I've got bologna sandwiches for your lunch," she says.

Lance is dead and I'm broken. I blubber into the telephone.

"I can get a substitute to take my class. I can come for a week, help you over the hard part. Like you did for me when your daddy died."

"You don't need to do that, Mama."

"It's what families do. I can be there late tomorrow."

"No, Mama. Please don't come. Madrina says you'll only stress me out."

You're a disrespectful little shit, Archer, but I saved your life. I fought with Iku and I won.

Finally, there is only the ocean. Boundless, ceaselessly energetic, cold. She tosses me around as if I were a jellyfish or a slimy knot of kelp. She is powerful but she is gentle. In the hissing flow of one huge broken wave, she washes me up on the beach. Alive.

FORTY-SEVEN

"The Chief's happy," Dixon said. I was downwind from him on Doc Sam's deck, envying the pleasure he got from his nicotine auto-intoxication. We sat next to each other, not across, in that manly way that makes it easier for straight guys to talk to other men. He kept his eyes on the horizon and addressed me sideways. "He never thought we'd wrap it up this fast."

"It's not over yet." I spoke to his profile and the smoke that drifted out of his mouth.

"Actually, it is. The DA charged Ernesto for all three murders, plus trying to do you."

Planters full of herbs edged the deck and when nobody was smoking, you could smell the rosemary and lavender once the sun hit mid-sky. I'd spent a lot of time out there since I got out of the hospital, most of it worrying in a low-grade way about how I was going to fix my life. "Ernesto didn't kill Madrina. You know that." After money and work, that her killer was still out there was high on the list of my anxieties.

"The shrink says he's in denial."

"You don't believe that."

"Doesn't matter what I think," Dixon said to the distant sea. "It's all about the jury now."

"Damn, I thought you were better than that."

"You're a real prick sometimes," Dixon said.

I didn't have the energy for a fight and he didn't have the inclination so we went to our separate corners, psychically speaking, and kept our mouths shut for a while. Then he took an envelope out of his pocket and tossed it down on the table. "This is for you."

I could see my name through the transparent window. The return address was *City of Oakland, Police Department*. Inside there was a check for $2135.71 and a stub that said, Consulting. I hadn't expected it and I was disappointed by how small it was, my latest variation on the half-empty/half-full conundrum. I called it the Fucking Broken Glass. "Thanks. I'll put it against my deductible."

"Good thing you have insurance."

"With insurance, I still owe close to year's salary."

"Holy crap," Dixon said. "When are you going back to work?"

"The doctor won't clear me yet and Don can't wait. If he lays me off, I can get unemployment plus the COBRA subsidy. If I move in here, that gives me six months to figure shit out." Did my life really suck or was I just feeling sorry for myself? Doc Sam said the world would look brighter once I metabolized the boatload of legal drugs in my system and put a little weight back on. Terry said bankruptcy was made for folks like me. Oscar said my scars were sexy. He was a shitty liar. In the interests of sounding less self-absorbed, I said, "How about the promotion? Did you get it?"

Dixon ground the little ball of ash and coal out in one of Doc Sam's planters. The result was olfactory vandalism. "Chief said I will."

"Congratulations."

He nodded. "I'll ask around if anybody's hiring."

"You know, I'm sitting here thinking, if I just use this check to feed So-and-So a goat and a couple of roosters, my luck is sure to change. I'm in danger of relapsing."

"Maybe you should study for the bar exam."

Good advice, I'm sure, and I'm sure it was well meant but it bounced right off me like the ball a kid throws against a wall, over and over, to annihilate loneliness on a slow afternoon. The problem was, we had no context. He made the father-shaped hole in heart ache, but he was not my father, or my uncle or anything more than a reasonably decent black guy with a deep voice and a touch of gray hair who'd wandered into my life. He would pass out soon enough.

"There's some stuff I have to do," I said. "Thanks for the check." We both stood up.

"You earned it."

"Say hello to your wife. To Leslie."

"She sends you her best."

"Back at her. I'll let you know if I hear who killed Michaela."

After one of those awkward handshakes—my good left hand meets his right—he headed back to Oakland. When I sat back down on the bench, it was in the spot he'd left some warmth behind. I stayed outside for a long time with Doc Sam's rainbow afghan wrapped around my shoulders, watching the sun move west and imagining I could hear the surf even though the beach was more than half a mile away, while I contemplated that age-old question: Is it really the future if you don't want to go there?

The sun got big as it approached the horizon and the air got cold enough to make me shiver. I could have given up, gone inside in search of warmth, but since I'd been staying at Sam's, I'd gotten almost superstitiously committed to being present at the precise moment the ocean swallows the sun. That night, I pulled the afghan up under my chin and inside the tent it made around me, stuck my left hand into the pocket of my windbreaker. Sometimes I find money I forgot I had in my pockets. That night, I found the paper I'd written on in the country jail. I took it out, unfolded it and read what I'd written to convince me I was still myself and that my mind was free.

She was my godmother.

Lance died.

I left her house.

Michaela is dead.

I am in jail, a prisoner in the human zoo.

If anything, I felt even sorrier for myself than I had then. With no one around to see me do it, I cried as the sun went down.

Doc Sam put her hands over my eyes, down the sides of my nose. Their heat extended from my forehead down to my jaw. I sucked in a long breath and blew it out. My body relaxed, aligned itself on the table and on the inside and Doc Sam felt the shift, acknowledged it with the tiniest whisper of a laugh. The Brahms she put on didn't do a lot for me but I liked it better than the quasi-Hawaiian New Age stuff that Lily Fusada

liked to play at Alta Bates. This had become the sweet spot of my con-
valescent days, an oasis of healing in a desert of invasive and expensive
medical procedures, care freely given and measurably effective. Corny as
it sounds, surrendered to a Reiki treatment, I felt loved and, by extension,
almost managed to love myself.

Doc Sam was impressed enough by my testimony and Lily's data that
she got herself attuned and was urging Pete to do the same. "There are
so many ways we can use this at the clinic. I wish I'd known about it
when Mom was dying."

Yep, it lowered my blood pressure, lessened my pain, improved my
blood flow and helped my wounds heal fast and clean. It helped me
detoxify. Somehow, I survived my hospital stay without pneumonia or a
deadly flu and I was ready for release a day or two sooner than the most
medically optimistic, fiscally conservative prediction.

"The establishment sees all that as anecdotal," Lily warned Doc Sam.
"The drawback is, nobody can patent Reiki. There's no real way to profit
from it. It just is."

Doc Sam moved her hands to the second position, over my ears, and
the warmth flooded in. In that little cocoon of personal silence, my life
was not materially different, but it seemed less dire. Doc Sam and Lily
assured me I did not have to feel beholden for their ministrations. They
did, however, expect me to get attuned myself and pass it on. If gratitude
is poison, that was the antidote they proposed.

"Under the circumstances, Arch," Terry said, "I'd rather take a deposition than have you testify in court."

"I don't mind going to court," I said. "In fact, I'd welcome the excitement."

For a while, he didn't say anything even though the phone conveyed
some ambient crackles and sighs. "And if you hadn't almost died, I'd welcome the chance to put you on the stand. But you know, you kind of look
like shit right now. I think I'd rather go with just your words."

"Thanks a lot."

"Don't take it personally, Arch. I need your story to convince the jury
that Carlos and Rosario were not fucking over the top fruit loops to think
that making ocha might save their kid's life."

"I hear what you're saying. I know what you need."

"Think of it as the Cult Defense."

My sigh sighed in Santa Cruz arrived full strength in San Francisco.

"Sorry, man," Terry said. "Just a little office joke."

"It's probably even funny."

"It makes us laugh. So, how about you come here late Tuesday afternoon, if you want to get out of the house. We'll tape the deposition and get some dinner. If you feel like it, you can stay at my place and head back in the morning."

"You sure you want an ugly house guest?"

"Lighten up, Archer. I'm talking about legal theater, not what happens between friends. We both know you'll get your gorgeous self back soon enough."

I told him I hoped it was true.

FORTY-EIGHT

＊

The court reporter was already set up in the conference room when I got to Terry's office, not the balding white guy I expected but a skinny Pakistani kid with hands that flew like birds over his keypad. The conference room itself was strictly non-profit, poorly lighted, mismatched and worn. After he captured the basics, Terry began his interrogation.

Q: You're HIV positive, aren't you?

A: I am.

Q: And when did you first learn of your positive status?

A: In 2000.

Q: You were initiated in the Afro-Cuban religion popularly known as Santería, is that correct?

A: Yes.

Q: When were you initiated?

A: In 2001.

Q: Mr. Barron, can you tell us why you chose to be initiated?

A: For my health.

Q: Why did you expect Santería to improve your health?

A: My godmother strongly suggested that it would.

Q: And you believed her?

A: There were a couple of godchildren in her house who had experienced dramatic remissions of AIDS-related cancers. Madrina strongly suggested it was due to her interventions.

Q: Have you experienced illness since your initiation?

A: Yes.

Q: Have you recovered?

A: I have.

Q: And do you attribute this to your godmother's actions on your behalf?

A: I don't know.

Q: Did your godmother believe that by initiating you, she saved your life?

A: I think so.

Q: Do you believe that getting initiated saved your life?

A: I don't know.

Terry signaled the court reporter to stop. "Archer, can't you do any better than that?"

"I don't think so."

"Damn it, don't you understand what I need here?"

"I do understand. How about asking me if I think Carlos and Rosario had reason to believe that making ocha saves lives? I could say yes to that."

Terry signaled the reporter that he was back on duty.

Q: Do you think Carlos and Rosario Mendoza acted reasonably in choosing to address their son's illness with initiation?

A: I believe they were doing what they believed was best for their sick child.

Q: Thank you, Mr. Barron. That's all for now.

At dinner, Terry seesawed between giddy and peevish, elated because he believed he'd win the case, angry that I'd not made a better witness. He kept urging me to have martini, a glass of red wine, an after-dinner drink. He kept asking me why I was such a damn prude about my testimony.

"You put me under oath," I said.

"Come on, Arch. You know how to play the game."

"I do. But I've purposely forgotten how to lie. It's not good for me."

"You really are a prick sometimes," he said, a sentiment that was in danger of becoming my theme song. *Archer Barron, Sometime Prick.* "You deposed a man who's sitting on the fence between faith and disbelief. What did you expect?"

"Something that would impress a jury."

"I think you lost me with 'you look like shit.'"

"That was *days* ago."

"Two of them."

"I still want you to come home with me." There it was, the bottom line. "Come on, Arch. You know you want to."

He was right, of course. I did.

Terry was fascinated by my scars. He looked and touched, kissed and licked with a tender intensity I found both exciting and weird. When I'd thought about spending the night at his apartment, I imagined another quasi-erotic sleepover. Even about that, I had mixed feelings. The prudish romantic in me wanted to be faithful to young Oscar, even though fidelity was not something either of us had put on the table. How could we? I was old, battered and broke while he was of the up-and-coming persuasion. There was nothing, really, to keep me from succumbing to Terry's ministrations.

Terry's ministrations, ranging from my eyelids to my toes and back again, were slow and artful. He worked the periphery until my center ached. Part of me felt guilty to be receiving and giving nothing back, but I convinced myself that there was time for reciprocity, all the time in the world. Terry was the *whitest* man I've ever been with. Around the edges of desire, I entertained strange thoughts: *We both loved Lance, maybe that's enough foundation for a life* and *Good thing I didn't die.* I wondered a little aimlessly about the relationship between lust and time. Then on far side of the meeting place of pain and wanting, he finally put his mouth around me. I exploded and then wilted, as if my nerves had been removed, my bones dissolved.

I woke up suddenly and in distress. I couldn't breathe and I couldn't see. I tried to push the pillow off my face, but my arms were spread wide and my wrists were shackled. I turned my head and found a small pocket of air between my collarbone and shoulder. Flesh on my chest, pressure on my face. My heart grasped the situation before my mind did and doubled the beat rate. Checking in with my lower body, it seemed my feet were tied together but not tethered to anything else.

"URRRRGHGHH." It was an attempt at communication, distorted by kapok. A corner of the pillow lifted and I gulped air.

"Awake, are you?" Terry said.

231

"What are you doing?"

"Punishing you. Actually, I'm glad you're awake. Why spare you suffering?"

"Have you gone crazy?" I still couldn't see him but once my own breath quieted a little, I thought I could hear his.

"Probably," Terry's voice said. "I've probably been at least a little crazy since you stole Lance."

I wanted to argue, to set him right. Hey, nobody gets stolen who doesn't want to be. On the other hand, I wanted to keep breathing.

"You stole him twice. Once when he left me, once when he died. Are you surprised I hate you?"

"You can get help," I mumbled. I heard him laugh.

"I don't think so. Besides, I don't want help. I want revenge."

"At least talk to me first. Let me see your face."

"You're stalling," he said, but he pushed half the pillow away, until I could see one mad blue eye.

"If you stop now, Terry, we can forget this ever happened. I won't hold it against you."

"I may be crazy but I'm not stupid." He chuckled. "I suppose you figured out by now I killed your godmother. The arrogant bitch."

Keep him talking, keep him talking. "How? How did you kill her?"

"I borrowed an X-Acto knife from an artist friend. I lost the blade and gave the handle back." Again, the laugh I'd never heard before. "If crazy Ernesto and his boyfriend hadn't come along, you could have admired my work. I did a good job."

"How did you know what to do?"

"I studied up on my anatomy, before. You really only have one chance."

You only have one chance. I flexed my shoulders and tried to lift my head. There was play, not a lot, but some. My legs were bound at the ankles. With enough thrust, I thought I could raise my hips and bend my knees.

"What did you learn?" I asked him.

"I learned where the carotid artery is," Terry said. "I nailed it, first try."

"How did you get close enough to try?"

"After you called and told me about Piri, I realized that someone had to stop Michaela. She was a death dispenser." For a moment he lifted the edge of the pillow far enough for me to see his whole face. "Willfully and not, I've infected my share of men. But I've never been proud of it. I decided it was time I stepped up and did something good for a change."

"You do good as a lawyer."

"I move a little energy around, that's all."

"Is killing me part of your crusade?"

He grinned down at me, a crazy angel. "No, it's entirely personal. I suppose I should get on with it."

"I'm in no hurry."

"Funny," he said.

"How did you get close enough to Madrina Michaela to use your X-Acto knife?"

"I called her up and made an appointment for a reading. Once I chatted her up a little, she remembered who I was."

One chance. I rehearsed the motion in my mind's eye.

"Want to hear the good part?"

"Of course."

"She counted up her shells and told me I'm a prisoner of ocha."

"I'm sorry, I couldn't quite hear you."

He gave me an odd look and then, as I hoped, drew his head a little closer to mine. Close enough?

"SHE SAID MAKING OCHA WOULD SAVE MY LIFE."

I took the shot, raised my joined legs and my neck in one fierce thrust, driving my knees into his back, slamming my forehead against his, imagining it was the thrust of an angry ocean that drove the blow. In one freak giggle of Newtonian physics, the countervailing forces broke him at the weak point. I heard his neck snap. Terry's eyes widened, then closed. He fell sideways across me. Blood dripped into my eyes from the laceration in my forehead and for a long time I just lay there, wondering if it wouldn't have been better if I'd died, too.

In the course of the hour or so I spent with Terry's cooling body, I said goodbye to everyone I ever loved who died. It was an indulgence and a comfort and probably still counts as the most perverse thing I've ever done.

Finally, I started looking for a way out of my bonds.

Terry's phone was on the night table. I couldn't reach it myself, but after a bunch of tries, I was able to use his limp arm as a kind of proxy and knock the phone onto the bed. I dialed nine-one-one and asked them to contact Jerry Dixon of the OPD. Then I fell into a deep sleep and didn't wake up until I heard his voice.

"Jesus, Barron, what have you done now?"

"I know who killed Madrina," I told him.

Once he and the other cop pulled Terry off me, we were all embarrassed by my nakedness.

ABOUT THE AUTHOR

JOYCE THOMPSON is the author of ten previous books, nine of them fictions. She is owner and president of Launchismo, a marketing services company. Thompson lives in the Oakland flats, where the barrio meets the 'hood.

CPSIA information can be obtained at www.ICGtesting.com
Printed in the USA
LVOW13s1857260314

379049LV00010B/1406/P